DECEMBER HEART

MERRY FARMER

DECEMBER HEART

Copyright ©2018 by Merry Farmer

This ebook is licensed for your personal enjoyment only. This ebook may not be re-sold or given away to other people. If you would like to share this book with another person, please purchase an additional copy for each recipient. If you're reading this book and did not purchase it, or it was not purchased for your use only, then please return to your digital retailer and purchase your own copy. Thank you for respecting the hard work of this author.

This book is a work of fiction. Names, characters, places, and incidents are products of the author's imagination or are used fictitiously. Any resemblance to actual events or locales or persons, living or dead, is entirely coincidental.

Cover design by Erin Dameron-Hill (the miracle-worker)

ASIN: B077K26MSD

Paperback:

ISBN-13: 9781983476716

ISBN-10: 1983476714

Click here for a complete list of other works by Merry Farmer.

If you'd like to be the first to learn about when the next books in the series come out and more, please sign up for my newsletter here: http://eepurl.com/RQ-KX

 Created with Vellum

CHAPTER 1

AYLESBURY, BUCKINGHAMSHIRE – MAY, 1879

May was the most beautiful month in the English countryside. Everyone said so. Meticulously tended gardens and sprawling, wildflower meadows alike glowed with fresh, colorful blooms. Trees stood tall, at their peak of green. Fragrant breezes blew from the budding fields into quaint and cozy villages. Neighbors seemed to be at their cheeriest, greeting each other with smiles and jovial conversation in the lanes between tiled cottages and thriving businesses.

But while everyone else was brimming with summery satisfaction, Mariah Travers bristled with unease. Every new spring ticked by as if scolding her. Each change of season and turning of the year pushed her further and further away from any hope of being her own woman, and deeper and deeper into spinsterhood. That fate wouldn't have been so terrible on its own, but being an unmarried woman past a certain age carried frustrating consequences with it.

"Ooh, Mariah! Look over there." Mariah's younger sister, Victoria, squealed and grasped Mariah's arm as the two of them passed through the center of Aylesbury on errands.

"What am I looking at?" Mariah asked. All she saw was the usual row of shops with goods displayed in the window, old Mrs. Murphy rushing the passel of farm children she taught for pennies down the street, and a trio of young men in red army uniforms chatting on the corner outside the pub.

"No, don't look," Victoria giggled, tugging on Mariah's arm as one of the officers glanced up and smiled.

Mariah was tempted to roll her eyes, but Victoria was only nineteen and had recently discovered that gentlemen's heads were easily turned by a fetching smile and a shapely figure. Mariah remembered all too well the sense of power that awakening had sparked in her, and felt far too keenly that her own power had died. Died along with Robert, God rest his soul.

"Quick." Victoria shifted from clutching Mariah's arm to holding her hand. "We should cross to the other side of the street so that we walk past them."

"But MacTavish's Books is on this side of the street," Mariah argued.

"It doesn't matter. We should talk to them. They're ever so handsome."

Victoria was already doing more than talking. Her smile grew wider by the moment as the three officers studied her, whispering amongst themselves. Mariah was quick to note that all three of them had their sights set on her sister. After the initial look, not one of them spared a glance for her.

"Victoria," she said, a wry note to her voice, "show some propriety. Even attractive officers prefer that young ladies not display themselves as if—"

"They're coming this way," Victoria gasped, ignoring everything Mariah said. "Oh. Oh my."

Victoria dropped Mariah's hand so that she could pinch her cheeks and smooth her skirt where it hugged the curve of her hips before flaring at her knees. Mariah had her doubts about the current fashion of tight-fitting skirts—mostly because it made walking with a long, purposeful stride impossible—but seeing the way her sister used the style to show off what she shouldn't to a group of strange men made her cheeks burn hot.

"Ladies."

They crossed paths with the officers at the intersection, across from the pub. All three of the young men seemed eager to make Victoria's acquaintance, grinning and bowing.

"Good afternoon," Victoria greeted them, batting her eyelashes.

With an inward sigh, Mariah shot a look of longing

past the officers to the bookstore. "Gentlemen." She acknowledged the men with a polite nod.

"We were just speculating," one of the officers with blond hair and a thick moustache began, "what sort of errand two such lovely young women would be on this fine afternoon."

Victoria giggled, blushing prettily. But then, everything Victoria did was pretty. "My sister and I were on our way to the bookstore."

"Sister?" Another of the officers with dark hair and eyes peeked at Mariah.

She knew in an instant what the man must be thinking. Victoria was youthful and fair and dressed in pink, while Mariah was gathering dust at the age of twenty-seven, brunette, and wearing purple to represent the end of a long period of mourning.

Victoria failed to see the subtle inquiry in the man's eyes. "Yes," she said. "This is my sister, Mariah, and I am Miss Victoria Travers." Bold as brass, she held out her hand for the three men.

Mariah ached with embarrassment at her sister's forwardness. They hadn't been formally introduced to the men, and although they were on the verge of the modern eighties and not the fussy twenties, Victoria's move was beyond the pale.

"It is a delight to meet you, Miss Victoria." The blond officer took her hand and kissed it. "I am Col. Nigel Scott."

"And I'm Lt. Gordon Banfield," the dark-haired man

said, taking her hand from Col. Scott.

"I'm Lt. Walter King," the third man, smaller than the others, but stockier, took her hand last.

Col. Scott blinked and turned to Mariah. "Miss Travers." He nodded.

Mariah fought to keep her smile in place. It shouldn't have hurt to be placed as second-best to Victoria, but there was a time when impetuous young men like these officers had rushed to make her acquaintance as well. Robert certainly had. But Robert was gone now, and with it the bloom off her rose.

"It is a pleasure to make your acquaintance, gentlemen," Mariah said, taking Victoria's hand when Lt. King let it go. "But if you will excuse us, my sister and I have quite a lot to accomplish today."

"Mariah." Victoria laughed, scolding in her eyes. "We couldn't possibly be so rude as to leave these kind men mere moments after making their acquaintance."

"Of course not," Lt. Banfield said with a wink.

Mariah arched a brow, instantly distrusting the gentlemen's motives. Particularly as two out of the three of them seemed more interested in Victoria's breasts than the conversation. Papa would beat all three of them within an inch of their lives, in spite of his age, if he saw the way they were behaving.

"That may be the case," Mariah went on. "But it is inadvisable to strike up a conversation with men to whom we have not been introduced by a trusted friend."

"Mariah," Victoria hissed, no longer trying to pretend she wasn't irritated.

"Tell us who your friends are and we'll get them to do all the formal stuff," Lt. King said.

"Well," Victoria began. "We're friends with—ouch!"

Mariah tugged her sister away from the officers, more certain than ever that they were up to no good, and that Victoria didn't have the slightest sense of danger.

"That was unspeakably rude," Victoria hissed as Mariah rushed them along the street and into MacTavish's Bookshop. "They were only trying to talk to us."

Mariah sighed, glancing out the window to make sure the men hadn't followed them. Sure enough, they crossed the street and entered the pub. She turned to Victoria. "My dear, a handsome face does not make for a handsome character."

"Maybe not," Victoria said, crossing her arms, "but you haven't smiled at a single man since Robert died." Her expression softened to concern beyond her years. "It's not good for you."

Guilt clenched Mariah's gut, but she couldn't let affection for her sister cloud the fact that Victoria was a poor judge of character. "Papa and Mama would be beside themselves if they saw you flirting with strange men in the street."

"I wasn't flirting," Victoria insisted. Her face instantly pinched in guilt. "Much. You hardly gave me a chance." Mariah fixed her with a hard stare. "And besides," Victoria went on, brimming with restless energy. "How am I supposed to meet any eligible men if you keep yanking me away from every prospect that comes through town."

"You don't know if they were eligible," Mariah told her. "And you'll have plenty of opportunities to meet suitable men through the appropriate means. You're only nineteen."

"You were only twenty when you got engaged to Robert," Victoria snapped. "Oh." She clapped a hand to her mouth, cheeks going pink with embarrassment. "I'm sorry, Mariah. I didn't mean to—"

"It's all right," Mariah sighed, moving away from the window. "I wish you all wouldn't be so anxious about mentioning Robert around me." She headed toward the counter near the back of the shop's front room.

"Yes, well, it's been five years since Robert died, but you're still...." She gestured to Mariah's dress.

"Purple suits me." Mariah said with a shrug. It did, but that wasn't the reason she continued to wear mourning for a fiancé who had died a fortnight before their wedding. It was easier for everyone in Aylesbury to see her as the grieving sweetheart beset by tragedy than to know that she was a slighted spinster whose fiancé had run off with a milkmaid, only to be struck by a speeding carriage in the middle of his flight. And for the sake of her own pride, it was less humiliating to think that every man from Aylesbury to London stayed away from her out of respect for a beloved, fallen friend than because she'd been stuck with a reputation for being frigid.

"Ah, Miss Travers, Miss Victoria." Mr. MacTavish greeted them as they approached the counter. "What can I do for you today? I have some lovely books of devotional stories you might be interested in."

Victoria turned up her nose and made a sound of disgust before being distracted by a stack of new, French fashion periodicals.

"I've been told that you have the new book of poems by the American, Walt Whitman, in stock," Mariah said, resting her hands on the counter and smiling.

Mr. MacTavish's smile turned from welcoming to condescending. "Now, Miss Travers. You know I can't sell you that book."

"What?" Mariah blinked. "Why ever not?"

He chuckled lightly, as he would to a child. "I think you know why."

"No," she insisted. "I do not."

Mr. MacTavish sighed. "The poetry of Mr. Whitman isn't appropriate for ladies such as yourself."

"I'm sorry?" Mariah blinked rapidly, shaking her head. "You've never had any trouble selling me books of poems before."

"Well, yes. There's nothing untoward in the poetry of Matthew Arnold or Tennyson," Mr. MacTavish explained.

"And there's nothing untoward about Whitman either," Mariah insisted.

Again, Mr. MacTavish chuckled as though she were an ignorant and foolish child. "I'm afraid you'll find that you're wrong about that assumption, Miss Travers."

Irate prickles raced down Mariah's back. "I'm wrong?" she asked, teeth clenched.

"You know full well that I cannot sell inappropriate reading material to unmarried women," Mr. MacTavish said.

"My marital state has nothing to do with my ability to read and appreciate poetry, Mr. MacTavish."

"But I would not be a responsible bookseller if I allowed such incendiary material into your hands, my dear."

Frustration boiled through Mariah. "It's a book, Mr. MacTavish. A single, solitary book. Surely the world will not fall apart if I read one book of poetry."

"I'm sorry, but I wouldn't be able to sleep at night knowing that I put reading material of that nature into the hands of an unwed woman."

The worst part was, he was sincere in his beliefs about what Mariah should or shouldn't be exposed to. As much as it made her want to stomp and shout, and as much as it twisted her stomach, Mr. MacTavish honestly believed he was doing the right thing.

"Perhaps you could have your father come in and purchase the book for you," Mr. MacTavish suggested. "I would feel right selling it to him, and if he deems it suitable to pass the book along to you, then so be it."

"No, thank you, Mr. MacTavish," Mariah said,

amazed that steam wasn't pouring out of her ears. "Come along, Victoria."

"Oh, but I'd like to buy this magazine," Victoria said, placing the periodical on the table.

"Yes, indeed, Miss Victoria." Mr. MacTavish smiled at Victoria with an indulgent happiness that brought Mariah to the edge of tears.

It was like looking through a glass and seeing the woman she had once been. The world was wide open to the young and pretty who didn't have a single ambition in their head beyond attracting a handsome mate. Mariah wished with all her heart that Victoria would find and secure that mate as soon as possible. Nothing was worse than the perpetual adolescence of a single woman left on the shelf. It wasn't just books of poetry. She could hardly go anywhere without her father's approval and a chaperone. At balls and parties, she was expected to stay seated at the edges of the room with the widows so that the younger ladies had a chance. And all because of the curse of having been born a female and having once failed at marriage.

"Come along," she said, holding the shop's door open for Victoria to walk through while leafing through her purchase. "If we hurry, we can still make it home while Mrs. Wentworth's tea cakes are warm."

"Mmm. I love it when the tea cakes are fresh from the oven," Victoria said with a grin and a lift of her shoulders. "The butter melts divinely."

Mariah tried to share her sister's smile, but her heart

wasn't in it. It was a glorious thing to have no other cares than whether the butter melted at tea or not.

"It's a shame that Mr. MacTavish wouldn't sell you a silly book," Victoria said when they were halfway home, walking amongst the larger houses inhabited by the more prosperous inhabitants of Aylesbury. Mariah was surprised that she'd been paying attention at the shop.

"It's nothing," she sighed, feeling as though, in fact, it were a very large something indeed.

"I don't know why you care so much about books anyhow." Victoria shrugged. "Not when there are handsome officers in town. I bet someone will throw a ball soon and they'll be invited. Ooh! A party would be just the thing right now. Ever since seeing this illustration here, I've wanted to remake my green dress in this style." She held open the page for Mariah to see.

"Ever since?" Mariah arched a weary eyebrow. "That long, eh?"

Victoria completely missed her sarcasm. She continued to chatter away about frills and flounces, skirts and bodices, and all of the things Mariah had once cared about but left by the wayside.

Her spirits were as flat as a platter by the time they reached home, which was why it came as such a surprise when her mother greeted them in the hallway with, "Mariah, your father and I would like to speak to you right away in the office."

"Papa's up?" Victoria asked, bursting into a smile.

Their father, Sir Edmund Travers, had been away in

London, attending Parliament, and had only just returned home late the night before. As a respected member of the House of Commons, his duties to country usually came before his duties to family, so it was an unexpected treat when he was there to lavish much-craved affection on his wife and daughters.

"Yes," their mother answered. "And we have something most exciting to talk to you about."

"Me?" Mariah exchanged a look with Victoria.

"Yes, you, dear. Now come along." Their mother hooked her arm through Mariah's and tugged her away, down the hall to her father's office.

"Tell me everything when you're done," Victoria whispered after them.

Mariah was too startled to reply, and before she knew it, she was standing in front of her father's desk as her mother shut the office door.

"Mariah, my dear heart," her father said, getting up as though he sat on a spring and coming around the desk to hug her. "My dear, sweet girl."

"Papa." Mariah hugged him back, soaking in every bit of the rare and wonderful hug. Suddenly, none of the frustrations of the afternoon mattered a bit. Her irritation was gone, and all she could feel was affection for her father.

"Now, Poppet," her father said, letting go of her at last. Mariah didn't even mind that he used the term of endearment he'd used when she was a tiny girl. "Let's sit down and have a chat. Your mother and I have something exciting to discuss with you."

Mariah glanced to her mother, whose hands were clutched to her heart in expectation. On top of that, she looked near tears.

"What's going on?" Mariah asked. "Is something wrong?"

"No, no. Far from it."

Rather than gesturing for her to sit in the chair in front of his desk in a businesslike manner, her father guided her to the long, leather sofa near the fireplace, his arm around her waist. Her mother came to sit on one side of her as her father sat on the other.

"I just want you to know that I'm very happy about this," her mother said. "And your father has my full support."

"Full support for what?" Mariah asked, half laughing, half crawling out of her skin with impatience.

Her father took a breath, then shifted to face her. "My dear, I've found a husband for you."

Mariah blinked, convinced she hadn't heard her father right. "I beg your pardon."

"I've found a husband for you," her father repeated as though the Queen had given him a medal.

Mouth open, Mariah turned to her mother. But where she'd been expecting confusion equal to her own, Mariah found only wide-eyed excitement. Her mother nodded enthusiastically and gestured to her father.

"You've found me a husband." Mariah blinked. "I didn't know I was looking for one."

"Well, you might not have been looking," her mother said, bearing a sudden resemblance to Victoria. "But all women need husbands. And we've been so concerned for you since Robert died."

"Yes, yes. Terrible business, that." Her father flushed and looked embarrassed.

"Besides, darling." Her mother rested a hand on Mariah's knee. "The life of a spinster doesn't suit you."

Mariah let out an undignified grunt of total agreement before she could stop herself. It was a little embarrassing to have what she knew so well pointed out to her, though. And by her mother.

"But...." She squirmed in her seat, glancing from mother to father. "How did this come about? It's not the Middle Ages, after all. Fathers don't simply go out and procure husbands for their daughters anymore."

"No, of course not," her father said, then burst into a smile. "It was a happy bit of coincidence, actually."

"Oh?"

"Yes, do tell the story, Edmund," her mother said with a girlish gleam in her eyes. "It's such a lovely story."

"Well," he said, "it all started about eighteen months ago—"

"Eighteen months?" Mariah shook her head. "And you're just telling me about it now?"

"About eighteen months ago," her father repeated,

with more emphasis, "a good friend of mine, Lord Peter deVere, expressed to me his wish to remarry."

"Oh?" Mariah searched her memory, but she couldn't remember her father ever mentioning a Lord Peter deVere before.

"Yes," her mother added. "His first marriage is such a tragic story."

Mariah pressed her lips together. No doubt her father had seen her romantic past as tragic as well and felt she and Lord Peter had something in common.

Her father held up a hand to brush her mother's interruption away. "Peter is a trusted friend, and his first wife, Anne, died without giving him an heir. I took the liberty of mentioning you, Poppet, and of putting you forth as a candidate to provide him with that heir."

"Papa!" Mariah pressed a hand to her suddenly hot face. "Please tell me you didn't present me to this man as breeding stock."

"No, no." Her father's brow furrowed, then his eyebrows popped to his hairline. "Oh dear, no. I didn't mean it like that at all."

"Thank heavens." Mariah pressed a hand to her thumping heart. She winced slightly and asked, "How did you say it?"

Her father shrugged. "Peter mentioned he needed to remarry. I said I had a daughter who would make a good wife."

Mariah bit her lip, not sure that was much better. "And he said...what?"

"He said he'd be interested in meeting you," her father said.

Mariah searched her memory once again, scrambling to remember if she had ever met anyone who might even remotely be the man her father was talking about. She'd had a season in London before Robert declared his intentions, but after his death, she'd stayed far away from town. She remembered quite a few young men, but her father's friends tended to be older. He was particularly close with a group of men who had served with him in the Crimean War, but that was ages ago. All of those friends served in either the House of Commons with him or the House of Lords, and Mariah had met them so few times that she couldn't match the bits and pieces of names she remembered to faces.

She shook her head, bringing herself back to the present. "If that conversation was eighteen months ago, why am I only hearing about it now?"

"Well, er...." Her father cleared his throat. "I may have mistaken the seriousness of Peter's intent for a while. Apparently, he warmed to the idea of marrying you right away and, uh, has had his heart set on it for all this time."

"But you didn't tell me?" Mariah wasn't sure whether to be offended or to laugh at the ridiculousness of it all.

"Your father is a very busy and important man," her mother reminded her. "He and his colleagues are engaged in a valiant struggle in Parliament to increase the rights of women throughout the country."

It was true. Her father was well known as a champion of property and personal rights for women in Great Britain. He and his friends were hard at work writing a bill that would extend a variety of legal protections to women—married women, that was—which they currently didn't have.

"But surely you could have found time to inform me that a man had determined to marry me, Papa," Mariah said.

"I wasn't aware of his level of intention," her father defended himself, red-faced with embarrassment.

"When did you become aware of it?"

Her father hesitated, cringed, then answered, "Three days ago."

"Three days?" Mariah nearly leapt from the sofa in alarm. "You found out three days ago that this friend of yours was serious about marrying me?"

"Yes." At least her father had the good sense to look sheepish. "The timing was my oversight entirely. But that doesn't mean I don't approve of the match. On the contrary. Peter is as fine a man as any woman could hope to marry."

"He is," her mother agreed. "I've met him. He's a kind and generous soul."

"But I don't know him," Mariah argued.

"Precious few women truly know their husbands before they are married," her father blustered on.

Mariah could have argued with him. Times had changed from when he and her mother were young, after all. But before she could form an argument, her mother blurted. "He's an earl, Mariah. The Earl of Dunsford. You would be a countess." She beamed with glee.

Mariah was speechless. She'd never been the sort to hunger for things like titles and wealth. All she needed to survive in life was a modest home and the freedom to read what she wanted to without being treated like a child. But to suddenly be offered the title and life of a countess? It didn't seem real.

"Peter has a lovely estate in Cornwall," her father explained. "Part of the property is on the English Channel, but the majority of it is inland. The deVere family have made their fortune through mining these last few generations. And Starcross Castle is listed as one of Southwestern England's most beautiful manor houses.

"Starcross...Castle?" Her last word came out as a squeak.

"I can picture you as the mistress of a castle," her mother said, clasping her hands to her heart.

Mariah's brain felt as though it were working through molasses. It was utterly impossible that an earl would appear out of nowhere, wanting to marry her and make her mistress of a castle by the sea. Her, poor Mariah Travers, forgotten and rejected, and on the verge of permanent spinsterhood. The notion of being pursued by a wealthy earl was ridiculous.

"When—" Her voice cracked, so she cleared her throat and started again. "When will I have a chance to meet Lord Peter?"

"Ah. Well." Her father shifted and tugged at his collar. "The thing is, he's coming tomorrow."

"Tomorrow?" Mariah's eyes went wide.

"Yes, and he's under the impression that the two of you will be married this Friday."

"*This Friday?*" Mariah could only gape for a moment before asking, "Why is he under that impression?"

"Because that's what I told him," her father confessed with a sigh, his posture slipping. "But if you don't want to marry him, I can call the whole thing off and send him on his way."

"But darling." Her mother grasped her arm, looking at her seriously. "You won't get another offer of marriage after this."

The room went silent. Mariah licked her lips, staring at her mother. The instinct to contradict her made a weak attempt to assert itself, but quickly withered. Her mother was right. At her age, it was unlikely enough that she would receive another proposal. But considering that almost everyone of their acquaintance knew she hadn't been good enough to keep Robert interested, the choice before her wasn't much of a choice at all. She could either marry this friend of her father's, whom she didn't know, or she could continue with her life of perpetual childhood, never fully admitted to adult society. It was a choice between freedom and the unknown or a lifetime of sameness.

"All right," she said, her voice barely more than a wisp.

"All right?" her mother asked.

Mariah glanced between her mother and her father. "I'll marry your friend, Papa," she said. "I'll marry him Friday."

"Excellent, Poppet." Her father let out a loud breath of relief and pulled a handkerchief from his pocket to mop his brow. "You had me worried for a moment there. I don't know what I would have told Peter if you'd said no."

"You won't have to tell him anything but yes, yes, yes," her mother said, giggling with joy. "Oh, this is wonderful," she sighed. "My daughter, a countess. And this means that you will be able to introduce Victoria to suitable, titled gentlemen as well."

"One thing at a time, Mama," Mariah said, cracking a smile at last and resting a hand on her mother's knee.

She probably would have an opportunity, as a countess, to introduce Victoria to a better class of men than she currently seemed drawn to. And it would be a formidable challenge to administrate a castle, as would be her duty. And providing Lord Peter with an heir? Well, she would worry about that particular duty when she had to, and not a second sooner.

CHAPTER 2

*H*ope was a sentiment Peter deVere had given up on more than a decade ago. Hope led to expectations, and when those expectations weren't met, it led to disappointment. And, at fifty, Peter was tired of being disappointed. He was tired of chasing dreams that never became reality, and he was tired of picking up the pieces of hearts that had been broken, especially his own. He was just tired.

So when the carriage his friend Edmund had sent to pick him up from the train station rattled along the sunny streets of the idyllic English village, past cottages with window boxes bursting with flowers and small, thriving businesses, he focused on the scenes around him, not what awaited him at Edmund's house. A group of children chasing a goose in the yard beside one of the cottages caught his eye and made him smile, but he was quick to tamp down the hope that by this time next year, he would have a child of his own to love and indulge. His expectations of a child had been disappointed so many times now that even such a joyful sight as children playing pierced him with pain.

He turned away from the carriage window, cleared his throat, and rolled his shoulders to shake some of the stiffness of travel from his limbs. He wouldn't let himself hope, but he could list the facts. Edmund's daughter was of child-bearing age. She was not Anne. And Anne's fifteen miscarriages had proven that he was, in fact, capable of siring offspring. It was not hope, but rather statistics which said that this time, things would be different.

That didn't stop the mantle of weariness from pressing down on him, though. This time *could* be different, but what if it wasn't?

The carriage slowed before turning into a half-circle drive in front of a moderately large house. Edmund did well for himself, but he was known for being frugal. His Aylesbury house looked comfortable, its gardens well-tended, and the footman that scurried to open the carriage door for him disciplined. But it wasn't the outer trappings of Edmund's prosperity that sent a jolt of wariness straight to Peter's gut. It was the neat, happy line of people waiting to greet him—Edmund, his wife Emily, and their two daughters. The younger was spritely and fresh, but it was the older daughter, his fiancée, that captured his focus.

Mariah Travers looked younger than he imagined she

would. Her oval face was lovely, with shapely lips and warm, brown eyes. She was a bit pale, but a healthy flush painted her cheeks. The purple dress she wore was fashionable and suited her coloring. She looked a bit nervous, which was unsurprising, considering the circumstances.

As soon as the footman had the steps in place, Peter cleared his throat again, brushed his fingers through his hair—he should have had it cut before coming, as curls on a man of his age were ridiculous and only emphasized how white it had become—straightened his jacket, then stepped down to face his future.

"Thank you," he murmured to the footman, then drew in a breath and started toward Edmund.

The girls looked right past him, still watching the carriage expectantly. Peter's heart sank in an instant.

"Where is he?" the younger daughter—Victoria, if he remembered correctly—asked. She frowned at the empty carriage, then turned to him. "Are you Lord Peter deVere's father?"

The sinking feeling in Peter's gut expanded to dread. "No," he answered, painstakingly polite, with what he hoped was an apologetic smile. He shifted that smile from Victoria to Mariah, hoping, praying she would forgive him for being old.

"Ah, Peter." Edmund stepped forward to greet him, more flushed than usual. His glance darted anxiously to his daughters as Victoria gasped. "Such a pleasure to see you've arrived in one piece."

"Edmund." Peter nodded and took his friend's hand.

A shake wasn't enough for Edmund, and Peter found himself drawn into an embrace. It gave him the split-second he needed to study his intended before having to face her directly.

Mariah's eyes had gone wide with surprise, and her blush deepened, but it was clear as day that he was not what she was expecting. Not by a long shot. Hope, once again, had descended into disappointment. Only this time, he was the disappointment.

"You remember my wife, Emily." Edmund let go of him and stepped back, gesturing to his wife.

"It's such an honor to have you in our home, my lord," Mrs. Travers greeted him with warmth that bordered on adoration.

"Please." Peter shook his head slightly. "Under the circumstances, Peter will do."

"Oh no," Mrs. Travers protested. "You are an earl. It *must* be 'my lord'."

Peter tried not to wince. "As you wish, madam."

"And these are my daughters," Edmund went on, gesturing to the young women. "Victoria is my youngest, and, of course, this is Mariah." He smiled at Mariah with a pride that Peter found admirable.

But before Peter could do more than make fleeting eye-contact with Mariah, Victoria burst out with, "He's ancient!"

Mrs. Travers gasped audibly. Panic flooded Edmund's eyes. But Mariah's reaction was the only one Peter cared about. Her reaction determined the course of the rest of his life. And she merely pressed her lips together, flushed harder, and glanced down in embarrassment. Peter had no idea if that embarrassment was for her sister or because of him.

"How do you do?" He fell back on the manners that had been drilled into him, both by his strict father and by his years of military service, standing straight and bowing crisply. Every nerve in his body was taut, until Mariah glanced up through her thick lashes and met his eyes. His heart thudded against his ribs, and he managed a smile.

"I'm quite well," she answered, bobbing an awkward curtsy, as if she weren't sure how she should be greeting him.

It wasn't the most passionate or smooth meeting of future spouses that had ever occurred, but at least it wasn't a total disaster. At least it wasn't—

"You can't marry him," Victoria whispered to her sister. She hid behind her hand, but her eyes remained locked on Peter, and she wasn't quiet enough. "He's an old man. He has white hair."

"Victoria, hush," Mrs. Travers snapped at her.

"But Mama, she can't," Victoria went on, trying not to move her mouth as she spoke. "She just can't. He's all wrinkled." She smiled politely at Peter, unaware that he'd heard everything she'd said.

He shouldn't have let the indelicate observations of a girl barely out of the schoolroom affect him, but he was only human. He squared his shoulders, trying to ignore the pang of self-consciousness squeezing his stomach.

Time was the enemy of all men, but he'd thought he'd done well fighting it. He stayed active and had kept his physique from turning soft, but he was well aware that he had lines around his eyes, and there was no denying his white hair.

"I can assure you, neither of my feet are in the grave," he replied, praying that his attempt at humor wouldn't make things worse.

Victoria snapped her mouth shut and blushed, embarrassed to have been overheard after all. Better still, a hint of a smile tugged at the corners of Mariah's lips.

"Of course not," Mariah said. "And please forgive my manners. It's a pleasure to meet you." She held out her hand.

Peter stepped forward and took it. The moment meant everything, and he struggled to know how to handle it. Should he pretend familiarity with her, since they were engaged? Should he show respect and keep his distance, or would that come off as too cold? Was she as repulsed as her sister, and if she was, could he, in good conscience, make her go through with the wedding? If they didn't wed, then what would he do?

All of those thoughts struck him within the instant it took to raise her hand to his lips and to meet her eyes. It was perhaps too formal and old-fashioned of a way to greet a modern woman, but he had to use every tool at his disposal to prevent Mariah Travers from despising him for not being younger. Because the more seconds that ticked by, the more his chest ached with that devil hope, and the more he wanted this union to work out. The only hint he had that he wasn't making a complete hash of it was Mariah's smile and the kindness in her eyes. Even if that kindness had a touch of pity in it.

"Well." Edmund clapped his hands, dispelling the tension of the moment. "Now that that's out of the way, why don't we all go inside and have a cup of tea?"

"Yes, that's exactly what we should do," Mrs. Travers agreed, taking her husband's arm. They started into the house, and Mrs. Travers nodded to Mariah, indicated the way her arm was joined with her husband's, then tilted her head to Peter.

Peter caught the startled flash in Mariah's eyes at the subtle command. "We don't have to," he whispered as he stepped to Mariah's side, meeting her eyes with a conspiratorial look.

She let out a relieved breath, and the two of them continued into the house side-by-side, not touching. Victoria brought up the rear, grunting in disgust.

Two questions battled for supremacy in Mariah's head throughout tea: what were her parents thinking and what happened to make Lord Peter deVere so sad?

"Of course, it will be several years until the bill is perfected enough to come before Parliament for a vote," Lord Peter explained the legislation that he was working on in the House of Lords. It was a variation of the same bill that her father was busy with in the House of Commons, a bill that would increase the rights of women. He sat in a stiff, upholstered chair diagonal from where Mariah sat wedged between her mother and father on the sofa. "We hope to do a great deal of good for a great many people once it comes up for a vote."

"How noble," Mariah's mother said. "Isn't that noble, Mariah?"

"Very." Mariah nodded. She sincerely believed it was, but it was next to impossible to concentrate on the particulars of lawmaking—even if the law would benefit her and every other woman—while coping with the surprise in front of her.

No wonder she hadn't been able to place a face to the name Lord Peter deVere when her father had unfolded her future the day before. She had been looking in the wrong generation. Lord Peter was close to her father's age, almost twice as old as she was. Although not quite. He was undeniably handsome for a man of ripe years. Though his face seemed worn, as though he had come through a harsh trial, his features were well-formed. His jaw and brow were strong, and his eyes were a brilliant blue that spoke of wisdom and cleverness. Victoria continued to grimace at him from the chair at the far end of the sofa as though he were one of the slathering, lecherous villains in the penny dreadfuls she read too many of. But the more Mariah studied him—furtively, out of the corner of her eye while his attention was on the conversation with her father—the more she felt that there was something more to him. He was intriguing and, in his own way, attractive.

"More tea, my lord?" her mother asked, tapping Mariah's side and prompting her to do the honors.

Mariah forced herself to hide her irritation at her mother's prodding and reached for the teapot. She glanced to Lord Peter, her brow raised in a silent question.

He hesitated, then answered, "Yes, please."

Mariah smiled and picked up the pot as he held out his cup and saucer. She had the feeling he didn't actually want more tea and was just being polite. She wasn't really in the mood to serve tea herself, come to think of it. As she poured lukewarm liquid into Lord Peter's cup, highly aware that she was right under her father's nose as she did, their eyes met. The sense that they were in this strange predicament together washed through Mariah, especially when he answered her smile with one of his own.

Perhaps he wasn't so old after all. The lines around his eyes seemed to be the remnants of a thousand smiles. Those eyes were a bright, crisp blue, and full of warmth and good humor. And intelligence. In spite of the fact that her parents hadn't offered any particularly interesting topics of conversation, Mariah could see that Lord Peter was a highly intelligent man. But it was the mysterious sadness that hung around him that intrigued her the most. Her father had said Lord Peter was a widower. Had he loved his first wife? Did he miss her?

"I know that Shayles is the big obstacle on your end," her father said, still talking about Parliament and legislation, oblivious to the silent exchange between Mariah and Lord Peter. "Just like Turpin is the opponent in Commons. It'll be quite the challenge overcoming their objections to giving the fairer sex any rights at all."

"Thank you," Lord Peter said softly, then sat back with his fresh tea and turned to her father. "All I know about Turpin is that Malcolm can't stand him."

Her father snorted. "Malcolm Campbell can't stand any Tory. But neither can I, come to think of it." Her father laughed loudly.

Victoria rolled her eyes and stopped Mariah from putting the teapot down with a quick, "I'd like some too." As Mariah poured for her, Victoria made a disgusted face, her glance darting toward Lord Peter.

Mariah fixed her sister with a scolding glare and shook her head before pulling the teapot away and setting it down. As polite as Lord Peter was being, Victoria was acting like a heathen.

"Men like Shayles and Turpin won't stop our efforts," Lord Peter went on. "At least not for long. Women have every bit as much of a right to maintain ownership and control of the property they bring into a marriage as men do."

Mariah's brow shot up, and she sat straighter. "Do you think so?"

He turned, addressing her as though she were as much a part of the conversation as her father. "Absolutely. There is no rational argument as to why a woman should not keep what is hers when she marries."

Mariah smiled, surprised that a man in Lord Peter's position would hold such a view. It wasn't lost on her that a man with views like that would make a fine husband indeed, but before she had a chance to let that encouraging fact settle into her stew of thoughts, her father blurted out, "You hear that, my dear? Marry Lord Peter and you'll be able to keep everything that's yours." He followed his statement with a laugh that had Mariah's face burning hot with shame.

To his credit, Lord Peter looked equally embarrassed. That raised her estimation of him even more.

"I don't have much that I would be in danger of losing by marrying," she said, glancing from her father to Lord Peter.

"Nonsense," her mother said. "There's the annuity from my family to think about."

"Two hundred pounds per annum is hardly enough to cause concern," her father cut in. "Why, Peter here will give her two hundred a week in pocket money, I'm sure." He laughed again.

Mariah's stomach churned with humiliation, but the hint of humor in Lord Peter's eyes stopped her from dying of shame. He wasn't laughing at her father, but it was evident he knew just how boorish he was being. Considering that the two were friends, he probably knew just as well as Mariah did that her father was only making a fool of himself because he was nervous.

"My father tells me that the name of your estate in Cornwall is Starcross Castle," Mariah said, shifting the conversation away from herself.

"It is," Lord Peter answered, seeming grateful for the change. "It's been in my family for generations now. The original castle was constructed in the sixteenth century, during Queen Elizabeth's reign, although many successive generations have made changes and additions to it."

"Oh?" Mariah asked before either of her parents could derail what promised to be the first relaxed topic of conversation since they'd all been seated in the afternoon parlor.

"The central part of the house is the original Elizabethan castle," Lord Peter explained. "With renovations. But the west wing was constructed during the reign of George II, and the east wing was my father's special project. I myself had the kitchens and servant's halls remade with modern conveniences about ten years ago."

"Your staff must appreciate that." Mariah relaxed her stance, leaning subtly toward him.

"Mrs. Harmon, the cook, thanks me at every opportunity she can get," he said, his smile betraying a fondness for his staff. "Usually with pies."

"Pies?" Mariah laughed.

"Cornish pasties are a specialty in our part of the country," he explained. "Mrs. Harmon is particularly skilled at their construction. It's a wonder I don't weigh three stone more than I do." He didn't wink, but his blue eyes contained the same spark as if he had.

"You seem perfectly fit to me," Mariah said.

Victoria snorted.

"Young lady—" Her father sat forward enough to temporarily block Mariah's view of Lord Peter. "—your manners have been sadly wanting today."

"Because I coughed?" Victoria balked. "It was just a cough."

"It was not just a cough," their mother hissed, attempting to be private and failing.

"It was. I swear it was." Victoria's glance shot to Lord Peter. Mariah needed every ounce of will power not to wince at the private exchange turned public.

Their mother sighed. "Your father should have sought out a husband for you as well," she murmured, but not quietly enough. "You need managing."

"I'm sure Papa can scare up another desiccated mummy in the back benches of Parliament."

"Victoria," their mother gasped, looking as though she might either weep or launch into scolding at the top of her lungs. "Behave yourself."

"My behavior is perfectly amiable," Victoria protested, sitting on the edge of her seat. "I am the only one here with my dear sister's best interest at heart. Whoever heard of arranged marriages these days?"

"Plenty of people," their mother said

"Hold your tongue," her father said at the same time. He could have been speaking to either woman.

"We all care very deeply for Mariah," her mother

said, a hard edge to her voice. "This is the last chance for marriage your sister will ever have."

"Lord Peter." Mariah stood, raising her voice to be heard above the mortification that was her family. "Would you like to see our garden?"

Lord Peter stood, setting his teacup aside. "Yes, I would be delighted."

"Right this way."

Mariah stepped around her father before he could rise, and gestured for Lord Peter to follow her out to the French doors at the far end of the room. She was shaking so hard with anger and humiliation that she had a hard time turning the key to unlock the doors.

"Allow me," Lord Peter said softly, opening the door for her. He met her eyes with a look that told her he had a few things he wanted to say, but as far as Mariah was concerned, he would have to wait his turn until she issued a thousand apologies for her dreadful family.

CHAPTER 3

As soon as the door was shut behind them, Mariah turned to Peter and said, "I'm so sorry." Her frustration was obvious, as was the fact that she was near tears.

Peter started to reach for her, but changed his mind about the propriety of touching her when they were unchaperoned. Even though they were engaged. Technically.

"Rest assured, I don't hold you responsible for the behavior of your parents," he said. He glanced over his shoulder at the doors and, unsurprisingly, spotted movement from inside. "Perhaps the other side of the garden would be a better spot to talk." He arched one eyebrow and darted a look to the door.

Mariah let out a heavy breath, her expressive mouth crooking into a grin. "Yes, we'd better."

They took a few steps along the brick path that

wound artistically through beds of spring blooms. Peter offered Mariah his arm, and was rewarded with a renewed feeling of confidence as she took it. More than confidence, a burst of warmth filled his chest and spread through him, loosening the tension from tea.

As they reached a trellis climbing with clematis that had yet to bloom, Peter glanced sideways to Mariah and said, "I'm not what you were expecting, am I?"

Mariah let out a short laugh and met his gaze with a wry twitch of her lips. "I wasn't expecting anything at all until yesterday."

"You weren't?" His back itched with foreboding.

Her weary smile grew, and she paused to turn to him. "My father only just remembered to tell me he'd arranged a marriage for me yesterday afternoon."

Peter's brow shot up. "Yesterday afternoon?" She nodded. "But he first mentioned you to me—"

"More than a year ago, I know." To her credit, Mariah laughed, though it was more ironic than amused. "He claims that he wasn't aware you were serious about the match until recently, and that he was too preoccupied with parliamentary matters to remember to tell me."

"That's—" Peter blew out a breath through his nose and rubbed a hand over his face. It didn't feel right to call Edmund ridiculous and flighty in front of his daughter, even though he had the feeling she would agree with him. At least complete surprise on Mariah's part was better than shock at finding him to be, as her sister had said, a desiccated mummy. "I'm sorry you've been put through all of this," he said at last, no idea what else he could possibly do to make up for the shock of the whole thing.

"It wouldn't be the first time my father let something slip his mind," Mariah said, pivoting back to his side and walking on. She led him toward a small gate set in a brick archway. On the other side was a path that meandered through a meadow toward what looked like a small river in the distance. "Papa is a visionary and a crusader. But the problem with giving all of yourself to causes you feel passionate about is that day-to-day details tend to fall by the wayside."

"Marriage is more than a detail," Peter said.

"Perhaps it would have been if I were as young as Victoria," Mariah said, a hint of sharpness in her tone. "Or if this were my first attempt at it."

"Yes, your father told me you were engaged once before, but that your fiancé died tragically."

"Oh yes. It was certainly tragic."

Peter frowned at the sarcasm of her statement. It was subtle, but definitely there, which told him there was much more to the story than he'd been told. He wasn't one to pry, though, especially when his past was colorful enough to paint a sunset.

Mariah didn't offer any further information about her previous engagement, so Peter moved on. "Seeing as you weren't told about me until yesterday, I would understand completely if you want to call off our engagement. Or if you want to declare that there never was one to begin with."

Mariah frowned, chewing her lip. "Thank you for your offer." She was silent as they walked a few more yards along the narrow path through the meadow, then said, "The thing is, my mother was right when she said you were my last chance to be married."

"Surely not," Peter contradicted her. She wasn't in the first blush of youth, but from what he could see, Mariah was pretty, intelligent, and far kinder than most women would have been in the situation she'd been thrust into. Any man worth his salt would be lucky to marry her.

She shook her head. "I'm seen as inferior used goods here in Aylesbury."

He flinched slightly. "Would it help if I assured you I would not hold any, ah, prior activity with your late fiancé against you?"

"No," she gasped, her eyes wide. "Oh, no, no, you mistake me." Her face flushed an appealing pink. "*That* is not what I meant at all. Exactly the opposite, in fact. Robert was involved with another woman during our engagement, and word got around that my inadequacies were the reason why."

Peter hardened his jaw in indignation for what he could imagine was the way Mariah had been treated. He knew how rumors could damage a woman's reputation, even if there wasn't a lick of truth to them. "It sounds to me as though this Robert did not deserve you."

Mariah looked away. "Perhaps not, but I fancied myself in love with him." She sighed, watching the flight of a crane as it took off from the side of the river at the far end of the meadow.

Peter remained silent, letting her have her thoughts. He couldn't say that he knew how it felt to love someone and to lose them. True, he had cared deeply for Anne, but theirs was a bond of duty, not passion, even though there had been affection involved. At least at first.

"Did your father tell you I was married once as well?" he asked, deciding to match her honesty with some of his own.

"He did." Mariah turned back to him, a look of sympathy in her eyes. "I'm sorry for your loss."

Peter lowered his head. "Anne was my father's choice," he admitted. He smiled wryly. "Most things in my younger days were my father's choice."

"Oh?" She adjusted the way her hand settled in the crook of his elbow, leaning closer to him.

That closeness gave him the confidence to go on. "My older brother, Arthur, was supposed to inherit the title and estate," he said. "I fully intended to pursue the life of a scholar. I had dreams of becoming a professor of history, or even literature, at Oxford."

"Really?" She brightened.

Peter was surprised. He would have assumed a woman would think having no ambition beyond teaching would be tedious. He nodded. "Unfortunately, Arthur was killed in a riding accident. That meant I was suddenly the heir."

"That must have been jarring."

He sent her a weary smile. "It was. Not only did it mean my ambitions in academia were over, my father also decided I should join the army in order to learn discipline and gain the contacts I would need when I became earl."

"Did he purchase a commission for you?"

"He did," he answered flatly. Although his resentment wasn't entirely fair. "I didn't hate the army," he went on. "I made a great many friends that have remained friends all these years."

"Like my father," she said.

"Indeed."

"Lifelong friends are hard to come by."

"True."

He drew in a breath of country air, reminding himself to be grateful for friends like Albert Tennant, Alexander Croydon, Basil Waltham, and Malcolm Campbell. They had helped him through more dark patches than he cared to remember.

"Father also decided that I needed a bride of suitable rank and fortune to be the mother of the future earl," he went on.

"And that was Anne?"

He nodded. "Anne was the youngest daughter of Adolphus Barkley, the Duke of Bedford. She was charming, accomplished, and widely regarded as a beauty. I knew her slightly, but it was our parents who decided on the union."

"That sounds familiar," she said with a smirk.

Peter chuckled. "Everyone thinks they know better than we do when it comes to matters of the heart."

Mariah blinked, then grinned up at him. He felt as though he'd said something that had won him points, but wasn't entirely sure how.

"Anne and I got along well enough," he went on, feeling more at ease as they reached the edge of the river. The path there was lined with stones and looked well-traveled. "Of course, war broke out in the Crimea, and suddenly my commission was more than just a formality."

"So you fought in the war?"

He nodded. "Fought, retreated, fought again, was wounded, fell ill, and nearly died in a flea-infested field hospital, just like most of the Englishmen caught up in that wretched travesty of a war."

"You were wounded?" She pressed a hand to her chest.

"Only a little," he said with a sidelong grin. "I have a scar on my thigh from where I was struck by shrapnel during an explosion. But you only get to see it if you marry me."

Mariah laughed. It was a clear, genuine sound, and it set him even more at ease. She didn't resent him. She didn't think he was repulsive. Her laughter said all of that and brought him face to face with his old enemy, hope.

That sobering thought wiped the smile from his face. "Anne was newly with child when I left for the war," he explained, "but she miscarried shortly after I left."

"I'm so sorry," Mariah said, squeezing his arm slightly.

He managed a half-smile. "She became pregnant again shortly after I returned home, but miscarried again."

He glanced down, the rest of the story sticking in his throat. It baffled him that even now, after all this time and all the disappointment he had endured, the pain was still as fresh as that letter he had received about the first baby while languishing in a Turkish hospital.

They reached a worn bench that sat under a spreading tree, and Mariah gestured for them to sit. She folded her hands in her lap and watched him with her full attention, waiting for him to go on.

"I don't suppose there's a delicate or sensitive way to put it," he said, watching a pair of ducks near the riverbank instead of looking at her as he confessed. "Anne never did give birth. But she was pregnant—" He swallowed, feeling ill at the thought. "—fifteen times."

Mariah gasped, reaching out to touch his hand.

Peter looked at her long, narrow fingers, then dragged his gaze up to meet her eyes. "It was difficult when she was young, but we kept trying, convinced next time would be different." He paused and looked back to the river. "As she passed thirty, however, each…failure had a greater impact on her health. Physical and mental." He closed his eyes. "Every doctor we consulted offered only one piece of advice: stop trying. And I begged Anne, pleaded with her to stop. But she refused."

Quietly, without pity or comment, Mariah slipped her hand into his. Peter opened his eyes, but he still couldn't bring himself to look at her.

"I did everything I could to—" He stopped. Now was not the time to confess to years of attempting to stay out of his wife's bed. He would have to explain far too many things about the darker side of the world, and himself, how he had failed Anne on every level imaginable in his attempts to save her. No one, least of all Mariah, should be forced to listen to those confessions.

"How did she die?" Mariah asked at last, her voice filled with compassion.

He shook his head. "The hemorrhaging from that last miscarriage was too much for her. She was past forty at that point, and never should have—" He shook his head. He was the one who never should have touched her again.

A long, heavy silence settled between them. The sounds of the breeze ruffling the grass and the ducks splashing in the river were soothing, but it would take a great deal more than the wonders of nature to bring solace to his disappointed heart.

"So you never had a child," Mariah said at last.

He shook his head.

"And you desperately wanted one."

He glanced to her in surprise only to find understanding in her eyes. "I need an heir or the estate and title will go to my nephew, William," he said.

"No, I think it's more than that."

Something warm and pulsing broke loose in Peter's soul. For so long, he had been able to convince so many people that his disappointment over remaining childless was for inheritance reasons only. It was widely recognized that his nephew, William, was an irresponsible reprobate and that he would likely ruin everything generations of the deVere family had worked to build if he inherited. Claiming that as his sole concern had spared him the awkwardness of being seen as overly sentimental in a world where men were prized for their aloofness and rationality. But Mariah saw through that, and because of it, Peter was seized by an aching need to have her accept their union, even though it had been presented to her in the most clumsy and shocking way possible.

"I will absolutely respect your wishes if you decide not to marry me," he said, pivoting to face her, their knees bumping. "I will not fault you one bit if you decide the surprise of this whole thing is too distasteful, or if you deem me too old to be a good match for you. But if we do marry, it must be with the understanding that we have children, or at least try." He couldn't discount the possibility that Mariah too would have miscarriage after miscarriage.

"So if you find me physically repulsive because of my age or in any way at all," he went on, "I will not force you to go through with this marriage. I would never force you to do anything." He hoped she understood exactly what he meant. "But sharing a bed would be imperative."

She took in a breath and squared her shoulders,

meeting his gaze—which had probably become far too intense—with a calm look. Then, completely unexpectedly, she burst into laughter. It lightened everything about her, turning her cheeks pink and making her brown eyes sparkle. Before Peter had a chance to be nervous, she said, "What a change to have a fiancé who *wants* to bed me rather than one who would rather tumble with a milkmaid in a barn."

As relieved as her statement made him, Peter cringed. "Is that what happened?"

"Yes," she all but wailed, blinking rapidly, as if fighting tears. She recovered quickly, gesturing as though brushing away the past. "But that was five years ago. I never thought I'd have another chance—" She pressed her lips shut and swallowed, looking up as her eyes grew glassy again.

Peter reached for her hand, but before he could say anything, she let out a breath and asked, "Will you let me purchase poetry by Walt Whitman?"

Peter flinched in surprise. "Walt Whitman?"

She blew out a frustrated breath. "Yesterday, shortly before I learned of your existence and our impending nuptials, I attempted to purchase a book of poetry, but was denied."

"Why would anyone refuse to sell a book of poetry?" he asked.

"Because the bookseller deemed it inappropriate for a single woman. Because in the eyes of the world, were I to remain unmarried, I would be nothing more than a perpetual child, always at the mercy of my father. I have been a child long enough, but I have no wish to jump out of the frying pan and into the fire."

Understanding dawned, and Peter nodded. "I seriously doubt any bookseller would deny Walt Whitman to a countess," he said, grinning. "Or anything else, for that matter. I certainly wouldn't."

She gulped, and a tear escaped at last. She was quick to wipe it away, beating him to it before he could indulge in the sentimental gesture of touching her face. "Then yes," she said. "Even though I didn't know about you until yesterday, and even though we just met, and in spite of the fact that my parents are being ridiculous in this whole thing—" She took a breath and smiled. "I would be honored to marry you, Lord Peter deVere, Earl of…oh, I've already forgotten."

"It's Dunsford," he laughed, taking both her hands in his. "But I insist, from here on out, you call me Peter. As a friend."

"All right," she said, still blinking up a storm as though to stop her eyes from leaking. "Peter. And it goes without saying that you call me Mariah. As a friend."

"Not 'your ladyship'?" he joked.

She laughed and shook her head. "No. Whatever we do, we must proceed as friends. Because I have a feeling we're going to need to combine our forces to survive my parents."

CHAPTER 4

The wedding would proceed. Mariah couldn't think of a single reason why she should reject Peter, and after his confession about his first wife as they sat beside the river, the sentimental part of her wanted nothing more than to marry him and wipe away the sadness of his past, like a heroine in a novel. Her parents were, of course, thrilled. And Victoria was beside herself with misery. But as unexpected and overwhelming as the whole thing was, Mariah was certain she was doing the right thing.

Which was all well and good when it came to sitting across the supper table from Peter and talking about the weather in Cornwall, but as Mariah brushed her hair out that night, the night before her wedding, wearing her nightshift and robe and nothing more, contemplating what was about to be asked of her on an intimate level, a cold burst of trepidation filled her.

"What am I doing?" she asked her reflection, her hands and hairbrush frozen mid-stroke. She glanced down at the loosely-tied ribbon holding the front of her shift together. In less than twenty-four hours, a man whom she'd never met before that afternoon would have every right to her body.

A knock sounded at her door, and Mariah jumped. It couldn't be Peter. He was unfailingly polite and wouldn't possibly anticipate their wedding vows—unlike Robert—or so she assumed—but Mariah trembled as she turned to her bedroom door all the same.

"Are you decent?" Victoria's impatient whisper sounded from the hall.

Mariah let out a breath and shook her head at herself, then stood. "Come in."

Victoria opened the door, rushed inside, shut the door behind her, and launched into, "You cannot marry him, Mariah. You absolutely cannot marry that decrepit old man." Her expression was filled with fiery determination, which, considering she too was in her nightgown and robe, painted quite a picture.

Mariah relaxed and crossed to hug her sister. "I know it's unexpected, and it will be a huge change when I move away so suddenly."

"It's not that." Victoria squirmed out of her arms and started pacing. "If you were marrying someone young and handsome, I'd be the first one in line to bless the vows and throw coins at your wedding."

Mariah crossed her arms. She couldn't argue that

Peter was young, so instead she said, "He's not as repulsive as you make him out to be. I found him quite handsome when we were on our walk." In fact, a bit of sunlight had improved his complexion immensely. That or else getting away from the awkwardness of her parents had done wonders for his state of mind.

"But that hair," Victoria protested. "The lines on his face. Ugh. Imagine what he looks like in other places."

Mariah instantly went hot, not only out of embarrassment over the mention of other places, or the fact that her sister's thoughts would head straight in that direction, but because when she had placed her hand on his leg for a moment during their heartfelt conversation, the muscle she had felt was firm and impressive.

But rather than letting her thoughts linger there, she said, "White hair can happen to a man—or a woman, for that matter—at any age. Michael Morgan was grey at the temples before he was twenty-five, like his father before him. And remember how the Johansen's poor maid, Henrietta, went completely white after her mother's house burned to the ground?"

Victoria made an impatient noise and waved her argument away. "He's old, and you know it. I cannot let my dearest, darling sister throw herself away to a gnarled old—"

"Please stop trying to compare Peter to a villain in a fairy story," Mariah barked, surprised at the vehemence of her tone and her defensiveness. "I believe he is a good, kind man who has endured a great deal of romantic tragedy in his life."

"Romantic tragedy?" Victoria snorted. "Now who's trying to make the man into a character in a fairy story? Lord Peter doesn't look as though he has a romantic bone in his body."

Mariah was certain her sister was wrong, although the only thing she had to base that on was her hope that it was so.

She opened her mouth to scold Victoria for her lack of manners, but there was another knock at her door.

"Mariah, it's me, Mama." A moment later, her mother opened the door and popped her head in. "Oh. Victoria. I didn't expect to find you here." She came all the way into the room, shutting the door behind her. She too was dressed for bed, with her hair covered by a floppy mobcap.

"I'm here trying to convince Mariah to put her foot down and refuse to let you and Papa drag her into this travesty of a marriage," Victoria declared, her chin tilting up.

Their mother started, blinking at Victoria as though she'd grown a second head. "Lord Peter is an earl," she said. "His fortune dwarfs our own."

Victoria let out a frustrated growl and flopped dramatically on Mariah's bed. "Why must everything be about money?"

"Because comfort in life and position in society are more reliable than affairs of the heart, my dear," their mother said, crossing to sit on the bed as well. She patted the space next to her, indicating that Mariah should join them.

"Mama, I do believe you read too many Jane Austen novels when you were young," Victoria scolded. "Single men of good fortune are *not* necessarily in want of wives. Particularly if they are old and shriveled and their prospective wives are still young and vibrant."

"Lord Peter is far from shriveled," their mother protested as Mariah sat gingerly beside her, wondering how much lower the conversation could sink. "He has taken very good care of himself, if what your father tells me is correct. He has never indulged in food or drink, has remained active in the administration of his land and mines, and is an important and respected member of the House of Lords."

"But he's so dull," Victoria sighed, leaning back on the pile of pillows at the head of Mariah's bed with a dramatic flourish. "The best years of his life are behind him. He'll be walking with a cane in no time, and poor Mariah will be responsible for wiping the dribble from his chin."

"Fifty is not a hundred," their mother snapped. "I myself am fifty-two."

Victoria gaped, sitting up suddenly. "You want Mariah to marry a man who is the same age as you?" She made a disgusted sound and buried her face in her hands.

Mariah cleared her throat. "Was there a specific reason you wanted to see me, Mama?"

"Yes, dear." Her mother grew suddenly squirrelish as she turned to face Mariah. "Seeing as it is the night before your wedding, I believe there are a few things we should talk about." Her eyes flashed with anxious mischief. "Victoria, it's time for you to return to your room."

Mortification threatened to swallow Mariah, particularly when Victoria threw her hands down and said, "Absolutely not. Under no circumstances will I leave this room. Especially if you are going to talk to Mariah about...about *married things*." Victoria's stubbornness took on a flash of curiosity.

"Victoria, you are not ready to hear what I have to say," their mother insisted.

"I think I am." Victoria's chin tilted up again. "I think I have every right to know what kind of torture my dear sister is about to endure."

"It's hardly torture," their mother said, her cheeks pinking.

The conversation wasn't going to end well or go smoothly, so Mariah let out a sigh, stiffened her spine, and said, "All right, Mama. Tell me everything I need to know to prepare for my wedding night."

"Victoria?" Their mother arched a brow at Victoria.

"No." Victoria pounded Mariah's pillow. "I'm not leaving. I will hear what you have to say."

Their mother threw her hands up. "Fine. On your head be it, then. But if you dare to share a single word of what I am about to say with your friends, and if word gets back to their mothers and therefore to me that you were the fountain of information on this topic—"

"It won't," Mariah said, tired of the endless prevarication the conversation had become. "Please just get it over with."

"Fine." Their mother cleared her throat, picked at the embroidery of her robe, and blushed even darker. "Well...." She cleared her throat again, then glanced from Mariah to Victoria, then back again. "Men and women are formed differently."

Victoria let out an irritated sigh. "We *know*, Mama."

Their mother snapped an irritated frown at her. "You may be aware of the outward characteristics, but there are different parts which are not displayed to the world."

"That's what I was talking about," Victoria replied in a tone that matched their mother's so exactly that Mariah was tempted to laugh.

"We've seen the differences in artwork, Mama," Mariah said, trying not to laugh.

"Yes, well." Their mother shifted uncomfortably. "Unless you've seen the kind of artwork I do not particularly approve of, you have only seen the male parts in a flaccid state. When aroused, however—"

Victoria made a choking sound and twisted to bury her face in a pillow. Mariah's face, neck, and entire body was hot with embarrassment, not only for her mother's awkward explanation, but from memories of Robert taking her hand and pressing it to his trousers. He had been anything but flaccid, and if he hadn't taken her by surprise, she might have had an entirely different response to his boldness. If she hadn't been too startled to be curious, then everything might have turned out differently.

"I think perhaps we should move on," she said, glaring at Victoria.

"I quite agree." Her mother cleared her throat yet again—Mariah wondered if she should offer her mother water—and took a breath, seeming to study herself. "When a man is aroused, he becomes turgid." Victoria snorted. Their mother scowled. "A woman, however, becomes viscous when aroused."

"*Viscous?*" Victoria raised her head from the pillow and gaped.

"In particular places," their mother went on, unable to look at either of them, and glowing so red Mariah was certain she could heat the room in winter. "The purpose of which is to provide lubrication when a man's member is inserted into a woman's...receptacle. That is, her most sacred vessel, encased between her legs."

Mariah winced.

"Is that the same thing as a cunny?" Victoria blurted.

It was Mariah's turn to make a strangled noise and bury her face in her hands.

"That is a filthy word," their mother said with a lofty sniff, then added, "But yes, it is."

"Oh," Victoria blinked, tilted her head to the side, then repeated, "Ohh," drawing the syllable out. The flash of understanding in her eyes was quickly replaced by fury. "That impudent snot!"

"Did someone speak that word to you?" their mother asked.

Victoria opened her mouth, then snapped it shut. "No." Her denial was too quick to be true. Before either Mariah or her mother could go on, Victoria erupted in a sound of utter disgust. "Mother! You can't possibly expect Mariah to submit to that ancient relic inserting his anything into any part of her. That's...that's...that's *barbaric*."

"I can assure you it's not," their mother said, her patience clearly at an end. "In fact, it's magnificent. The experience is far and away my favorite way to spend an evening. When done right, a woman experiences the most glorious explosion of pleasure throughout her entire body."

"Really?" Victoria arched a brow and crossed her arms, clearly doubting everything her mother said.

"And for your information, young miss, a man does not have to be fresh out of the schoolroom to produce that thrilling sensation. Quite the contrary."

"Mama, I don't think you—" Mariah tried to settle her mother.

But the woman was on a roll and kept going with increasing enthusiasm. "Men might slow down a bit and need increased stimulation for a longer amount of time as they age—which is quite all right with me, as it allows us both to take our time—but women can take pleasure in a great many things with an ever-increasing enjoyment as we grow older. Particularly when there is no longer any worry about getting with child. And believe you me, my dear, I'm sure you'll find that a more experienced man knows quite a few ways to make your time together exquisite. Besides which, once you have had many years to learn each other's likes and dislikes, every night will be—"

"Mama!" Victoria's eyes went wide and she sat bolt-upright. "You're talking about you and Papa, aren't you?"

All of the energy behind their mother's impassioned lecture scattered into pink-faced guilt. "Well, what your father and I do when we are alone is none of your concern."

"Disgusting," Victoria hissed, then followed it up with a sound as though she were going to be sick. "The two of you are relics. How could you?"

"Someday, my dear, you won't be asking that question," their mother said, her jaw clenched.

Victoria continued making horrible sounds and shaking her head as though trying to get the image out of her mind. Mariah attempted to be circumspect about the whole thing, but when she imagined herself ardently embracing Peter, her mind's eye conjured up images of her parents. Naked.

She grimaced and waved her hand as if trying to dispel the images. "Just tell me if it hurts," she said. "I've been told it hurts." She wasn't about to implicate their maid, Hannah, who had painted a grim picture of what went on between men and women all those years ago, when Robert was still alive. Mariah doubted Hannah had first-hand experience of the whole thing to begin with.

"The first time can be a bit of a shock," their mother admitted. "If a woman's hymen hasn't already been torn while riding or during some other vigorous activity."

"Good lord, what's a hymen?" Victoria asked.

Both their mother and Mariah ignored her. Thankfully.

"I didn't experience *that* much pain," their mother went on. "I was far more preoccupied with surprise over how the whole length and girth of it felt moving deeper and deeper inside of me."

"You're right," Victoria shouted, leaping off the bed. "I shouldn't have stayed to listen to this." She marched halfway across the room, then turned to scowl at their mother. "Mama, I shall never think the same of you again."

With a final upward tilt of her chin, Victoria turned and marched to the door, then out of the room.

Mariah let out a breath of relief as soon as she was gone.

"You'll do fine," her mother said, patting Mariah's leg, then standing herself. "Lord Peter strikes me as a kind man, and fit as well. He'll know what he's doing. All you need to do is trust him, and I'm sure you, like me, will find yourself enthralled with the new activity, and that you'll welcome it every time he makes advances." A flash of mischief brought a smile to her mother's face. "And you *are* allowed to initiate it yourself, if you so choose. Don't ever let anyone tell you otherwise."

"I won't?" Mariah still wasn't sure what to do with all of the information that had been imparted to her.

But after her mother left, she was still bristling with confusion and embarrassment. How was she supposed to trust a man she didn't know with something so intimate? Even if the marriage bed was as delightful as her mother implied—and the images of her parents together continued to supersede all else when she thought about it—how could she not break apart with nervousness the first time Peter attempted to touch her? And if Peter rejected her the same way Robert had when she flinched....

She got up and walked to her washstand, splashing cold water on her overheated face. It was one thing to stand in front of a clergyman and say "I do," but actually being married, and with hardly any warning, would be the biggest challenge of her life.

Another fit of incredulous shrieking filtered down through the ceiling. Peter did his best not to cringe. Or laugh.

"What are those women talking about up there?" Edmund asked, swirling brandy in his snifter.

"Something tells me it's better not to know," Peter answered, although he had a few guesses. The voice behind the shrieks was Victoria's, not Mariah's, and if everything he'd heard and endured during the afternoon and evening held true, she was probably waging a full campaign to convince her sister to call off the marriage.

Peter sank deeper into his chair and finished off the last of his brandy with an exhausted smile. Mariah wouldn't call off the wedding. He barely knew her, but he knew that much. When Victoria had whined and railed, Mariah had calmly accepted. Where Victoria was flighty and impetuous, Mariah had been circumspect and thoughtful. It didn't take a wise man to see the intelligence in her eyes earlier. And the respect she'd shown for Anne as he related his sad tale to her, well, that had won him over fully.

"Thinking about tomorrow?" Edmund asked, an impish gleam in his eyes.

"Yes," Peter admitted.

Edmund let out a contented sigh. "You have no idea how happy I am to see Mariah settled. She means the world to me."

"I can imagine." Peter sent his friend a tired smile. "Daughters are precious gems." His smile faded into anxiety. And hope. Always hope, as if it were a disease he could never quite be cured of.

Edmund chuckled. "Mark my words. It'll be your daughter someday too, you'll see."

"When I'm nearly eighty," Peter mumbled.

Edmund snorted. "You'll be fitter and sharper at age eighty than any of the rest of us will be in five years' time."

"I'll believe that when I see it." Peter saluted his friend with his glass, then leaned forward to set it on the low table in front of them.

"Of course you will," Edmund chuckled. "You'll have a young wife to keep you on your toes." He downed the last of his drink.

Peter was too exhausted and warm from the brandy to object. "I have you to thank for that."

"It's my pleasure." Edmund smacked his lips and put his glass down as well. "Although I should thank you for relieving all of my worries for her."

"Worries for Mariah?" Peter cocked his head to the side, studying his friend. The more he could learn about his soon-to-be bride the better.

Edmund heaved a sigh. "She's far too headstrong and intelligent for a spinster's life. And if you ask me, she was too good for that rotter, Robert."

"Yes, Mariah told me a few things about her late fiancé in confidence this afternoon." Although Peter was sure there was much, much more to learn.

Edmund snorted. "Robert didn't appreciate her. He would have been better off with Victoria, except that she was barely thirteen when he died. Mariah needs to be more than an ornament on a man's arm and a body to warm his bed."

"Does she?" Peter's curiosity was piqued.

"By all means, give her something to do down there in Cornwall," Edmund went on. "If she feels useful and challenged, she'll be the light of your world."

"And if not?"

Edmund hmphed. "Then you'd be better off letting your nephew, William, inherit the estate."

Peter scowled. "I'd sooner dissolve the estate and give it to the good people who work for me."

"Surely William can't be as bad as all that."

"Worse." Peter sighed, tempted to ask for another snifter of brandy. "Not only has he squandered his mother's fortune and accumulated debts while in America last year, I have reason to believe the money he owes his creditors in London is well beyond what he's confessed to."

"You don't say." Edmund sat back and studied Peter as though watching a particularly riveting play.

Peter shook his head. "The whole point of his jaunt to the States last year had more to do with fleeing creditors and searching for a rich wife than seeing the sights."

"Did he find a wife?"

"No. He couldn't even do that properly. Instead of taking his pick of wealthy young heiresses, he targeted Lady Cecilia Patterson."

"You're joking." Edmund burst into a deep laugh. "Young William thought he could wheedle his way into Cecilia's affections? Why, she's a minx of the first order."

"You don't need to tell me."

But Edmund went on with, "She seduced half the men of our *fathers'* generation. Oh, William." He continued to laugh, slapping his knee.

"It gets worse," Peter went on. "Not only did he fail to marry what he thought was a wealthy widow with one foot in the grave, in addition to the debts that he's still trying to conceal from me, there's a chance that he was instrumental in the death of a young woman who had been posing as Lady Cecilia's maid."

Edmund's laughter stopped abruptly. "Good Lord. William is a murderer?"

Peter winced. "There's no proof." But he wouldn't put it past his nephew to have a hand in the death of someone he felt was beneath him.

Edmund shook his head. "Far be it from me to recommend cruelty, but you should consider turning your back on the young man before it's too late."

"That's just it," Peter went on with a frown, "I can't. William is my responsibility. He has been ever since my brother Will died."

"We all feel a responsibility toward the younger generation."

Peter shook his head. "It's more than that. It's written into my brother's will."

"How so?" Edmund frowned.

Peter let out a breath. "Will knew he was dying. He also knew that his son was a rogue. I promised that I would always have a place for William, no matter what, but Will wanted that set in stone. We drew up a legal document in connection with his will that states I will always provide a home for William at Starcross Castle, come what may. The agreement says that if I turn William out or refuse to give him shelter at Starcross for any reason, he will inherit half the estate, whether I have a son or not."

"But that's ridiculous," Edmund said.

"My brother knew what I didn't, that William is beyond reform. I think he knew William would waste the money he inherited from his mother and lose her family's estate, which he has."

"So what is William doing now?"

Peter shrugged. "Last I heard, he was in London, taking full advantage of all my townhouse has to offer. And racking up more debts, no doubt. I keep paying the ones I know about, which I hope will keep him away until Mariah is well and truly settled at Starcross Castle. It's the debts I don't know about that worry me."

"Yes, I can imagine." Edmund arched an eyebrow. "Is Shayles involved?"

Peter tensed. "Not as far as I know." But even the mention of Theodore Shayles made his blood run cold. Not only was the man his and his friends' chief opponent in the House of Lords, it was well known in certain circles that Shayles owned an establishment, The Black Strap Club, with a particularly devious reputation. If William were involved with Shayles, there was no telling how far he'd sunk.

"You will keep Mariah safe, won't you?" Edmund asked when Peter had been silent for too long.

"Yes, of course." Peter tried to smile. "Once she becomes my wife, she will be my first priority and greatest concern."

Edmund let out a contented chuckle. "I knew there was a reason I suggested this marriage. I predict you will have a long and happy union."

"I certainly hope so."

There was another shriek above them and a thump. Someone—Victoria by the sound of it—said something, then marched across the room, slamming the door. Edmund let out a breath and rolled his eyes. "I suppose I should figure out what to do with that one next."

"If worse comes to worst, send her to Starcross Castle."

"Really?" Edmund asked as though he couldn't believe anyone would willingly take that on.

"Mrs. Wilson will straighten her out right away," Peter joked.

Edmund laughed. "Your housekeeper is a formidable woman."

"I have a feeling my house will be known for its formidable women in no time," he said, then pushed himself out of his chair. "Now if you will excuse me, I think I'll try to get a good night's sleep."

"Absolutely." Edmund stood and thumped him on the back. "You've got a big day ahead of you tomorrow. We all do."

CHAPTER 5

Despite his most valiant efforts, Peter did not sleep well that night. He argued with himself that everything had worked out. He was about to marry a beautiful, intelligent woman who did not despise him—despite not knowing about him until well past the eleventh hour—and with a little luck, in a year's time, he could have the heir he so desperately needed. He would be a father at last.

But ever since mentioning William in his chat with Edmund, Peter's doubts had grown. His nephew was a bounder and a cad. William's voyage home from New York had been catastrophic for Peter's friend, Captain Albert Tennant. Albert's ship had been sabotaged and burned, and had sunk at the mouth of the English Channel. No one could prove that William was involved, but the signs were all there.

Was he a fool for bringing Mariah into a situation that could be dangerous for her? William had his eye on the Dunsford title and estate, his obvious feelings of entitlement growing with every year that Peter had remained childless. Was he being naïve to think that William would accept his new wife without protest, or that he would sit idly by once Mariah was pregnant?

He finally nodded off in the small hours of the morning, but William continued to prick at his conscience, even as he woke, washed, and dressed for his wedding day. As he shaved, unsatisfied with the careworn face he saw in the mirror, he resolved that whatever it took, he would guard Mariah against any threat William presented. And he would pay whatever he could to keep William distracted in London.

The Travers family was in a frantic state by the time he made his way downstairs. Mrs. Travers was haranguing the family maid about simultaneously fetching breakfast for Mariah to take in her room, and packing up all of Mariah's earthly belongings, putting the maid into a state of near panic. Victoria took one look at him as he walked into the breakfast room, then burst into a fit of tears and fled.

"Don't mind them," Edmund told Peter as he helped himself to a light breakfast from the offerings on the sideboard. "Weddings have a way of driving women mad." He saluted with his coffee cup from the far end of the table, and proceeded to tell Peter all about every article he was reading in the morning's paper.

After breakfast, Peter excused himself to run an errand in town. He was surprised to find that his wedding was the topic of gossip on every street corner.

"Out of the blue, it is," a grocer's wife told a customer as she set out the day's produce in front of her store. "Miss Travers didn't have the slightest clue she'd been affianced."

"None at all?" the customer balked.

"Sir Edmund forgot to mention it." The grocer's wife laughed.

"Blimey. If I forgot to mention a whole entire fiancé to my Bess, she'd likely beat me over the head."

And then, up the street, Peter caught the edge of a conversation in MacTavish's Bookshop.

"Apparently, he's some lord her father dug up in Parliament," a middle-aged man said to the bookseller, leaning on the counter. "Old and grizzled, he is."

"Edmund Travers has never seemed like the type who would shove his daughter off on a crony with one foot in the grave," the bookseller replied with a frown. "He loves those girls."

Peter searched for the book he wanted to purchase, then brought it to the counter.

"I'm just telling you what I heard," the middle-aged man said. "Mind you, none of us thought Miss Travers would ever marry. Not after Robert."

"God rest his soul," the bookseller said, then turned to Peter. "That'll be one pound fifty, sir."

The middle-aged man straightened and nodded to

Peter. "Here. What do you think about old men marrying young girls?"

A grin tugged at the corner of Peter's mouth. "I'm not the right person to ask."

He focused on the bookseller as he wrapped the book in paper, but the middle-aged man went on with, "Are you married?"

Peter took his pocket-watch out, opened the cover to check the time, then said, "In about two hours I will be."

Realization dawned in the middle-aged man's eyes, and he burst into laughter. He slapped Peter on the back. "Good luck to you then, my lord. And you're not so old as all that."

Whether it was the exchange at the bookshop or the other rumors flying around town, by the time Peter arrived at the parish church with Edmund and the special license he had procured in town, a small crowd of curious onlookers had arrived. As he waited with Edmund at the front of the church, a surprising number of people filled the pews. By the time Mariah appeared in the doorway at the back of the church, her mother beaming on one side and Victoria weeping on the other, the church was nearly filled.

The ceremony was simple. The tiny church had an organ, and Edmund left Peter at the front of the church to rush back and escort Mariah to the altar while a hymn played. Victoria stood up with her sister, but couldn't bring herself to look at Mariah or Peter. Edmund handed

Mariah off to Peter, then shifted to the side to serve as his best man. The whole thing had an air of the ridiculous about it, which was only made worse when he met Mariah's eyes.

She smiled at him. Victoria wailed behind her. Then Mariah snorted, almost as if sneezing. Peter flinched and blinked, concerned that something was wrong with her, that she would back out, leaving him at the altar. But then her eyes crinkled at the corners, her cheeks flushed pink, and her shoulders shook.

"Are you all right?" he asked, slipping his arm into hers and taking a step toward the vicar, who waited for them, Bible in hand, with an air of celestial patience.

"No," Victoria groaned, and Mariah choked again.

Peter grinned, seized by a sudden tickle. Mariah's eyes sparkled. She pressed her lips firmly together as if... as if trying not to laugh. He could feel the tension of it rippling off of her. She held a small nosegay of flowers in her free hand, but as the vicar cleared his throat to begin the ceremony, she swallowed an explosion of laughter and raised the flowers to her face, unable to do anything but press the back of her wrist to her mouth.

It was contagious. As the vicar began with, "Dearly beloved, we are gathered here together in the sight of God and friends to join this man and this woman," Peter could hardly keep a straight face.

He ventured a sideways glance at Mariah as the vicar launched into a scriptural explanation of the beauties and benefits of marriage. Mariah must have felt him looking and stole a glance, meeting his eyes. Whether it was Victoria weeping behind them, the spectacle of the church filled with curiosity seekers, or the general absurdity of the marriage, that fleeting look broke both of them.

Mariah struggled to contain a peal of laughter as the vicar said, "Therefore, if anyone knows of any lawful impediment, let them speak now or forever hold their peace."

Behind them, Victoria muttered, "Oh, blast it."

Mariah laughed outright, and Peter was helpless but to break down with her. His whole body shook with unexplainable mirth, and his heart felt as though it had grown too large for his chest. That feeling only doubled when he snuck another peek at Mariah and found her grinning up at him, tears of jollity in her eyes. He reached over to lay his free hand on top of hers as it rested in the crook of his arm and tried to blink away his own silly tears.

"Do you, Lord Peter Charles Horatio deVere, take Miss Mariah Travers to be your lawfully wedded wife, to have and to hold, from this day forth, until death do you part?"

Somehow, Peter mustered the nerve to turn to Mariah and say, "I do," without dissolving into a fit on the spot. Thank God they had opted for the shorter version of the vows.

"And do you, Mariah Travers, take Lord Peter Charles Horatio deVere to be your lawfully wedded husband, to honor and obey, from this day forth, until death do you part?"

Victoria squeaked, but Mariah answered, "I do," barely getting the words out before Victoria groaned. That set Mariah over the edge, and she laughed openly, her shoulder pressing into Peter's as she sagged to the side.

Behind them, a chorus of giggles grew amongst the congregation. It seemed only right, even though it was the last thing he would have expected. But why shouldn't the crowd of curious townsfolk laugh with them? It was better than laughing at them.

"Then by the power invested in me by God and the Holy Church, I now pronounce you man and wife. You may kiss your bride."

Peter let out a breath that sounded more like the sort of sigh that ends a bout of raucous laughter and turned to Mariah. She was still giggling, which was a damn sight better than weeping or shrinking away from him in horror. He leaned close and brought his lips to hers before either of them could lose the joyful feeling that so much laughter brought on, and was pleasantly surprised by the spark he felt. She seemed surprised as well, and swayed toward him when he straightened. Her whole face shone as though she'd found a new penny by the side of the road and was eager to see what it could buy.

As he turned with her to face the congregation and walk out of the church as man and wife, he swore to himself that he would be worth the price she paid.

. . .

It came as a surprise to Mariah that, in spite of the fact that three days before, she hadn't known it was about to happen, she enjoyed her wedding day. At least, once she got through the first few hours of fussing, fretting, and tears. None of which were hers or her doing. Her mother had driven Mariah to distraction as she dressed her, groomed her, and fixed her hair as though she were a small child or a doll. But the result was more impressive than she'd have been able to accomplish on her own. And even though she didn't have a white dress—or any new dresses, for that matter—her mother had dug deep into her wardrobe in the middle of the night, found a rose-pink frock that Mariah had worn before Robert's death, and stayed up letting the seams out and embellishing it with lace.

At the other end of the day, after the ceremony—which, she had a feeling, would make her giggle every time she thought about it for the rest of her life—a wedding breakfast that proved Mrs. Boyce, their cook, was worth every penny they paid her, and an afternoon filled with visitors dropping by unexpectedly to wish them well—or to gape at Peter, she suspected—Mariah was once again alone with her mother, this time as she was undressed and prepared for the one part of the whole marriage deal that left her frozen with trepidation.

"Remember what I told you last night," her mother said, taking the pins out of Mariah's hair as she sat on the bed in one of the guest rooms at the far end of the house. Not only was Hannah busy packing up Mariah's room, her mother had insisted that she and Peter would appreciate the privacy of being well away from the rest of the family for the night.

"I remember," Mariah said, trying not to let the dread show in her voice. How could she ever forget the vivid picture her mother had painted of her own marriage bed?

"Just trust Lord Peter, and you'll be fine." Her mother finished with the pins, then took a step back and studied Mariah, her expression full of sentiment. If Mariah didn't know better, she would have said her mother was near tears. "My own, sweet girl," she sighed, as if Mariah were on her way to the guillotine.

A soft knock at the door cut off any last-minute questions Mariah might have been tempted to ask. She stood, brushing the front of her robe and flushing with self-consciousness.

"Come in," her mother said, pressing a hand to her heart.

The door opened, and Peter peered cautiously into the room before opening it wider and stepping in. "I hope I'm not interrupting anything."

"No, oh, no." Her mother sighed, then stepped forward and lifted onto her toes to kiss Mariah's head. She then turned and headed for the door. "Take care of my darling baby," she told Peter, her voice cracking at the end. She let out a watery sigh that reminded Mariah of

Victoria's weepy dramatics, then left, shutting the door behind her.

And with that, Mariah was alone...with her husband.

She pried her eyes away from the door and glanced cautiously to Peter. He was wrapped in a maroon robe tied at the waist. The cuffs and legs of his pajamas were clearly visible at the sleeves and below the bottom. In spite of herself, Mariah let out a sigh of relief. She wasn't sure how she would have reacted if he'd been obviously naked under the robe. He'd brushed his hair as well, and if the clean, spicy scent was any indication, he'd shaved again before coming to bed.

She wasn't sure how long she'd been studying him before he cleared his throat and said, "Well. Here we are."

Mariah swallowed and focused on his face. "Here we are." A distinct tingling started in her hands and feet and spread quickly inward. It centered in her frantically thumping heart and in the part of her that she was desperately trying not to think of as viscous.

"Listen," Peter said, taking a step toward her.

Mariah gasped and took a step back. Instantly, she felt like a heel. "I'm sorry," she said, pressing a hand to her face. "I'm so sorry. I didn't mean to flinch like that."

Peter chuckled, holding up both of his hands. "I don't blame you. I understand."

"It's just that this might be the most awkward situation I've ever been in," Mariah rushed on.

"I can't recall very many situations in my own life

that were more awkward," Peter agreed. "Although I was caught weeing on a statue of Cromwell my mother had in her private garden when I was five."

Mariah burst into laughter. Once it started, just like at the ceremony, she couldn't make it stop. "I can only imagine."

"I'm not sure you want to."

"Oh, but I'm sure you were adorable."

"My mother didn't think so."

There was a pause. They both stood where they were, Mariah giggling and Peter smiling.

Before things could grow any more awkward, Peter said, "I don't think it's a good idea for us to place too many expectations on each other tonight or to rush into anything."

This time, when he took a step toward her, she didn't flinch or flee, she merely said, "You don't."

"No. We've got all the time in the world to reach the point where we're ready."

Mariah smiled. It was a far cry from the pressure Robert had heaped on her. "I suppose we do."

"So why don't we just start by sharing a bed tonight," Peter went on. "Believe me, that takes enough getting used to in itself."

"It does?" She followed him with her eyes as he walked around to the other side of the bed, and removed his robe, revealing simple, blue pajamas.

"Absolutely. For example, how do I know you won't steal all the covers while I'm asleep?"

Mariah laughed and peeled down the bedcovers in question. "Victoria and I used to share a bed when we were younger. She was the cover thief."

"Why am I not surprised?" he said with a wry grin.

She liked him. It shouldn't have come as a surprise, but then again, everything about the situation was different than she expected it to be. Not that she'd been given the time to form expectations. She shrugged out of her robe, laid it over the closest chair, and climbed into her side of the bed as Peter slid into the other. There were plenty of pillows behind them, and in no time, they were lying side by side, the coverlet pulled up to their shoulders. It was a cool night, but not cold, and the breeze wafting through the open window was filled with the scent of May flowers.

Mariah chuckled to herself. "May-December," she said.

"I beg your pardon?" Peter turned his head to her.

"I was just thinking about the May flowers you can smell in the garden."

"And the December fool lying in the bed beside you?"

Mariah smiled, settling onto her side. "You're no fool."

"But I am December to your May. Is that what you're saying?"

"I like December," Mariah shrugged her free shoulder. "December is full of excitement, Christmas, New Year's Eve, and all sorts of celebrations."

"It's not cold and lifeless and, what was the word? Desiccated?"

Mariah rolled her eyes and hid her face in one hand for a moment. "Please forgive Victoria," she said, peeking between her fingers. "She's nineteen and full of herself and the idea that all men of worth are strapping young bucks in officer's uniforms."

"She's not wrong," Peter said, a hint of mischief in his eyes. "I cut quite a figure in my red coat when I was twenty, or so I'm told."

"I'm sure you did." Mariah grinned.

"I still have it, you know."

"Have what?"

"My red coat. My entire uniform, actually. I would have brought it to be married in, but I gave up my commission a decade ago. I'll dig the coat out of mothballs and try it on for you when we get back to Cornwall, if you'd like."

A shivery thrill zipped down Mariah's spine at the thought of Peter in an officer's uniform. She blushed and dismissed her moment of excitement as something worthy of Victoria, but said, "I'd like to see that."

"Speaking of which," he went on, shifting as if trying to get comfortable. His knee bumped into hers, and she didn't pull away. "You looked lovely today."

"Did I?" She blushed, then glanced at the exposed skin above the top button of his pajamas.

"Of course you did," he chuckled. "You're a beautiful woman."

She hummed in assessment of his statement. "I haven't thought of myself that way in years."

"Why not?"

She shrugged. "It doesn't matter whether you're pretty or not when no one looks at you that way."

He let out a surprisingly firm breath. "I'm not so sure I like the way people have treated you in all the years that I didn't know you."

His words were as good as a caress, and the pulse of warmth deep in Mariah's gut grew. "People have expectations of single, young women who are still on the marriage market," she said. "And they often have expectations about widows, even young widows. But no one knows what to do when a fiancé dies so shortly before a wedding. Therefore, no one has ever known how to approach me or where I fit since then. And it doesn't matter one way or another if a woman is beautiful when she exists in a permanent limbo."

She'd lowered her head during her explanation, and Peter surprised her by caressing her cheek and lifting her face to look at him again. "It matters to me."

She smiled, and was certain he could feel the heat of her blush against his palm. He had fine hands too, strong with long fingers. The warmth inside of her pulsed and expanded, and she had to resist the urge to scoot closer to him.

"Were you close to your mother?" she asked, eager to keep the conversation going, but completely inexperienced when it came to talking to a man while in bed, their bodies mere inches apart. "When she caught you weeing on Cromwell, that is."

He laughed. The vibration shifted his legs closer to hers. "I adored her, of course. All boys adore their mothers."

"Did you still adore her when you grew up?" she asked, remembering how she had thought she was too grown-up and sophisticated to show affection to her father when she was in her teens.

Peter's expression turned sad. "I'm sure I would have, but she died in childbirth with what would have been my younger sister."

"Oh, I'm so sorry." On instinct, she reached out and touched his chest. His heart thumped against her fingers. Propriety begged her to pull her hand back, but she didn't.

"It was a long time ago," he sighed, gently placing his hand over hers. "I was ten at that point, with one older brother and one younger brother."

"Two brothers?" She blinked. "I thought you only had the one, the older brother you told me about."

"No," he said. "Arthur was my older brother and died while I was at university. But I had a younger brother too, Will."

"Don't tell me you have another sad story in your past." Her heart squeezed for him, which had the paradoxical effect of making the rest of her pulse with life.

"Not to worry," he said. "Will lived well into adulthood. He served in the army as well, although he managed to avoid the war by taking up an appointment in the Transvaal. He married and had a son, my nephew, William."

Something about the way he spoke of his nephew told Mariah the relationship wasn't a happy one. That didn't make her feel any less as though she were within arm's reach of a tragic hero.

"Will died of a fever six years ago," Peter went on. "I still miss him."

"I'm sure you do." She hesitated, feeling as though the small space between them were buzzing. Part of her wanted to slide her arms around him and give him the hug she felt that he needed so badly, but the rest of her enjoyed the curious energy of their current position too much.

"You seem quite close with your parents," Peter said with the same sort of urgency to keep the conversation going that had prompted her to ask about his mother.

"We are a close family," she said, then laughed. "Sometimes a little too close."

"Oh?"

She shifted a bit, as if to share a secret. The movement brought more of her legs into contact with his and her torso close to his, although their arms still formed a barrier between them.

"You saw the way Victoria is," she said, arching a brow.

"I did," he answered with a twin arch.

The two of them shared a grin reminiscent of the

moment of connection they'd had as they laughed during the wedding ceremony.

"She's only bold like that because, at times, Mama treats us both more as her friends than as her children."

"Isn't that as it should be?" Peter asked.

Mariah blinked in surprise. "Not according to traditional wisdom. Children should treat their parents with respect and awe, or so the books will tell you."

"I would rather love my children and be loved by them in return," Peter said.

The warmth filling Mariah coalesced into a throbbing ache. As soon as she realized the exact location of that ache, a wealth of other sensations sizzled through her. She did her best to ignore them in favor of the conversation.

"I usually prefer that myself," she said, trying to maintain eye-contact with Peter, but unnerved by the depth of...something new in his expression. "But you should have heard her last night."

"What did she say?"

Her breath caught in her lungs as she realized the corner she'd painted herself into. She swallowed. "Actually, she was attempting to explain what I could expect tonight."

"Oh?"

It was one, tiny syllable, and yet, to Mariah, it felt as though someone had just thrown a dozen logs and a packet of gunpowder onto the fire. Every nerve in her body bristled, anxious and impatient, and utterly irrational. She wanted him to kiss her. She wanted him to demonstrate all the things her mother had said, from turgid to viscous. And she still didn't really know him. Worse still, his heartbeat grew faster and harder under her hand as if he knew exactly what she was thinking, what her body was feeling.

She cleared her throat. "I asked her if it hurt, and she said it didn't really. Only that she was distracted by the sensations."

His lips twitched, and a downright devilish gleam filled his eyes. As exciting as December could get. Christmas Eve exciting. "What sensations would those be?"

She worked to hide the trembling that the ache inside of her was starting to cause with a smirk. "I expect you're experienced enough to know all about that."

His eyes sparked and danced as though he enjoyed every minute of her discomfort. "I know," he said. "But I've always been curious about what mothers tell their daughters and whether it's anything useful or complete rubbish."

"Oh, I think what my mother had to say was useful," she said, her voice a tad too rough.

"Really?"

He moved his hand gently over her stomach to rest on her side. The simple movement sent lightning through her veins, leaving her throbbing with curiosity. She should be fighting it. She really and truly should be fighting it.

Instead, she whispered, "What does viscous mean?"

"You don't know?" In the dim light of the lantern on the bedside table, Mariah was convinced she could see the blue of Peter's eyes turn a deeper shade, near sapphire.

She wet her lips nervously. "I know what it's supposed to mean."

"But you'd like to know more?"

She nodded, her breath catching in her throat.

His hand slipped from her side to her hip. "Are you certain?"

He was asking for permission. She nibbled her lip and nodded again.

He drew in a breath and reached farther down her thigh, grabbing a handful of her nightgown and drawing it up over her knees. Then he shifted closer to her, nudging her to her back. The movement was small, but to Mariah, it felt like the undulations of an earthquake. He circled her kneecap with his long fingers, then drew them slowly up the inside of her thigh.

Her body melted into a riot of sensation as his hand moved upward. The ache in her core was so intense it drove her to distraction. Her legs moved apart with each inch he traveled up the smooth flesh of her thigh, but it wasn't until she realized that she was the one moving them, willfully giving him access to touch her more and more intimately, that she let out a squeak of shock. Only, it didn't sound like shock at all. It sounded far more primal, and Peter sucked in a breath at the sound.

At last, his hand reached the juncture of her thighs, and she gasped as he came into contact with the most intimate part of her. Her mother had been right. The burst of pleasure that his touch caused was like nothing she'd ever experienced before. It was like standing too close to a fire or a tree as it was struck by lightning. More than that, it was like discovering parts of herself that she hadn't known existed. His fingers did more than brush, they delved. He rubbed and teased and tested at first, then he slid two fingers inside of her, deeper and deeper, stroking her within. Every movement was slick and smooth, like silk, because her body had made it so.

His hand continued to tease and enflame her, and his whole body moved closer. He nuzzled the side of her head, breathing in the scent of her hair. That was when she realized his breath, like hers, had grown ragged and shallow. The heat radiated from them both like a furnace. More than that, she suddenly became aware that the hot, hard thing pressing against her thigh was him.

She let out a passionate sigh, but the sound instantly frustrated her. It was supposed to be words. She was supposed to be telling him that she took it all back, that they should do much more than simply sleep in the same bed that night. That in spite of the ridiculousness of her mother's explanation, she wanted to feel that part of him inside of her. Even if she hardly knew him. He was her husband, after all, and this was their wedding night.

And then his hand pivoted slightly, and in addition to stroking her on the inside, his thumb made contact with a part of her that might as well have been a flashpoint. In no time at all, the furnace of energy that had built inside of her exploded like a clock wound too tight, and throbbing waves of ecstasy crashed through her. Her inner muscles squeezed around his fingers, and he made a sound that was half triumph, half surrender as she arched against him.

The waves of pleasure began to lessen, but the tension radiating from him felt as though it had just begun. He withdrew his hand from her cunny—it didn't matter that her mother had said it was a crude word, in that moment, it fit—and brushed it over her curls to rest his palm against her lower belly. Of all things, that kept the wild, wanton feeling inside of her burning hot.

"Did you like that?" he asked, a tender note of hope in his voice.

"Yes," she panted. And, seeing in an instant how awkward things could become again if she didn't grab the bull by the horns, so to speak, she rushed on with. "I think I would like it more if we were both naked and it was more than just your hand."

He moved so fast that if she hadn't been so saturated with pleasure, she would have laughed. He swept her nightgown up over her head, throwing it to the side. Then he knelt and frantically worked the buttons loose on his night shirt, popping the last one in his haste to remove the thing. He tugged at the string tying his bottoms, and as soon as he pushed them down, his staff sprung up eagerly. Mariah bitterly regretted that the lantern was behind him and that everything she wanted to see was in shadow.

She, apparently, wasn't in shadow, though. After kicking his bottoms off, Peter paused, gazing down at her. Never had Mariah been so aware of being naked, and never had she enjoyed it so much. Her legs were still slightly parted, and the part of her that he'd made sing continued to ache. Her breasts tingled and her nipples were taut as he gazed at them.

"You're more beautiful than I could have imagined," he whispered.

She wet her lips, wishing she could think of something equally tender and wonderful to say to him. The only words she managed to form were, "Isn't there supposed to be kissing?"

It worked like a charm. He lowered himself to cover her, their bodies touching everywhere, She spread her legs apart farther as he settled between them. The hair on his chest tickled her oversensitive breasts. But it was the surprise of magnificence when their mouths met that sent her right back to the edge of bliss.

It was their first kiss, minus the brief peck at the altar. It was the first kiss she'd had since the ones Robert had impatiently stolen. And it was everything she'd dreamed a kiss could be. He parted her lips with his, demanding, but more because he couldn't hold himself back than from any desire to conquer. His tongue slid along hers, giving her the sensation that they were joined. She wanted more and more of their kiss, never wanting it to stop.

At the same time, his hand brushed up her side to close around her breast. That too was a powerfully delicious sensation. She arched her back to urge him on. He squeezed just enough to make her sigh and raked his thumb across her nipple. All the while, the deep, aching need to be filled threatened to overwhelm her.

He broke their kiss at last with deep, desperate pants, nuzzling her cheek and the side of her head. "I can't," he started, but switched to, "I need...." Even then, he couldn't go on. His hips shifted between hers.

She felt a press of fullness where he had touched her before, but only had a split second to realize his erection was much bigger than his fingers before he entered her. And yet, it was the most divine sensation she had ever felt. She gasped with awe as every last bit of awareness in her focused on the feeling of him stretching and filling her. If there was a moment of pain, it was by far eclipsed by the wonder of being joined with him. It felt so perfect that emotion overwhelmed her.

And then he started to move. It was glorious. Her heart soared as he moved in and out of her, building her pleasure higher and higher. She couldn't hold back the sounds that ripped from her throat to match what her body was feeling. It just kept getting better and better as he moved faster and faster. And, God help her, she felt a whole new level of wanting, of craving, of desiring to be one with him like this. She wanted him and the sensation he was firing in her so thoroughly that it consumed her. And when the explosion of pleasure happened again, she welcomed it like the earth welcomed the first burst of dawn and color and life.

He reached the climax of his pleasure shortly after she did, which was another revelation. She knew nothing about men's bodies, but had a feeling she was poised to learn everything as he tensed and shuddered, then gradually slowed and collapsed in exhaustion on top of her. The sensation was uncanny and wonderful. She loved the weight and heat of him over her so much that even when he was limp and panting, she wrapped her arms and legs around him to feel everything that she could.

"Yes," she sighed as she caught her breath. "Yes, yes, yes, and yes."

To which he answered a simple, exhausted, "Good."

She tried not to, but she laughed anyhow. Everything felt so wonderful that she couldn't help herself. And rather than feeling like things had reached a satisfactory conclusion, she buzzed as though they were only just beginning. She spread her hands across his back, feeling his muscles. She wriggled her hips against his, squeezing her inner muscles where he was still lodged inside of her, much softer now.

He laughed with her, his body shaking in the most delicious way. "Wait, wait," he panted, rolling to the side, much to her regret. "I'm not as young as I once was. Let me rest for a bit, and then we can do it again."

"Good," she repeated, snuggling against him and

pressing a kiss into his shoulder. "Because, as it turns out, my mother was right about a great many things."

And, she suspected, her father was right when he hatched the idea that the two of them would be a good match.

CHAPTER 6

The one thing Peter hadn't counted on in his improbable marriage was not the possibility that Mariah would be biddable in bed. Her willingness was one of the possible scenarios he'd considered, even hoped for, before entering their room the night before. The thing that he hadn't expected was the intensity of self-consciousness when the two of them joined the rest of her family for breakfast the next morning.

"Good morning," Mrs. Travers greeted the two of them with a cheery smile as he and Mariah stepped into the breakfast room.

Like a sentimental boy, Peter had held his new wife's hand all the way from their bedroom, through the halls, and to the breakfast room, but he dropped it just before rounding the corner. He risked a glance at Mariah only to find her blushing up a storm, her face twitching and contorted as she tried not to laugh. He would never be able to keep a straight face while she dissolved into giggles, so he was forced to look at her mother and reply, "Good morning, madam."

"Ah. There you are at last," Edmund said from the head of the table, reading his paper and sipping coffee, a congenial smile on his face, as though it were an ordinary morning with a guest in the house. "Did you sleep well?"

Mariah turned quickly toward the sideboard, snatching up a plate and scooping a fried egg off the platter, her lips pressed tightly together and her face blazing.

"Quite well," Peter answered with his best attempt at banality, though his face and neck were hot. Not as hot as his entire body and soul had been mere hours before. Mariah had surprised him with her enthusiasm all through the night, and he had surprised himself with a vitality he hadn't felt in years. In fact, he felt like a man half his age even now, and loaded up his breakfast plate with enough food to build up his energy for what he hoped would be repeated that night.

The awkwardness continued once Peter and Mariah were seated at the table. Edmund seemed oblivious to the undercurrents of embarrassment that halted their conversation. But Emily kept smiling and smiling until she grew misty-eyed as she studied her daughter.

"Oh, my dear, I'm so happy for you," she squeaked at length, dabbing at her eyes with her napkin. "I was so worried, but I see now there was no need."

"Thank you, Mama," Mariah mumbled, then hid her

pink face by taking a long sip of tea. Peter was afraid she would choke as her shoulders shook with merriment.

Across the table from them, Victoria let out a loud sigh and slumped in her chair. "All is lost," she whispered, adding a second, overdramatic sigh.

Peter wanted to rest his hand on Mariah's leg under the table. He wanted to take her hand again. The urge to be in physical contact with her was overwhelming. But he held back, cutting up his sausages and searching for some topic of conversation that would not draw attention to the fact that he and Mariah had thoroughly enjoyed their wedding night. He would indulge in the newfound infatuation he felt for Mariah as soon as the two of them were alone.

"I don't like this kerfuffle Turpin and his cronies have started over women's employment," Edmund said, turning a page of his newspaper, then folding it and setting it down. "I especially don't like the way he's dragging the church into it."

"Unscrupulous men always attempt to drag the church into politics when they need to be seen as angelic while doing something diabolical," Peter replied, grateful beyond measure to talk about work. "The sad part is that they'll sway the common people to their cause by claiming the moral high ground."

"Makes you wonder about the wisdom of extending the franchise," Edmund sighed, cutting into an egg on his plate with the side of his fork.

"I thought you were in favor of extending the franchise, Papa," Mariah said. "To women as well."

"I'm not sure we're quite ready for *that*," Edmund replied with a proud grin for his daughter.

The awkwardness of having everyone in the room know what had transpired in the night gradually dispelled as Edmund and Mariah launched into a discussion about voting rights. Peter added his bit, but was far more interested in learning how educated and opinionated Mariah was on the subject. She held her own against her father, citing some of the same arguments he'd heard on the floor of Parliament. His fascination with her grew.

He was on the verge of joining the discussion and offering some contrary opinions just to see how Mariah would react, when the family's butler, Graves, appeared in the doorway with a silver salver in his hand, and cleared his throat.

"What do you have there, Graves?" Edmund asked, turning to the man.

"An urgent message has come for Lord Dunsford, sir," Graves informed them.

Peter nodded, taking the letter from Graves's outstretched salver.

As soon as he opened it, his body tensed and a headache formed at his temples.

"What is it?" Edmund asked.

But it was Mariah's quiet look of curiosity that prompted him to tell all. "It's a message from Mr. Snyder, the butler at Starcross Castle. It seems there's been an emergency at the chief mine on my property."

"What kind of emergency?" Mariah asked.

Peter's frown deepened as he read the rest of the letter. "The mine produces copper, or at least it did." He let out a breath, rubbing one hand over his forehead and putting the letter down. "It seems that, as we feared, the copper vein is exhausted."

"What does that mean?" Mariah pressed a hand to his knee under the table, just as he'd wanted to do with her earlier.

"It means that the livelihood of a great many people could be in jeopardy if a new vein isn't discovered," he said, meeting her eyes with seriousness. "It means that I need to return home as soon as possible."

"Then we should go at once," she replied, absolute certainty in her eyes.

He studied her, looking for any sign of fear or anxiety. "You wouldn't mind leaving your family and going off with a near stranger so quickly?"

She blushed and lowered her gaze. "We're hardly strangers at this point."

If they hadn't been sitting at a breakfast table with her parents and sister watching, Peter would have pulled her into his arms and kissed her until she sighed the way she had the night before. As it was, he cleared his throat and turned to Edmund. "I hope you would not think it cruel of me to leave so soon and take Mariah with me."

"Of course not," Edmund said, taking up his cup and

finishing the last of his coffee, then declaring, "We'll get everything settled and be off with you at once."

As he pushed back from the table, Victoria groaned, "No! You can't banish Mariah to perdition so soon. Why, she's barely married at all."

The look Mariah sent her sister contradicted the statement, but all she said was, "It's all right, Victoria. I'm in good hands."

Peter did his best not to dwell on the images of where his hands had been through the night and where he wanted them to be later. In spite of the multiple times they'd made love, he'd only just begun to learn her shape and show her all the ways they could take pleasure from each other. But thinking about the lessons to come wouldn't do him a lick of good when the future of his estate was in question.

"It shouldn't take me long to pack," he said, spearing a sausage so that he could gobble down the rest of his breakfast. "I can venture out and purchase tickets and telegraph my valet at Starcross Castle while you organize your things, my dear."

Beside him, Mariah blushed and smiled. He realized he hadn't called her by a pet name yet. It felt natural and sweet.

"I couldn't possibly pack up everything in one day," she said. "But if it's all right," she turned to her parents, "I could put together enough to travel with and have you send the rest along to Starcross Castle as soon as it's ready?"

"Yes, of course, my dear," Emily said, standing and looking ready to organize an army campaign. "We'll have Hannah arrange it all at once."

The rest of the morning passed in a swirl of activity. The Travers house buzzed like a hive as the servants packed both his and Mariah's things. He could easily have handled his own suitcase, but as long as Graves was there to help, it meant he could make arrangements not only for the tickets, but for an overnight stay in Winchester, halfway along their journey. It was the best he could do to divide their journey into two parts, considering the short notice and infrequency of trains traveling all the way to Truro, the closest station to Starcross Castle.

It was with a sense of the surreal that he found himself saying goodbye to Edmund, his friend and now his father-in-law, shortly after noon as Mariah hugged and kissed her mother and sister farewell.

"This is the most awful thing ever," Victoria wept, clinging to Mariah. "I won't be able to eat or sleep from worrying about you. I'll wither away to nothing, and then who will want to marry me?"

Mariah rolled her eyes, but hugged her sister all the same. "You'll survive," she said. "And you can come visit whenever you want."

"Can I?" Victoria perked up a bit.

Mariah turned a questioning look to Peter.

"Of course you can," he answered with a smile that was more suitable for a child than his wife's sister.

Minutes later, the conductor called for all to board, Peter and Mariah shuffled into their first-class carriage, the door shut behind them, and they were off.

"Well," Mariah said with a sigh, settling onto the seat by his side. "This has certainly been the most startling and eventful forty-eight hours of my life."

Peter chuckled, stretching out his arm over the seat behind her shoulders. "It might just be the most eventful for me as well."

"Which means we're bound for smooth sailing from here on out," she said, settling closer to his side and leaning her head against his shoulder.

The simple gesture set his heart to singing. Mariah didn't have to show him the least bit of affection. Theirs was not a love match, after all. How could it be, under the circumstances? But the tenderness and the trust that she had shown him touched him far more deeply than he could have imagined, awaking a fierceness and protective instinct within him that he hadn't felt since the war. He would do anything to make sure her faith in him was justified.

The train ride from Aylesbury to Winchester passed in a blur. Mostly because both Peter and Mariah were so exhausted that the rocking of the train lulled them to sleep only a few miles into their trip. The sun had already gone down when they arrived in Winchester, but the station was manned with porters who were willing to transport their baggage to the Winchester Royal Inn. Mariah looked as vague and bleary as he did when they arrived at the hotel, so Peter wasn't quite prepared for the concierge's question.

"Will that be one room or two, sir?"

"I beg your pardon?" Peter frowned.

"One room or two?" the concierge repeated. "For you and your daughter."

Peter exchanged a glance with Mariah. Her mouth twitched, and the sleep fled from her eyes, replaced by amusement.

"She's my wife," Peter said, gazing at Mariah with far more fondness than he had any right to show.

"We were married yesterday," Mariah told the concierge.

"Oh?" The concierge's expression switched from confusion to a knowing look that bordered on lewd teasing. "Well then, that's a whole other kettle of fish. Wait right here and I'll see if our honeymoon suite is free."

"Honeymoon suite?" Mariah glanced to Peter in question.

He shrugged. "I don't know. I suppose most hotels and inns have them these days."

It was a fair enough assumption, but by the time he and Mariah were led up several flights of stairs to a room near the top of the inn, he was beginning to question the wisdom of admitting to being newly married.

The room was a sight. The high, four-postered bed at the center of the room was decorated with a maroon velvet coverlet and an explosion of heart-shaped pillows. The furniture was all carved in an elaborate, Rococo style with fat, naked cherubs carved on the edges of the bedposts and the table and chair set against the wall. A large mirror faced the bed and was angled in such a way that left no doubt about what one was supposed to view in it. And to top it all off, the large, framed artwork all around the room depicted classical scenes of the Rape of the Sabine Women.

Mariah slapped a hand to her mouth at the first sight of the room and didn't move it away, or stop shaking with laughter, until well after Peter had requested supper be brought to the room and kicked the concierge out.

"Oh my," she said through her giggles once they were alone, taking in the full luridness of their surroundings. She stared at one of the paintings that left nothing about sexual congress to the imagination and said, "I suppose this is the artwork Mama doesn't approve of."

"I'm not sure it's the kind of artwork anyone's mother would approve of," Peter said, moving to stand beside her, his hands behind his back, debating whether he should do something about the blood rushing to his groin. He couldn't very well make love to Mariah now, the second they were secure in their hotel room. They had to connect in other ways too if their marriage was to be a success.

She turned to him, her eyes bright with mirth. "Have you ever done that?" she asked, pointing to a Roman who had one of the Sabines bent forward over a log while he took her from behind.

Peter cleared his throat. He nodded at the painting.

"Yes." Then he nodded at several of the other painted couples. "Yes, yes, yes, almost, yes, and I think I would probably throw my back out."

Mariah burst into laughter, clutching her stomach. "Oh dear. What does it say about us that I've hardly been able to stop laughing since we stood in front of the vicar yesterday?"

He let go of his last attempt to stay serious and sober, and drew her into his arms, holding her close. "I hope it says that we will have a long and happy marriage, full of good humor and easiness with each other."

A flash of shyness joined the humor in her eyes as she glanced up at him, but whether she was intimidated by him or not, she slid her arms around his waist. "I hope it means that as well. Although it probably means we will forever be laughing at each other."

He returned the sentiment with a lop-sided smile. "Just as long as nobody else is laughing at you." His seriousness returned. "I don't want you to be a laughing stock, Mariah."

She blinked, tilting her head slightly to the side. "Why would I be?"

He arched a brow. "A man as old as me marrying a woman as young as you?"

"First of all—" She settled into his arms with a rigidity that said he was in for a scolding. "—I'm not as young as all that. I was on the shelf when you found me."

"Which I find hard to believe," he said, brushing his fingers across her pink cheek. He was rewarded by the shiver he felt pass through her and flattered himself to think that it was a shiver of desire.

"Secondly," she continued, her voice deeper. "You're not as old as you think you are."

"I know how old I am," he said, settling his hand at the top of her neck so that he could trace the line of her jaw and her lips with his thumb.

"I think you may have your numbers wrong," she replied. "I have been given tangible proof that you are neither feeble nor desiccated, and that your faculties and powers of endurance are in full working order."

He certainly felt powerful with her in his arms. "That is because I am borrowing vitality from you, my dear," he said, gazing deeply into her eyes, eager to discover whether she would ignite the way he hoped she would, or if she would be intimidated when he gave free rein to what he was feeling.

She hovered somewhere in between, her eyes flashing with fire while her body trembled in his embrace. He hadn't burned for a woman the way he did with Mariah for a decade. He'd assumed he was long past the point of losing control when it came to his passions, that Anne's insistent attentions, which had sometimes bordered on punishment, had killed his body's ability to eclipse his mind. But at that moment, he wanted to strip Mariah bare and work his way through every one of the outlandish positions depicted in the artwork around them.

And then his thumb stroked too close to her lips. She

flicked her tongue against the pad of his thumb, then sucked it inside of her mouth. The daring move made his cock jump with need as images of her doing to it what she was doing to his thumb hit him.

He moved his hands to cradle her face, then slanted his mouth over hers in a kiss that could leave her in no doubt of what he wanted from her. She made a sound of acceptance...just as there was a knock at the door.

She jumped, pulling away from him, her face red and her chest heaving.

"Supper service," a man called from the other side of the door.

Peter cleared his throat and tugged at the bottom of his jacket, glad he'd hadn't removed it yet for all that it hid, then marched to the door.

"Hope I'm not interrupting anything," the young porter bringing their supper said, wiggling an eyebrow.

"Not at all," Peter replied in what he hoped was a threatening voice.

"I'll just bring this in, shall I?" Without waiting, the porter wheeled in a cart with two covered plates on it. He winked at Mariah as he moved the plates from the cart to the table. "Many happy returns on your nuptials." He then turned to Peter and muttered, "You lucky old dog."

It was a good thing for the porter that Mariah covered her mouth in a fit of giggles. If she'd been even a little bit put out by the man's teasing, Peter would have grabbed him by the collar and thrown him bodily from the room.

Instead, he simply said, "That will be all," and arched a disapproving brow at the man.

"Right." The man winked and headed for the door. "I expect you'll be wanting to get started. On supper, I mean." His tone implied he meant everything other than supper. "There are some items you might be interested in over in the drawer there, but let us know if you need anything *special*."

"Thank you," Peter growled, and shut the door hard once the man stepped out. He locked it with a satisfying click, then blew out a breath, shaking his head.

"This I have to see," Mariah said, rushing for the drawer the porter had indicated. She tugged it open, then gasped, holding a hand to her mouth.

"Do I even want to know?" He winced as he crossed to join her and peeked into the drawer.

It contained a variety of cords, from velvet to rough rope, a few masks, and a long, rectangular box.

"What do you suppose that is?" Mariah giggled, pointing at the box.

"I have my suspicions," Peter said, his voice flat. He pulled the box to the front of the drawer and lifted the lid. Sure enough, it contained a larger than life, marble replica of male genitalia.

Mariah rolled with laughter, gripping his arm and burying her face against his shoulder. "What mad world have I crossed into by marrying you?" she said gasping for breath. "It's like I took wedding vows then stepped through the looking glass into a universe of, shall we say, *intimacy* that I never knew existed."

Peter cleared his throat and shut the box as well as the drawer. "Oh, this world exists, all right." He took her hand and led her over to the table and their supper, the most normal thing in the room. "In general, one needs to ask for this kind of accommodation deliberately."

"But there are people who actually seek out this kind of silliness?" she asked as he held her chair out, then tucked it into the table before sitting across from her.

"Believe it or not, yes." He removed the covers from their dishes to find, in addition to the beef he had ordered, a hefty helping of oysters. He wasn't sure if he wanted to roll his eyes or laugh along with her. "This is tame by comparison to some of the things I've seen."

"Really?" she asked, fascinated.

He wasn't sure how he felt about her curiosity. Though in truth, he was ridiculously aroused by her openness. He just wasn't sure if he should be.

"It's all well and good when rational adults enter into this sort of silliness, as you call it, freely and willingly, but I've seen far too many instances where coercion was involved, both inside and outside of marriage." Again, he couldn't shake the lengths Anne had gone to in her restless pursuit of the child she was never going to have. He cleared his throat. "It is part of what my friends and I have been working to have included in the law we are attempting to form in parliament, though there is so much resistance to even talking about what women are subjected to in this way that I doubt we'll be able to include provisions against coercion in the bill."

He realized too late that he'd spoken to her the way he would speak to a male colleague, with far too much candor. Her smile had vanished, and her eyes gone wide.

"I'm sorry," he said with a sigh. "I'm not used to keeping my conversation delicate. I shouldn't have embarrassed you that way."

"No, it's all right," she said, taking a small bite of her supper. "I...I just hadn't imagined what things are like."

He studied her carefully as he ate, figuring her vague statement covered a great many things. Her late fiancé might have given her a glimpse of the possibilities between men and women, both good and bad, but he knew enough to know he had been the one to actually open her eyes. He was probably a cad for finding immense satisfaction in that knowledge.

"I'm hoping that Snyder was exaggerating the urgency of the situation at the mine," he said, deliberately steering the conversation in an entirely different direction.

"Do mines run out frequently?" she asked.

"Not frequently, but there are a finite amount of resources in the earth," he said. "I won't know until I've spoken to my foreman, Mr. Sinclair."

The mood between them relaxed, and they continued talking about mines and mining, then the estate in general as they ate. There was only time to share the basics of mining with Mariah in the amount of time it took them to finish their food, but Peter was surprised that she seemed to digest what he was telling her. Edmund's words about giving her a purpose came back to him. It occurred to him that he could involve her in something more serious than redecorating the castle or choosing flowers for the garden.

"Now, do we leave this all here tonight or do we ring for the porter to take it away?" Mariah asked as they finished their meal.

"Please let's not call him back again," Peter begged.

Mariah laughed. "Agreed. I suppose we should get some sleep, then. We've an early train tomorrow, right?"

"Ten thirty." He stood, offering her a hand and helping her to stand as well. "Do you need help getting ready for bed?"

"I might," she answered, mischief in her eyes.

In an instant, they were right back where they'd been before the porter knocked. The delicious sense of blissful madness rushed through him again, and instead of letting go of her hand, he tugged her close.

"I'm sure I can help in a great many ways."

"Oh?"

The single word was an invitation, and he brought his mouth to hers, first with a light kiss, then with increasing ardor. He couldn't remember the last time kissing a woman had been so enjoyable. Or the last time undressing a woman had been a treat instead of torture. It was heavenly to undo every button of Mariah's traveling dress, exposing her warm skin and kissing it in the process. He kissed her shoulders as he pushed her sleeves down, then paused to kiss her wrists and hands as he tugged her bodice off.

He shrugged out of his jacket and shirt as she undid her skirt and petticoats and laid them aside, then was back with his body pressed to hers for more kisses before they continued. The ridiculous bed was high enough off the floor that he lifted her by the waist and sat her on the edge. It wasn't lost on him that she was suddenly at the perfect height for replicating the position she'd pointed out in the painting. All he would have to do was flip her to her stomach and dispose of her drawers. But there was a time for a quick tupping and a time for something much slower and more sensual. So he pulled off her garters and rolled her stockings down, kissing her knees, calves and toes as he did.

"Who would have thought knees could be so nice," she sighed, leaning back on her elbows as he slipped her second stocking off.

"You have no idea how gratifying it is to hear you say that," he said, draping her stockings over the back of a chair, then unfastening his trousers.

"Ooh, do I get to see you this time?" she asked, unhooking her corset.

His moment of disappointment as she finished undressing herself was eclipsed by the thought that she wanted to look at his body.

"You didn't see last night?" he asked.

She shook her head. "The lantern was behind you. What I saw was in shadows."

He responded to that by letting his trousers drop and kicking them to the side, displaying all. And for some ridiculous reason, he felt as green and self-conscious as a youth standing in front of her, naked and aroused. Her eyes went straight to his erection, and her cheeks pinked.

"I had all of that inside of me?" she squeaked, eyes wide.

"And you liked it, if I recall," he said, joining her on the bed and helping her dispose of her chemise and drawers. "Quite a bit."

She shivered as he stretched over top of her, which made him want to be inside of her again, and soon. But he was determined to take his time, particularly since, chances were, she was still sore from the night before.

He should have pushed aside most of the ridiculous pillows covering the bed and slipped between the sheets with her, but the uncanny notion that the velvet coverlet felt uncommonly good against the bits of him that weren't in direct contact with her made him careless.

"Do I get to touch it?" she whispered, looking up at him with an impish glint in her eyes.

"Love, you can do whatever you want with it," he growled, taking her hand and guiding it between them. "And if you don't know what to do, I have a few suggestions."

Even though he was the one taking the lead, he still

gasped when her hand cradled him. More so since she gasped too, her eyes bright with excitement and desire.

"Like this?" she asked, moving up and down his length with short, quick strokes.

"More like this." He guided her with longer, slower movements that had him hard and aching under her touch.

"Oh, I like that," she hummed. "I like that quite a lot."

"So do I," he replied, unable to hide just how much.

"You do," she said with a relish that made her touch so much more potent. "That just makes me want to learn all the ways I can get you to make that expression."

"What expression?" He moved his hand away, leaving her to caress him on her own, and balanced on his forearms above her.

"This one." She squinched her face up in a ridiculous expression that he found thoroughly arousing.

"Is that so? Because I seem to recall you looking something like this last night." He made a face that was a vague approximation of the ecstatic wince she'd worn as she cried out in pleasure.

She laughed. "I'd like to make that face again, if you please."

"All right," he said with mock warning. "You asked for it."

He closed his hand around her breast and lowered his head to take her nipple into his mouth. She sighed with pleasure, and her hand squeezed his cock. He almost regretted that he had to shift out of her reach to give her breasts the attention they deserved. As far as he was concerned, it was a miracle that she was so sensual with him, that she responded to his touch with enthusiasm.

He breathed in the salty scent of her skin as he kissed and suckled her breasts. He'd always been fond of breasts, and now hers in particular, and could have spent all night with them, but there was more to explore. He slid down the velvet a little farther, hooking a hand under her knee and lifting it to the side so that he could kiss the soft skin of her thigh. Mariah writhed with pleasure, her hands digging into the coverlet. He didn't suppose she was aware of the view she was giving him of her glistening sex as she moved her other leg restlessly to the side. He reveled in it, though, kissing closer and closer to the heart of her.

She sighed and writhed as he drew close enough to feel the heat of her against his cheek and to smell the musk of her desire. It was a blessing that no one had taught her not to enjoy sex. It whispered to him that they could gain so much more than the child he desperately wanted by being together this way. He would do so much more than fill her with seed, he would drive her wild with pleasure.

His mouth reached her wetness, and he traced his tongue along her opening. She cried out, her thighs tightening. "What are you doing?" she panted. Her hands moved from the coverlet to grab handfuls of his hair.

He probably shouldn't tell her how devastatingly

good it felt to have her pulling his hair while he went down on her. At least, not yet. "I'm doing this," he said, then resumed his mouth's work.

She was perfect, sweet and salty, and so hot. She made glorious sounds as he licked and suckled her, and blessedly, she gripped his hair harder and harder. He could feel how close she was to coming, but he pushed on relentlessly instead of bringing her to the brink and pulling back over and over until she begged him for release. They'd save that for another day. Instead, he circled her clitoris with his tongue until her panting grew desperate. When she cried out as her body convulsed, he felt like the most powerful man alive.

He couldn't wait to join with her. He slid up her body, hooking her knees with his elbows and bending her into a position worthy of one of the paintings around her. She wasn't quite flexible enough to rest her ankles on his shoulders, but the position she did manage left her spread and open for him. He pushed inside of her, groaning with pleasure at the way she took him in and tightened around him. She squeezed him so perfectly that instinct took over and had him thrusting with more energy than he thought he had, over and over until the friction was beyond exquisite.

As had happened the night before, he climaxed before he expected to, the hot ball of energy at the base of his spine bursting into a flood of pleasure. The joy of spilling his seed inside of her went beyond anything he'd experienced before, so much that he cried out wordlessly, completely undone. All the while, she sighed and mewled beneath him with genuine enjoyment. It was so good that he never wanted it to stop.

Except that the afterglow was almost as good as the orgasm. He dropped, spent, to her side, rolling her with him so that they could remain entwined. And even though he knew in seconds that he would fall asleep out of pure exhaustion before he could tell her how beautiful or wonderful she was or how much she meant to him, everything felt right. He tumbled into sleep with her in his arms, resting her head against his shoulder and whispering his name on a pleasured sigh.

THERE WERE FEW PLACES WHERE LORD WILLIAM deVere felt more in his element than London's Black Strap Club. Shayles provided excellent food and drink, the décor was fittingly dramatic, and the occasional plaintive, female scream that echoed through the walls from one of the other private rooms was exactly the sort of spice to make a night interesting.

"You wouldn't scream like that, would you, sweeting?" he asked the woman hard at work between his spread legs in a hoarse, panting voice.

The woman leaned back, her mouth breaking free with a slick pop. "No, my lord." Her eyes were round and vacant, just the way he liked it. Her ankles and wrists were tied, and while that made it difficult for her to balance on her knees as she was, the sweet thing managed somehow.

William sat up slightly from the specially-designed, padded chair and slapped the darling across her pretty face. "I didn't tell you to stop."

"N-no, my lord," she squeaked. She leaned gingerly forward, mouth open, attempting to catch his bobbing erection without hands.

William moved his hips, making her task even harder, and laughed at the sight of her trying to catch him. When she failed, he slapped her again. "Get on with it."

"I'm trying, my lord," she sniffled pathetically.

"Oh, here." He fisted his hand in her hair and held himself until her mouth closed around him again. She squealed and then choked as he drove deep, holding her head with both hands and forcing the action he enjoyed so much.

The sounds of the whore's muffled protests, coupled with the sensation of her mouth, had him rushing toward the edge when the door flew open, banging against the wall. Two of Shayles's bouncers marched into the room.

"What is the meaning of this?" William shouted.

One of the bouncers stepped forward, looping his meaty hands under the whore's arms and pulling her back. She gasped in relief and sobbed as the bouncer unlocked her chains and carried her out of the room.

"I paid for that," William growled, making no attempt to hide his red and rigid cock from the remaining bouncer.

"No, you didn't," a softer, cooler voice said. A moment later, the slim, handsome figure of Oscar Lawrence appeared in the doorway.

William leapt up from the chair, reaching for a nearby robe to cover himself. "Lawrence," he laughed nervously. "What brings you here?" His mouth twisted into an anxious smile.

Lawrence brushed the sleeves of his fine jacket, his expression as mild as a summer day. "I hear felicitations are in order."

"Felicitations?" William trembled as he threw the robe around his shoulders and tied it at his waist.

"On your uncle's marriage." Lawrence smiled. His eyes flashed with wrath.

"My uncle's…he's not married. He's well past anything like that," William said.

Lawrence's brow inched up almost imperceptibly. "You weren't aware? He married a Miss Mariah Travers yesterday."

Itching panic spread down William's spine. "Yesterday? How would you know?"

"Shayles has eyes everywhere," Lawrence said, still smiling pleasantly. "He keeps track of his interests, you know."

"What interest does Shayles have in my uncle?" William hunched forward and hugged himself to stop the trembling. His groin ached with unspent arousal.

"In your uncle himself?" Lawrence shrugged. "Parliamentary rivalries, mostly. With Lord Dunsford as the

DECEMBER HEART

source of your income and future prospects? Everything."

William couldn't breathe as stark fear spilled through him. After a twenty-year marriage with no heirs, he had been certain his uncle would die childless and the Dunsford title and estate would come to him. He'd counted on it. Every single one of the vast debts he'd rung up in recent years used his status as heir to the Dunsford estate as collateral. But if his uncle had married, if the woman he'd shackled to his decrepit leg was of child-bearing years, that collateral was gone.

"Yes, I think you see the situation we're in," Lawrence said, tilting his head to the side and sniffing. "I believe the money you owe Shayles stretches deep into the six-figure range?"

"I can pay him," William snapped, feeling the color drain from his face. "He'll have his money. I'm still the heir, no matter what this new little chit thinks."

"She's the daughter of a respected MP, you know." Lawrence studied his nails. "Young."

The message was as clear as if Lawrence had spelled out how babies were conceived and calculated the odds of a new heir by Christmas.

"You'll get your money," William insisted. "Shayles will get his money."

"Yes, well, you may think that—" Lawrence sniffed, then clasped his hands behind his back, smiling again. "—but Shayles believes you're a substantial liability now. In fact, he believes the only use you can serve at this point is as an example for others who may attempt to withhold what they owe."

William swallowed hard. "What do you mean?" he croaked.

Lawrence shrugged. "You have the summer to pay your debts in full—"

"I can't possibly—"

"—or you will pay with your life."

Lawrence smiled.

A chill shot down William's spine. "He can't do that."

"I assure you, he can," Lawrence said.

He turned to the bouncer, who had watched the entire conversation with his jaw clenched and his fists balled, a look of pure hatred in his eyes. William swallowed again. There were rumors that the Black Strap's bouncers actually cared for the whores employed there, and that they didn't look kindly on club members who liked things rough.

"Escort Lord William to the door," Lawrence ordered the hulking man. He turned back to William. "Repay all of your debts in full or put your affairs in order."

"But that's not enough—"

Lawrence ignored him. He turned and strode from the room as if moving from one exhibit in the National Gallery to another. The bouncer remained behind, growling.

"All right, all right." William feigned annoyance, but inside his bowels had turned to water. He rushed to dress, fumbling every article of clothing as he did. Shayles was asking the impossible of him, but what stuck in William's craw even more was his uncle's audacity. How dare the old fool marry again and put his life at risk? And who was Mariah Travers anyhow? He would have to find out all he could about her as soon as possible. And once he did, there was really only one course of action open to him. He would have to get to Starcross Castle as soon as possible, taking an overnight train if he had to, so that he could give his uncle a piece of his mind and get what was his.

CHAPTER 7

Mariah had never imagined it was possible for one chapter of her life to end and another to begin with such sharp definition. By Sunday evening, as she sat drowsily by Peter's side in the carriage his butler had sent to pick them up from the train station in Truro, the life she'd lived for twenty-seven years in Aylesbury seemed like a dream. Except she wasn't sure she was awake. Exhaustion infused her, from her boggled mind to her deliciously sore body.

She should have been distressed by the soreness of her muscles, and other important areas, considering how she'd come to feel that way. She should have been scandalized at the speed with which she and Peter had become so intimate. But whether it was the whirlwind of travel and change or the fact that the things she and her new husband had done in bed were unbelievably pleasurable, she didn't know and, frankly, didn't care. It was almost as if she'd known Peter her whole life.

"We're almost there," he said softly, kissing her forehead.

She'd fallen asleep against him yet again. At some point, he'd put his arm around her. It was cozy, intimate, and natural. She smiled and drew in a breath, pushing herself to sit straight and half regretting it.

"Sorry I'm such a sleepy-head," she said with a yawn.

"You have every right to be," he told her. It was dark in the carriage as the sun had gone down just as they disembarked from the train, but she could still make out his tired smile and the way he looked at her as though she were a treasure. He reached out to brush a lock of hair from her cheek.

Had Robert ever looked at her like that? She'd known him for years, but she wasn't sure he had. And here Peter had only known her for days, but he treated her as though she were a cherished lover. Yes, her life had taken an unexpected and definitive turn. One she was determined to appreciate to the fullest. Nothing would get in the way of this new life she was so enthralled with.

The carriage slowed and turned. Peter glanced out the window beyond her and nodded. "There it is."

Mariah turned to the window, eager to get a glimpse of her new home. But all she could see were a series of windows glowing with dim light, and a great, dark space. There wasn't enough light for her to decide whether she thought Starcross Castle was beautiful or bulky. But the looming expanse of it filled her with an eerie sense of the unknown.

The carriage circled around a drive, drawing up beside a long set of stairs, before which a line of uniformed servants stood waiting to greet them.

"It's nice of them to greet us so late at night," Mariah said. "And on a Sunday. Don't servants usually have a half-day on Sundays?"

"Yes," Peter answered, shifting so that he would be ready to step down from the carriage when the door was opened. "It's kind of Snyder to bring them out to greet us like this, but I'll have to have a word with him about respecting their free time."

Mariah smiled at the consideration Peter showed, although as soon as one of the footmen opened the door and Peter helped her down, she wondered if she was the reason for the full turn-out from Starcross Castle's staff. Even in the dark, she could see the eager expressions of everyone from the stately woman who must have been the housekeeper to the young maid at the far end of the row. It was flattering to think that she could garner so much attention.

"Welcome home, sir." The imposing figure of the butler, Mr. Snyder, stepped forward from the line to bow to Peter.

"Snyder." Peter greeted the man with an equally respectful nod, then smiled on to the housekeeper and another man who was dressed slightly better than the others. "Mrs. Wilson." He nodded. "Wright."

"Shall I take your things up to your room, sir?" Mr. Wright asked. Mariah put two and two together, realizing the man must have been Peter's valet.

"Yes, please," Peter said. "And if you would have Miss—that is, Lady Dunsford's things taken to the countess's suite, I would appreciate it."

Mariah nearly stumbled. Lady Dunsford. The countess. Somewhere in the maelstrom of surprise weddings and nights spent discovering the wonders of bodily pleasure, she'd completely forgotten that she was now a countess. And Lady Dunsford at that. She really had stepped into a whole new life.

Mr. Wright motioned for two of the footmen to retrieve the trunks from the back of the carriage, and to take them into the house. Peter took Mariah's hand, leading her on.

"Mrs. Wilson, may I present my lovely new wife to you, Mariah deVere, Lady Dunsford."

"How do you do, my lady." The housekeeper dropped into a low curtsy that had Mariah near to panicking.

The woman was as old as her mother, and Mariah's instinct was to show her the respect she would to an elder. But she was a countess now, and countesses didn't show respect to servants.

Well, she would show respect, whether she was supposed to or not. "It's a pleasure to meet you, Mrs. Wilson," she said, taking the older woman's hands as if greeting an old friend.

Mrs. Wilson blinked in surprise, smiled, then schooled her expression as though smiling were against the rules.

"I expect that the two of you will want to meet as soon as possible to discuss the running of the castle," Peter said.

"Yes, my lord," Mrs. Wilson answered, then turned, still somewhat baffled, to the younger woman standing beside her. "This is Ginny, my lady. She will be serving as your personal maid. That is, unless you already have one."

"I don't," Mariah said, then turned to study Ginny.

The young woman seemed a bit overwhelmed, but wore a broad smile. She had blonde hair secured under a cap, and a pretty, round face. Mariah liked her at once.

"My lady." She curtsied.

"I'm sure you'd like to come inside and relax after your travels, my lord," Mr. Snyder said. "Perhaps a bath for Lady Dunsford and supper for both of you?"

It took Mariah a moment to remember that Mr. Snyder was talking about her. "Oh. Yes, a bath would be lovely." She didn't know whether to look to Mr. Snyder or Mrs. Wilson or Ginny.

Ginny was the one who curtsied. "I'll see to it right away, my lady." With a final smile, she turned and rushed into the house.

"And I'll see to supper." Mrs. Wilson hurried after her.

Peter hooked her arm through his and escorted her up the stairs and into the house.

"I've never had so many people rushing about to do things for me," she whispered to him.

"But your parents have a maid and footman," Peter whispered back.

"Yes, they mostly saw to the house while we saw to ourselves."

Peter chuckled. "Don't try that with Snyder, Wilson, and this lot. They'll be mortally offended if you don't allow them to wait on you hand and foot."

Mariah laughed and started to say, "I doubt that," but at that moment they crossed through over the threshold and into the castle's front hall.

The air left her lungs and her mouth hung open as she looked around. Her family's house in Aylesbury was nothing to scoff at, but the immensity of the room she found herself in—only a front hall at that—was as grand as any she'd ever set foot in. It was easily two stories tall, maybe more, with a grand staircase of warm, polished wood that split halfway up, leading to two wings, one on either side. The floor was marble, but had been covered with a vast, Turkish rug. At least four doorways led off to various corridors and side rooms. On top of that, the walls were hung with paintings that ranged from portraits to landscapes, some of them in the style of well-known masters. In fact, Mariah was certain that one of the landscapes was by JMW Turner.

"It's amazing," she said, still looking around.

"It's home," Peter replied.

She dragged her gaze down from the paintings and looked at him. He was studying her with as much appreciation and excitement as she felt for the castle around her. His look brought heat to her face and, of course, made her want to laugh.

"You're going to have to stop looking at me like that," she murmured, leaning closer to him so that the swirl of servants who had burst into motion around them wouldn't hear.

"Like what?" He led her on to the stairs and up to the left.

"Like I'm more interesting than the art," she said, then added, "Is that a Vermeer?"

Without checking to see which painting she had nodded to, he said, "Yes. And you're far more interesting."

She shook her head, feeling warm all over—and more than a little guilty for enjoying his appreciation so much. Particularly if it would lead to more of what had kept them from getting sufficient sleep for the past two nights.

The flash in Peter's eyes hinted that he was thinking the same thing, but it came to an abrupt stop when Mr. Snyder caught them at the top of the stairs.

"My lord, there's something you should know," he began.

Peter stopped, facing his butler with a slight frown. "Is it about the mine?"

Mr. Snyder hesitated. He shot a quick glance to

Mariah, then cleared his throat. "No, my lord. You should know that Lord William arrived this morning."

Mariah was surprised that lightning didn't strike as Peter's expression and mood changed so quickly. He tensed, shifting back to the serious, anxious man she'd first met four days ago. She hadn't realized how quickly or thoroughly he'd changed into the relaxed, ardent man she'd spent the last two nights with.

"Where is he now?" he asked Mr. Snyder, his frown growing darker.

"Not at home," Mr. Snyder said. "I presume he took himself into Truro, to one pub or another."

Peter nodded. "Which room is he staying in?"

Mr. Snyder cleared his throat and glanced down for a moment. "I insisted he take the Lion Room, in the east wing. I assumed you and your new bride would not want to be disturbed."

"Thank you, Snyder," Peter said with the sort of gravity that was usually reserved for death or wars.

He started to lead Mariah on, but Mr. Snyder stopped him with, "My lord, he wasn't happy."

"No, I don't suppose he would be," Peter said, his tone laced with foreboding.

They continued down a hall lit by gas lamps in sconces on the wall to a door near the end.

"Lord William is the nephew you told me about?" Mariah asked, already knowing the answer.

"He is," Peter mumbled, his frown as deep as ever.

He turned the handle and pushed open the door. "I was hoping he'd stay in London."

As soon as her eyes settled on the room before her, all thoughts of nephews drifted right out of her head. The room Peter escorted her into was like something out of a fairy tale. It was decorated in shades of rose and violet, exactly in line with a fine woman's taste. The bed was sumptuously fitted out with quilts, pillows, and curtains that hung from the tall canopy. A matching wardrobe and vanity, along with a pair of comfortable-looking chairs were spread through the rest of the room. A fire was already crackling merrily in the fireplace, and Ginny was there, directing a pair of maids as they filled a brass tub.

"I hope you don't mind," Peter said, nodding to the tub but leading Mariah on to another door at the far end of the room. "The next project I'd like to undertake in the castle is installing modern plumbing and bathing facilities."

"I don't mind at all," Mariah said, eager to see what new wonder was behind the door at the far end of the room.

It turned out to be a dressing room the likes of which she had only dreamed of. Her trunk had already been brought to the room, and looked ready for unpacking. Yet another door stood open at the far end of the dressing room which led to a second, more masculine dressing room. It had much more of an appearance of use, and right away, Mariah breathed in Peter's scent.

At the far end of that room was another bedroom,

obviously his. It was decorated in dark blue, with paintings of the sea and exotic ports. It had much more of an air of being used than her room—at least, she presumed it was her room—had. The furnishings were more worn, and several small personal items sat on the fireplace mantel and on a small desk near the window.

Mariah took it all in with the same sense of wonder she'd had while studying the front hall. This was Peter's inner sanctuary, the room that was most private to him. He probably had an office somewhere else in the house, but this room was distinctly his. Everything from the colors to the scents to the trinkets on the desk and side table were just as intimately him as the sight of his naked body.

A small, old portrait of a woman, sitting on the mantelpiece, caught her eye. Anxiety shivered through her.

"Is that...." She felt too awkward asking if the portrait was Anne to finish the question.

"My mother," Peter answered, walking her to the mantel.

"Oh." Relief rushed through her, which brought with it a twinge of guilt. She shouldn't feel jealous of the wife Peter had lost years ago, especially when she'd been left with the impression that all hadn't been right between them.

"And this is my father, my older brother, Arthur, and younger, Will."

Mariah studied the portraits, which also formed a

short history of photography. There was a distinct family resemblance between all of the men, but Mariah also found some of Peter's facial features in the portrait of his mother.

It was only after she realized she was looking at almost all of Peter's family, and that all of them were dead, that her heart squeezed in her chest. "You must miss them."

His only answer was a weary smile.

Mariah's sense of treading on sacred ground increased as she looked around. She glanced back toward the door to the dressing rooms. "Was that Anne's room?" she asked, cursing herself for sounding like it mattered to her.

But to her surprise, Peter answered, "No," and lowered his eyes. Something dark and disturbing seemed to hang over him. "At least, it wasn't for the last ten years or so of our marriage."

"Why...." she started, but pressed her lips shut when she saw the warning not to ask in his eyes. It was more than a warning. It was a haunted look, one of misery. It made the sadness she'd seen in him at their first meeting pale in comparison.

A soft knock sounded from the dressing room, and Ginny poked her head cautiously around the corner. Peter took a step back from Mariah and straightened. Mariah wanted to move with him, to hold him until he felt safe telling her what he was thinking.

"My lady." Ginny cleared her throat. "Your bath will be ready momentarily. Would you like help undressing?"

Mariah glanced to Peter, who nodded subtly and walked over to his desk. There would be a time to talk, but not yet. She started toward the dressing room with a smile for Ginny.

"Yes, that would be lovely, thank you."

The bath turned out to be exactly what Mariah needed to soothe her sore muscles. But having a few minutes alone after days of being by Peter's side also gave her a chance to reflect on her situation. She was happy, overwhelmed, and grateful that her father had thought to promise her to Peter, even if he should have told her about the match sooner.

Other thoughts poked at those contented ones, though. Why had Peter reacted so seriously when Mr. Snyder told him his nephew was home? What was it about the younger man that made Peter so unhappy? And was it just Lord William, or did the memory of his first wife have something to do with the unease that Mariah could see he felt? Come to think of it, why had Anne only used the room that adjoined his for the first part of their marriage but not the last?

Her bathwater cooled before she came up with any answers. She climbed out of the tub on her own and dressed in her nightgown and robe, then braided her own hair rather than calling Ginny back to help her. She wasn't used to anyone helping her to dress, other than enlisting Victoria to fasten a few gowns whose buttons she couldn't reach. It felt anticlimactic to climb into her new bed without at least saying goodnight to Peter, though, so rather than crawling between the covers that Ginny had turned down, she tip-toed through the dressing rooms and poked her head into Peter's room.

For a brief moment, she saw him before he saw her. He sat at his desk, wearing a look of fierce concentration. His head was bent over whatever he was reading, which highlighted his white hair in the lamplight. The light and his frown also accented the lines on his face. It struck Mariah how much experience of life he had. Much more than her. She'd spent two days lulling herself into a belief that she knew him completely. She'd given everything she had to him, trusted him with the most intimate parts of herself. But the man she spied on, with the cares of the world sitting on his shoulders, once again felt like a complete stranger to her.

Then he looked up, and the stranger was once again the man she'd married.

"You're still up?" he asked as she walked slowly toward him. "I was sure you'd go straight to bed after your bath."

She shrugged, leaning against the side of his desk. "I wanted to come say goodnight."

His smile heated, and he reached for her, settling her across his lap. Prickles of uncertainty raced down her spine in spite of the tenderness of his embrace. Did she know him? Did she really know him?

"Is something wrong?" he asked.

Self-consciousness enveloped her, but rather than admitting to her uncertainties, she asked, "Do you not get along with your nephew?"

He let out a long sigh, resting his forehead against her shoulder for a moment. When he looked up at her, every bit of the weariness that he'd had when she first met him was there.

"William is a difficult person. He was against me marrying, obviously, as any child of ours will be my heir, usurping him. But he is my responsibility. I had an agreement with his father, my brother, to always give him shelter at Starcross Castle if he asked for it."

She believed him, but sensed there was more. "You're worried that he will cause trouble?"

"I am," Peter admitted with a long exhale. "But it's not anything you need to concern yourself with."

"Really?" She arched a brow. "You're telling me that a man in this house has reason to resent me, but I shouldn't worry about it?"

"I'll keep you safe," he said.

Mariah smiled, even as a shiver went down her spine. She liked feeling protected, but the thought that she needed protection was unsettling.

"It will be all right," he said, then stood, taking her with him. His mood had shifted, though Mariah had the feeling it was a deliberate shift, designed to make her think about something else. "Now. I have something for you."

"For me?"

He crossed to the dressing room, but before she could follow him in, he returned with a small parcel. "I intended to give this to you on our wedding night, but we were distracted." The look he gave her sent a wave of excitement sizzling across her skin. "It isn't wrapped, but I hope you'll still like it."

"I'm sure I will," she said, recognizing the small book he held out even before she took it. Her heart thrummed in her chest and excitement filled her. "Walt Whitman."

He grinned, stepping toward her with a triumphant grin. "Of course, it would have been more of a prize if you were able to buy it from MacTavish's bookshop yourself."

"Oh no, this is wonderful." She smiled up at him, and the way he watched her almost made her want to throw the book aside and fling herself into his arms. Which was unsettling in itself, since, a minute before, she'd been uncertain whether she knew him or not. She glanced to the book, tracing her fingers over the imprinted title. "Leaves of Grass."

"We could read a bit of it together, if you'd like." He moved close enough to rest his hands on her waist. The spark she'd grown so familiar with over the last two nights was back. That was the part of him she knew.

Her grin grew teasing as she peeked up at him. "You know what's in these poems, don't you?"

"I might have read one or two...or all of them before." His expression turned downright sultry.

From serious stranger to ardent lover, all in a matter of minutes. Mariah suddenly doubted whether she had the mettle to keep up with her new husband and his moods. Although, as he brought his lips to hers and kissed her in the way that ignited showers of sparks deep in her core, she ceased to care.

"Maybe some other night," she sighed when he ended their kiss. "I don't think I could possibly concentrate on poetry at the moment."

"Me either." He plucked the book from her hands and tossed it on his desk before sweeping her in his arms and carrying her to his bed.

She shed her robe and nightgown as he undressed, and when he climbed into bed with her, their bodies twined together as though they were meant to be one. But before they could do more than kiss and warm the sheets, he stopped and glanced down at her with an expression that was suddenly serious.

"What is it?" she asked.

He took a long time to answer, his frown deepening as if in confusion, his thoughts so intense that she could practically see them in his eyes.

"I want to ask you something," he said at last, as hesitant as she was curious.

"You can ask me anything." She caressed his cheek, which was rough with stubble. She had the uncanny feeling that their positions had reversed and he was suddenly the anxious one.

"Would you," he started, paused, bit his lip, then continued. "Would you consider sleeping in my bed?"

"Tonight?"

"Every night."

Her heart raced, and the sense that he was asking something deeply important, something that made him feel vulnerable, struck her. But it was such a simple question. It was obvious, really. Her parents slept in her mother's room, even though her father technically had a room of his own. Before seeing the rose and violet room, Mariah had always assumed married couples slept together. Had it not been that way with Peter and Anne?

"Of course," she answered, feeling a paradoxical burst of pity for him.

"Good." He let out a relieved breath, and bent to kiss her.

She wrapped her arms and legs around him, needing to embrace him, even if she didn't understand why. It was easier to give her body to him and to share pleasure than it was to comprehend the mysteries of who her husband was. She only hoped that in the morning, as their lives together truly began, she would finally get to know the man she'd married and figure out how she fit into his life.

CHAPTER 8

Sometime in the night, as was usual for him after the times Anne had forced her way into his bed, Peter rolled to his side. But a strange, new sensation greeted him when he woke. Not only was the other side of the bed not cold and abandoned, Mariah lay curled against his back, one arm thrown over his side. Her breath warmed his shoulder.

His chest ached with a sudden poignancy that came close to devastating him. Mariah hadn't retreated to the sanctity of her own space. She embraced him in her sleep. He could feel the silken softness of her curls against his backside. He was instantly aroused and growing harder by the minute, but it was his heart that throbbed the most.

When was the last time someone had hugged him? Not a cursory embrace from a friend or Anne's frantic clinging as she urged him to come inside her, or even the cloying grasps of the women he'd tried to take as mistresses, but failed to when guilt overwhelmed him. The last time that anyone had put their arms around him of their own volition, motivated only by affection...must have been his mother. And she'd been gone for almost forty years.

He swallowed the sigh that attempted to escape from his throat. It shocked him. Why on earth was he weeping at the knowledge that everything he had longed for was nestled softly against him?

He twisted, rolling Mariah with him and reversing their positions. It was his turn to spoon her, and nothing had ever felt so heavenly. She sighed with contentment, hinting that she was awake, but he didn't speak, barely moved. He considered lifting her leg over his and entering her, but that would be too much. In spite of the throb of his arousal, all he wanted to do was hold her, breathe in the scent of her, love her.

Love her?

He'd worry about that unfamiliar sentiment later. For the moment, he buried his face in the pillow of her hair, still fragrant from her bath the night before, and concentrated on the beat of his heart against her back.

"Are we going to get up?" she whispered.

"No," he murmured in return. "We're going to stay like this forever."

"Oh," she sighed happily, wriggling against him, making herself comfortable.

The rub of her backside against his erection was

heavenly torture, but still he made no move to seek out satisfaction. The act of lying with her in a state of blissful arousal was enough for him. Although perhaps she needed something as well.

He moved his hand between her legs, satisfied beyond measure to find her wet. But he was in no hurry to bring her to orgasm. He closed his eyes and breathed deeply as he teased her with a gentle touch. She remained silent, the raggedness of her breath his only clue that she was awake and alight.

And he was happy. Happier than he'd been in ages. It had come out of nowhere. All he'd wanted was a woman to give him an heir. But this, this was heaven. Mariah's shallow breaths turned into pleasured sighs, and she arched into his hand. This wasn't a futile attempt to erase failure after failure after failure. This was a moment. This was now. This was the two of them, taken by surprise, by each other, building something that could be so much more than anything he'd ever had.

He would protect this with his life, his soul.

"I need you inside of me," she whispered, trembling with that need.

He didn't hesitate. He took hold of her thigh, guided her to shift positions, then pushed inside of her. The sound of acceptance that rippled from her went straight to his heart. He took his time, reveling in the sounds of pleasure she made, drawing out the moment. They could be so much more than a means to an end. He could feel it in the way she moved with him, finding and matching his rhythm. They could be partners, lovers, everything.

He would keep her safe. He wouldn't fail her as he'd failed Anne, as he'd failed himself. If he had to bring down the stars to do it, he would shelter Mariah from the world's cruelty.

She came with a rending sigh, bringing him to the brink of completion. As her body relaxed into satisfaction, he withdrew, rolled her to her back, then continued thrusting as he gazed down at her. The acceptance that radiated from her was enough to push him to the edge, and he came with a glowing burst of warmth that took his breath away. It was beautiful, wonderful, precious.

They slept a while longer, still snuggled together, but eventually, reality invaded. Mariah showed reluctance to leave his bed—which was the most charming thing he'd ever been privy to—then returned to her room to dress. He washed and dressed as well, but they met for another lingering kiss in his room before heading downstairs to the breakfast room.

"Are you ready to face the day, Lady Dunsford?" he asked, stealing one last kiss.

"I am, my lord," she answered with a flick of her brow. "Oh, I just want to fetch a shawl. You go ahead without me."

Like a schoolboy with his first crush, he watched Mariah rush back through the dressing room. He shook his head and chuckled, then made his way downstairs.

And, like too many dreams, his ended with a withering crash of reality.

"So, Uncle. Where's this wife of yours?"

William was already seated at the table in the breakfast room. His hair was unkempt and he needed a shave. He wore only a vest above his shirt, but at least his clothes were clean. A pang of regret hit Peter as he moved to the sideboard to fix a plate from the breakfast offerings. He should have done a better job of guiding William after Will's death. He wanted to be a father himself, but he'd failed miserably where his nephew was concerned.

"Mariah is on her way down," he answered without looking at William.

"That slow and decrepit, is she?" William snorted. "But then, I suppose the only women who would have an old dog like you were the spinsters gathering dust on the shelf."

Peter frowned as he carried his plate to the table, but didn't reward William with a reply. The young man was likely baiting him into losing his temper, something that had become William's favorite pastime since learning he could inherit half of Starcross should Peter kick him out in a fit of pique.

"I heard that this Mariah of yours had a man but couldn't keep him." William shook his head and made a sound of mock sympathy. "And now she's stuck with you."

Davy, one of the footmen, slid silently up to the table to pour a cup of coffee for Peter. The dark, ferocious instinct to protect Mariah from William's vicious brand of gossip all but killed Peter's appetite. He couldn't let his nephew see that his insults had hit their mark, so he kept his face perfectly impassive, pretending he didn't care. It was harder than it'd ever been.

"It's a shame, though," William went on.

"What is?" Peter sipped his coffee, checking on the headlines of the newspaper at his place.

"That my creditors snapped their purses closed so quickly the second they heard about your marriage."

Peter glanced up at his nephew with a frown.

"Oh yes," William went on. "It seems I've suddenly become too much of a risk, now that my claim to Starcross Castle and its riches is in question."

"That's not my problem." Peter took another sip of coffee, his pulse racing.

"Isn't it?" William seethed. A moment later, he chuckled, leaning back in his chair. "I think my creditors have more faith in womankind than I do. What kind of woman would stoop to marry the likes of you, after all?"

Peter didn't acknowledge the jab.

"As far as I can see, after a twenty-year marriage that produced no children, the only thing you have to offer a woman is a title and its trappings."

"Get to your point, William," Peter said with a fake sigh.

"Write to my creditors and tell them you did not marry to get an heir. Assure them that I am still in line to inherit, and that this new wife of yours is for show only."

Peter's only response was a single, raised eyebrow.

"It *is* just for show, isn't it?" William leaned forward, worry pinching his face. "You can't actually be so stupid that you'd inflict your poisonous seed on another woman. Not after what you did to Anne."

Peter couldn't hide his wince fast enough. He buttered a piece of toast, pretending to read the paper.

William's smarmy attempts to get under Peter's skin shifted to genuine anger. "Lawrence said my debts would all be called in if your new wife has a son. They've started taking bets on when your new heir will be born."

Peter's gut clenched in alarm. Oscar Lawrence was one of the most notorious money-lenders in London, but that was only the beginning. Lawrence was little more than a shill. The real power behind that particular, seedy empire was none other than Theodore Shayles. And if Shayles was involved, it was likely that William was nothing more than a pawn to get to him.

If he'd known Shayles was involved and his progeny was the stuff of wagers, he would have thought twice about marrying Mariah. But now that his heart was involved, there was no going back.

"Come on, old man," William pushed on when Peter was silent too long. "Tell me what this new wife of yours is like."

"She could tell you herself," Mariah said, sweeping into the room.

Panic flooded Peter. Mariah stood beside the sideboard with a look of defiance for William. She was radiant in her indignation, but she didn't know what she was walking into.

"This is Mariah," he said, pretending not to be interested. Inwardly, he prayed that Mariah would sense his caution and stay as far from William as she could.

She glanced his way with a curious frown. He met her eyes and tried with all his might to communicate the danger in front of her without words, but her expression grew more confused.

And then it was too late.

"Well, well." William stood, sauntering up to Mariah. "Hello, auntie."

"Mariah, please fix your breakfast then come have a seat by me," Peter said, showing no emotion, nothing William could capitalize on.

"I—" Blinking, Mariah glanced from William to Peter with a look of shock. "I haven't been introduced to your nephew."

The panic pulsing through Peter grew hotter. "Mariah, this is my nephew, Lord William deVere," he said, gesturing with his fork but not getting up. "William, my wife, Lady Mariah deVere, Countess of Dunsford. Please show her the respect she is due."

"Yes, uncle," William said and studied Mariah with far too much salaciousness.

Mariah did a double-take and stepped away from William. She went to the sideboard to make a plate for herself, her confused look deepening. Peter breathed half a sigh of relief, but his nerves remained on edge as

William continued to watch her. He rubbed his jaw and bit his lip with open lust.

"That's enough," Peter barked, glaring at him.

"I was just being friendly," William tossed back at him. He returned to his seat with a chuckle, his eyes never leaving Mariah.

"*My wife* deserves your respect, not your friendship." He glared at William until the whelp looked up at him.

A predatory smile spread across William's face. "Well, if she means that much to you."

Peter's jaw clenched so hard his teeth hurt. He'd been too careless too quickly. William had spotted his weakness. He sent a wolfish grin in Mariah's direction as she brought her plate to the table and sat. Peter had to do something, and he had to do it immediately.

"She's the countess," he said feigning indifference and focusing on his breakfast. "She deserves the respect befitting her rank."

"Yes, Uncle," William said, his tone mocking.

Peter pretended the matter was settled and went through the motions of eating, but the food was like ash in his mouth. He should have packed Mariah up and taken her to his London house the moment he discovered William was at Starcross Castle.

ONCE, WHEN MARIAH WAS A CHILD, SHE'D STUMBLED across a hornet's nest while playing near the river. The sensation of sudden fear and the urgency to get away that she'd felt then was a little too close to the tension that buzzed throughout the breakfast room. But what brought her up short wasn't Lord William's lascivious greeting, it was the harshness in Peter's eyes. That and the fact that he had commanded her to get her breakfast and sit down as though she were a child.

The snap of resentment that raised in her was second only to her utter confusion that he would speak to her like that and look at her the way he had, almost as if she'd done something wrong and he was scolding her. What had happened to the man who had held her so tenderly early that morning and had made love to her so sweetly?

"What brings you to Starcross Castle, Lord William?" Mariah asked, falling back on politeness. "I thought you lived in London."

"I heard my uncle had married, and I wanted to be here to meet my new aunt," William said, arching an eyebrow at Mariah and biting his lip.

Mariah blinked rapidly, hardly believing William's shockingly inappropriate advances. But Peter didn't seem to notice, or if he did, it was as if he didn't care. Mariah did her best not to be hurt, but she couldn't help it.

"It's downright cruel, you know," William said when no one immediately responded to him.

"What is cruel?" Mariah asked, since Peter seemed more interested in his eggs than the question...or her.

"To shackle such a pretty, *young* woman to this crumbling ruin."

The only indication Mariah had that Peter had heard

the comment was a tightening around his mouth and eyes.

"You sound like my sister, Victoria," Mariah said, imitating Peter and focusing on her meal. Peter must have been pretending indifference for a reason, and until she had a chance to ask him what that reason was, sense told her it was best to follow his lead.

"Sister?" William perked up. "You have a sister?"

"She's nineteen," Peter said without looking up.

"Even better."

Mariah frowned at William's tone. "Are you married, Lord William?" she asked. She knew the answer, but figured it was safer to get the man talking about himself than prying for details about Victoria.

"No," William answered with a snort. "You would never find me with a marital noose around my neck. Well, until the time comes to get an heir."

There was too much bitterness in William's voice and the way he glared across the table at Peter. Mariah suddenly saw what Peter had told her about William being his heir for now in a new light. It wasn't just names on a family tree. To William, it meant more. A shiver shot down her spine.

"I suppose I should start searching for a wife soon, though," William went on. "Uncle here isn't getting any younger and, well, a nubile young bride is useless when the groom has ancient piping."

Mariah nearly choked on her toast. Surely William

couldn't be so crude as to bring up a subject like that at the breakfast table.

"Hold your tongue," Peter said with surprisingly little interest, glancing at his newspaper. His cheeks reddened.

William grinned. "I'd be happy to do the job for you, if you'd like."

"I said, hold your tongue." At last, Peter looked up, glaring at William.

Mariah watched the silent exchange between the two men, her tea cup suspended halfway to her lips. Peter was furious, and William...well, he looked as though he'd discovered a secret. He couldn't think that Peter was incapable in bed, could he?

The whole jumble was too much for Mariah's brain to tackle in the midst of so many other changes. She sipped her tea at last, deciding it would be better for everyone if she sat back, observed, and learned the terrain before charging off into it.

After several minutes of silence, Mr. Snyder strode into the room. He waited until Peter acknowledged him, then said, "My lord, Mr. Sinclair is here to speak to you about the situation at the mine."

Peter glanced to Mariah, worry creasing his brow, then flashed a look to William. He glanced back to her with the stern look of command he'd worn earlier. Mariah frowned. What was he trying to tell her?

"Would...would you like my help with Mr. Sinclair?" she ventured.

"No," he said, a little too fast. Her spirits sank. "Perhaps you could meet with Mrs. Wilson about the running of the house as she requested."

"Oh...all right."

"Tell Mr. Sinclair that I'll be with him shortly." Peter focused on Mr. Snyder, ignoring Mariah completely. He wiped his mouth with his napkin, then stood, heading out of the room with Mr. Snyder in tow.

Frustration killed the last of Mariah's appetite. Reason told her to trust Peter, but her heart felt bruised. They had been getting along so well. Was that simply the honeymoon state, and was this new coldness the way their marriage would progress? But no, that didn't seem right at all. She didn't like not knowing the rules of the game they were playing.

"Interesting," William said. He had slumped sideways in his chair and was watching Mariah while rubbing his lips.

"The trouble at the mine?" she asked, knowing full well that wasn't what he meant.

"No. You." He shifted suddenly forward, staring at her with an intensity that caused Mariah to drop her fork. "I thought you'd be much older, much...dustier."

"I'm sorry to disappoint you." She picked up her fork, but her hand shook too much to continue eating.

"You have no idea," William mumbled. He shifted to lean one elbow on the table and asked, "Has my uncle been able to get it up yet?"

"I beg your pardon?" Mariah flushed hot, unable to meet his eyes directly.

"Twenty years without producing an heir, you know," he said as if she did know. "I can't blame all of that on my dear, departed Aunt Anne."

"I...um...that doesn't have anything to do with me."

"Then let's talk about you," William went on. "I heard a rumor in London when I asked around about you that you're quite the cold fish. That your dear, late fiancé looked for entertainment elsewhere because your doors were closed, so to speak. I assumed it was because you were a tired old prude."

"Sir, I am appalled that you would speak to me like this." Mariah pushed back her chair and stood. She started to leave the room, but William leapt up and blocked her way.

"Just tell me if my uncle is capable so I know whether to be worried about my inheritance or not." He lifted a hand to trace the back of his fingers across her cheek.

Mariah recoiled in disgust. "Leave me alone," she hissed, trying to dodge around him and out the door.

"I see," William said with a triumphant hum. He took a step back, grinning. "So you are frigid. Well, then, I don't have as much to worry about as I thought."

Mariah rushed past him, but pride kept her from fleeing without having the last word. She turned back to William, her fists balled at her sides. "Your uncle informed me that you were a difficult man, but the least you could do is behave like a gentleman around his wife."

"And the least you could do is respect the fact that I was here first." He narrowed his eyes at her. The look made Mariah's blood run cold, but at least any hint of lust had vanished. "You can have the castle and the title, and all the pretty clothes and balls you want, but just you make sure you keep your legs crossed, auntie dear."

He blew her a kiss, then marched past her and off down the hallway. Mariah pressed a hand to her stomach to keep from being sick. She was shaking as well, and hated every bit of how William had made her feel. She wanted to run to Peter to tell him everything that William had said. But Peter was meeting with his mine foreman, and she couldn't shake the way he'd dismissed her throughout their short, uncomfortable breakfast.

The only thing she could do was gather her wits and go off in search of Mrs. Wilson. But as she left the breakfast room, a hollow sense of being dropped alone in the middle of the wilderness went with her.

CHAPTER 9

*P*eter was halfway across the front hall on his way to his study, where he received visitors on business, when he stopped with a wince. He'd handled the situation at breakfast terribly. Instead of feigning indifference to Mariah, he should have made absolutely clear to William that if he harmed a hair on her head, there would be consequences. But he had been so used to closing off his emotions whenever Anne was in a state that it had come all too naturally in the present situation. William had assumed he didn't care about Anne and left her alone. And Anne had always been less likely to have one of her fits without him adding fuel to the fire. But Mariah had reacted as though she were hurt.

He rubbed a hand over his face and turned back to the breakfast room. The least he could do was to explain his motivations for wearing a mask in front of William. Mariah was intelligent enough to understand the tactic.

Although, if he explained why he felt it was necessary to manage William like he was planning strategy for a military campaign, he'd have to explain the debts William owed and to whom he owed them. Was it worth burdening Mariah so soon in their marriage, or could he figure out a way to demand William leave so that he didn't have to tell her?

He had to tell her, of course. He blew out a breath and started back to the breakfast room.

"My lord."

Peter clenched his jaw in frustration and turned to find Douglas Sinclair and young Owen Llewellyn watching him from the hallway that led to his study. Both men's faces were drawn with worry, telling him the situation with his mine was worse than he'd imagined. His heart urged him to go back and rescue Mariah from William and to explain, but his head and his sense of duty to the estate tugged him to deal with Sinclair first.

"Is there something I can help with, my lord?" Snyder—who had followed him and stood patiently to one side while Peter's thoughts roiled—asked.

Peter frowned, pursed his lips, then said, "Yes. Go back to the breakfast room and make sure that William doesn't interfere with Mariah in any way."

"Understood, my lord," Snyder answered with a look that confirmed he understood everything.

Snyder went back, allowing Peter to move forward. "Apologies for the delay, gentlemen," he said striding across the hall. He forced his posture straighter and put on the air of complete confidence the men who worked for him needed to see. "Come into my study and tell me what's going on at the mine."

The men followed him into the large room lined with bookcases that served as his study. It'd been one of his favorite rooms in the castle since he was a boy. Back then, it had been the library, but when he'd inherited the castle and its contents, he'd moved his father's desk and several leather-upholstered armchairs into the room. Half of it retained the feeling of a library, complete with cozy chairs placed next to windows where one could spend a quiet afternoon reading, and the rest was designed for receiving guests and handling business.

He gestured for Sinclair and Owen to take seats in the leather armchairs while he crossed to sit behind his desk.

"Well, my lord, it's like this," Sinclair began in his thick, Cornish accent. "It's the Carleen mine. We've seen this coming for a while, but the situation is worse than any of us anticipated."

"I see." Peter sat back in his chair, steepling his hands and tapping his index fingers against his lips. The gesture called to mind the sweetness of Mariah's kisses. She'd been shy and unstudied that first night, but she'd been a fast learner. She had yet to take the lead and seemed more content to remain passive, but he could sense a fire inside of her that told him it wouldn't be long until she was making demands of him.

As long as they weren't like Anne's demands.

A shot of ice pierced his gut and he blinked, snapping to attention.

"—can try other means to follow the exhausted ore, but frankly, my lord, I don't see us finding more copper."

Peter cleared his throat, embarrassed at letting his thoughts pull him away from the business at hand. Mariah was his current obsession, but the mines, the estate, were his duty.

"What about the Trescowe mine?" he asked, frowning in an attempt to stay focused and serious.

Sinclair glanced to Owen. The young man sat forward on the edge of his seat. "The copper we've been able to find at Trescowe never held a candle to what Carleen was able to produce, my lord," Owen said. Youthful enthusiasm and the need to show that he was worth the faith Peter had put in him was evident in his every word. "That mine is still producing, but the quality and quantity aren't enough to fetch the price at market that the estate requires to fulfill its needs.

"I see." Peter nodded. "What do you suggest we do?" He was as eager to see what his former footman could do as Owen was to show him.

"It's clear that we need to find a new deposit of ore," Owen said. "I've been surveying the extent of the estate for the past several weeks, and although it hasn't been enough time to discover anything comprehensive, I have a few suggestions for potential locations to dig."

"And I think it would be a wise investment to hire a professional surveyor to come in and study the estate, my lord," Sinclair said, glancing to Owen with a hint of disapproval.

Perhaps Owen had overstepped a little, but Peter couldn't blame him. He was young, eager, and he too had a young wife to impress. He and Millie, the American girl Peter had hired to be a maid as a favor to an old friend more than a year ago, were getting along quite well, and they had a new baby, if he wasn't mistaken. Perhaps someday that child would be a playmate for his own offspring.

If he had offspring. The last look he'd had from Mariah wasn't exactly tenderness and passion. And yet, the thought of not sleeping with her in his arms that night caused an ache in his gut that he wasn't willing to live with. He needed to find her and explain everything as soon as possible.

"My lord?"

Peter blinked, coming back to the present. "Hmm?"

Sinclair's expression changed from worry to a sly grin. "Ah, my lord. Felicitations on your recent wedding."

Owen drew in a breath and nodded, as though just remembering. "Yes, congratulations, my lord."

"Thank you." Peter sent the men a sheepish smile. "Apologies if my mind is elsewhere. I can assure you, though, that the situation with the mines will have my full attention."

"I remember how it was when Phyllis and I were first married," Sinclair went on. "It's hard to stay focused on anything but your bride."

"I won't let it put the mine or any of your livelihoods in danger," Peter promised the men, leaning forward and resting his elbows on his desk. Even if Mariah had more to contend with than most brides. Perhaps there was a way to kill two birds with one stone. "I like your idea of sending for a surveyor to assist Owen in his search for new ore deposits. I'll send my nephew back to London to interview likely candidates at once." Sending the young man on an errand wasn't the same thing as banishing him from the house.

Sinclair and Owen exchanged less than enthusiastic glances. In fact, they looked downright disturbed at the prospect.

"I have a few fellows in mind already, my lord," Sinclair ventured. When Peter frowned, he rushed on with, "But if you think it would be good for Lord William to be involved, I'm sure there are other possibilities in London I haven't considered."

Peter let out a breath and lowered his head to stare at decades' worth of ink stains on the blotter covering his desk. He had to get rid of William somehow. He was inclined to hire whomever Sinclair recommended as surveyor, but William didn't need to know that. He didn't need to know he was being sent on a fool's errand. He just needed to leave.

"Send me the details of the men you'd like to hire," he told Sinclair. "I may send William to London regardless, though."

"Yes, my lord." Sinclair nodded.

There was little else to discuss, though Peter did ask for a quick report of the situation and morale of the men in his employ. When he was satisfied that all was as well as it could be for the time being, he stood and walked the men to the door.

"Let me know if there is anything else I can do in the meantime," he said as Snyder came forward from his daytime position near the front door to show the men out.

"Thank you, my lord."

Snyder took over the task of seeing the men on their way as Peter turned to head back to his study. He was relieved beyond measure when Mariah marched into the hall before he could seclude himself to think about things. She wore a deep frown and seemed out of sorts, but at last, he'd get a chance to talk to her and fix what he'd stupidly broken.

LIFE AS A COUNTESS IN CHARGE OF A CASTLE DID NOT begin well for Mariah. In her attempt to get away from William and seek out Mrs. Wilson, she'd gotten lost in the maze of rooms that was Starcross Castle. It wouldn't have bothered her, except that instead of marveling over each new room she found herself in, she constantly looked over her shoulder, worried that William had followed her.

By the time she stumbled into the front hall and spotted Peter heading across the large room as though he knew where he was going, she was almost relieved.

Almost. The twist of ambiguity his treatment of her in the breakfast room had given her kept her from running to him.

Instead, he spotted her and abruptly changed directions, striding across the hall to meet her.

"There you are," he said, taking her into his arms for what ended up being a stiff hug. Stiff because she was so taken by surprise. He glanced around the hall as if searching for someone, then rested a hand against her cheek and kissed her.

Mariah's heart leapt for joy at the kiss, but confusion wouldn't let her enjoy it fully. "What's going on?" she asked, taking a step backward and out of his arms. "What was that all about at breakfast?"

Peter let out a breath, rubbing a hand over his face, and proving that she hadn't been imagining his odd behavior in the process. "It's William," he said, glancing around the hall once again.

Instead of launching into an explanation, he took Mariah's hand and led her across the hall to a room just off one of the corridors. It was half library, half office, and all Peter. Aside from his bedroom, of all the rooms at Starcross Castle that she'd seen so far, this one was most filled with his signature.

He brought her to an old, comfortable-looking sofa near a massive fireplace, whose mantel was decorated with army memorabilia and items that looked Turkish, and sat with her, their knees touching.

"I don't trust William," he began.

"Neither do I," Mariah quickly agreed.

Peter looked startled for a moment, then wary. "Did he behave himself after I left?"

"No," she answered with far more energy than she'd intended.

Peter blew out a breath and pressed his hand to his temples. "I was afraid of that. I had hoped that Davy's presence in the room would stop him from being...William."

Mariah frowned. She'd hardly noticed the young footman standing in the corner during her conversation with William, but that only doubled her alarm. Any man who wasn't afraid of how the servants would talk was a proverbial loose cannon.

"He's threatened by me," she said. "Well, *was* threatened by me."

Peter narrowed his eyes. "What do you mean?"

Mariah sighed. She would much rather have forgotten the whole incident, but Peter was her husband now, and though she had no experience with husbands, she knew one was supposed to tell them everything. "He believes there are—" She cleared her throat, suddenly self-conscious. "Difficulties in the bedroom between us."

He arched a brow, a sly, provocative grin pulling his mouth sideways. "We both know that's not true."

She met his grin with one of her own, warming as though her blood were moving again after being frozen with puzzlement. "Yes. Well." She lowered her eyes to study the way their hands were twined together, growing more and more aware of how close they sat to each other.

The reality of their situation swung back and hit her, and she took a breath, looking up and going on. "He warned me that he was here before me, and told me that I was welcome to the title and trappings of nobility, but to stay out of your bed."

"Damn his hide," Peter growled.

"Why?" Mariah asked. "What's going on?"

"William owes a great deal of money. It seems his creditors cut him off when they learned that I remarried—"

"Because if we have a son, William won't inherit and won't have any money to repay them," Mariah finished.

"Exactly."

"He's a grown man. Doesn't he have any other sources of income?"

Peter shook his head. "He had an estate and an income from his mother, but he's already lost them to pay creditors. I'm sure he sees his position as my heir as his last hope."

She let out an irritated breath. "Well, that's too bad for him. I'm finally married, I enjoy our time together, and I look forward to having as many children as we decide we want."

Peter burst into a smile of warmth and longing, but it faded all too soon.

"Beware. William is like a bloodhound," Peter said

with a bit too much condescension. "He sniffs out the things that matter to people and uses them as weapons."

"I can take care of myself," Mariah said.

"In this situation, I'm not sure if you can," Peter replied.

Mariah huffed, her back going straight. "I did not risk my happiness on a surprise marriage just to be treated like a child by my husband."

"I'm not treating you like a child, Mariah." Peter rubbed his temples, tension rippling off him. "But you don't know what you're up against with William."

"If your nephew is such a problem, then why not send him away, banish him from your life?"

He met her eyes with a surprising flash of guilt. "I can't."

Mariah blinked. "What do you mean?"

"I mean that I can't," Peter went on, shaking his head. "I am legally bound to provide a place for William to live."

"No one can be legally bound to keep someone in their house."

"It was an agreement I made with my brother as he lay dying. It was codified in his will and mine. If I banish William from Starcross Castle or disown him in any way, he inherits half the estate, whether I have a son or not."

"I see." Mariah bit the inside of her lip. "And why would you agree to something so outrageous?"

Peter closed his eyes with a wince. "Because I was young and foolish when Will lay dying. I believed I could make a difference in William's life and character. Will knew his son much better than I did, but cared about him nonetheless. We argued. He was certain I would reach the end of my tether and attempt to wash my hands of William, and so the damnable agreement was made."

A strange mix of compassion for Peter's attempt to please his brother and frustration that the brother in question had so obviously importuned him before dying knotted Mariah's gut. "So no matter how difficult he is, we can't ever send him packing."

Peter answered with, "William has been my responsibility for all these years, and for all these years, I've failed him. I would like to believe that it's not too late for him to reform."

"And you think having him near will reform him?" It didn't seem likely or even possible. But then again, the sum total of her experience with the young man was twenty minutes over breakfast.

"I should have been a good enough influence to begin with. If I hadn't failed—"

"Uncle, we have to talk." William burst into the room before Peter could finish. He turned the corner, then stopped cold, his mouth hanging open when he spotted Peter and Mariah sitting together.

Peter instantly dropped Mariah's hands, pushed away and stood, facing William with his back straight and all expression erased from his face. "What do you want, William?"

It was hard for Mariah not to be hurt as he pushed

her away. But worse than the sting of being shut out was the worry that their whole marriage would be like this, constantly treading on eggshells around William to avoid losing half of everything to him. She stood and stepped away, wishing she knew more about Peter, enough to trust his actions.

"I've come to talk about my allowance," William said, his tone distracted. Mariah stole a glance at him over her shoulder. Unfortunately, William was studying both her and Peter as though he were reassessing his earlier assumptions about them.

"Mariah," Peter snapped. "Go put your riding habit on. I don't have time to show you the entire estate, but if you must get a look at your new home, then we'll make it quick."

Her heart raced as she fought not to feel slighted. She hadn't said a thing about seeing the estate, but if Peter thought this was the best way to deal with his nephew, then she'd try to play along. For now.

"Yes, my lord," she mumbled, then turned to rush past him and William, her head lowered.

When she reached the door, she paused to glance at Peter. He lifted his chin and narrowed his eyes. A chill went down her spine. The overall effect was terrifying. Every bit of softness was gone from Peter's expression. The lines and crags on his face stood out, making him seem like a particularly vicious judge. She only hoped that the look was part of his act for William's sake.

Mariah fled from the room, but instead of heading straight upstairs to her bedroom, she whirled around to press her back to the wall, listening to see what Peter would say.

"Your allowance is sufficient," Peter said. Mariah heard footsteps and assumed he was moving.

William made a scoffing sound. "You give me pennies when you should be giving me pounds, Uncle."

"You cannot keep racking up debts the way you have been." The sound of paper being shuffled told Mariah he'd moved to his desk.

"And you cannot do something as underhanded as marrying without asking me first."

"My personal life is none of your business," Peter replied in a bland mumble.

"It is if it makes my creditors see me as a risk."

"You *are* a risk." Peter let out an exasperated breath, which accompanied the sound of papers being thrown down. "Why are you so fixed on being my heir? Why don't you follow my example and find a wife yourself? There are plenty of American heiresses who won't care if you're a rogue."

"I have no desire to marry."

"No," Peter said, sarcasm thick in his tone. "You never were one to solve your own problems."

"I can solve my own problems," William argued. "I'm attempting to do that right now."

"By interfering with my personal life?"

"By claiming what is rightfully mine." He paused for

a moment, then said. "If I can't do it one way, I'll just have to do it another."

Mariah frowned. Peter must have had a similar reaction, since he didn't reply right away.

"You are not entitled to any of this," Peter finally said.

"But my creditors—" William stopped abruptly, growling with frustration. "I don't think you understand the position I'm in or what I'm capable of, Uncle."

"On the contrary," Peter said, his voice as dark as Mariah had ever heard it. "I believe I understand your position better than you do. And I repeat, it is up to you to solve your own problems."

"What kind of heartless bastard would put his own pleasure above the life of someone he's responsible for?" William growled.

Mariah expected another grave, commanding reply from Peter, but was shocked when he shouted, "How dare you?"

She flinched. She'd never heard that intensity of emotion from anyone in her life. It caused her skin to break out in prickles. Any intelligent person would run from that kind of fury and pain, but William charged on with, "You were the death of her, and now you'll be the death of me."

Mariah swallowed, her mouth going dry. William could only mean Anne.

"And probably your pretty new wife too," William added.

"I'm done talking about this," Peter said, his voice

quieter but still thick with emotion. "I have a mission for you. I need you to go to London to find a competent surveyor to—"

"Are you throwing me out?" He seemed far too delighted by the prospect. "You know what happens if you throw me out."

The room went so silent that Mariah held her breath for fear of being discovered. William's problems were bigger than she'd thought. And apparently, Peter's were too.

"I'm not throwing you out," Peter said at last, his voice hoarse. "You will always have a place under my roof, as your father and I agreed."

"It sounds as though you're finally giving me the old heave-ho, and I'm sure my solicitor would agree," William said.

"I'm not—"

"All I want is for my debts to disappear and my line of credit to be open again," William interrupted.

"Then find a way to pay your own bills."

"Oh, I think I have. Which of us do you think will buckle first, Uncle?"

More silence. Mariah's heart beat so loud that she feared the men would hear it.

After what felt like an eternity, Peter said, "I won't discuss this now. I have to show Mariah the estate."

Mariah pushed away from the wall and hurried out into the front hall as quickly and quietly as she could. She knew the signs of a conversation coming to an end, and it would be a disaster if she were discovered eavesdropping. There didn't seem to be anything she could do but run to her room to change into riding clothes, as she'd been ordered. There didn't seem to be anything that could be done about the threats and accusations William had made either. At least, not until she knew more about what was behind the harsh words and accusations she'd just overheard.

CHAPTER 10

Mariah was fortunate to find Ginny in her dressing room, brushing out her dresses as she unpacked them.

"Good morning, my lady," she said with a curtsey. "Can I help you with something?"

Mariah let out the breath that had been trapped in her lungs since overhearing Peter and William's conversation. "Yes, I need to change into a riding habit."

"Right away, my lady."

Mariah sank into the small chair in the dressing room while Ginny sorted through the jumble of her clothes, some already hung in their new places, some still in the trunk. If William refused to leave Starcross Castle, then Peter would have to continue acting outwardly cold to her. And after seeing how fierce he could look when he was in a temper, she wasn't sure she was ready for that.

Beyond that, what had William meant by saying Peter had been the death of Anne?

Of course, the answer to that was obvious, considering the way Anne had died. But surely that wasn't Peter's fault. Although, it did take two people to conceive a child.

"Is something the matter, my lady?" Ginny asked as she drew Mariah's riding habit out of her traveling trunk. "If you don't mind my asking," she quickly added.

Mariah studied the young woman for a moment. At home, she would have shared her thoughts with Victoria, even though her sister was young and flighty. Ginny seemed older and wiser, and in spite of being Mariah's maid, she could be a much-needed confidante.

"What do you think of Lord William?" she asked, standing and starting to undo the buttons of her morning dress.

Ginny was silent, but her pinched look of disgust told Mariah everything she needed to know.

"That bad?"

Ginny's cheeks pinked. "There are many things that I could tell you that I shouldn't."

Mariah smirked. "If I guessed, would you be able to nod?"

A flash of a grin pulled at Ginny's lips, and she bobbed her head once.

"Is he disrespectful toward his uncle on a regular basis?" Mariah asked.

"That I can tell you openly, and the answer is yes."

Ginny paused, then added in a whisper. "Downstairs, we're appalled by it."

Mariah's brow shot up as Ginny helped her to step out of her dress. "So the servants like Lord Peter, then?"

"Oh yes, my lady," Ginny answered with genuine enthusiasm. "He's kind, fair, and a wonderful man to work for."

Mariah smiled at that. It confirmed everything that she thought she knew about him, but had begun to doubt at breakfast. "I rather like him myself," she said.

Ginny smiled as she draped Mariah's dress over the back of the chair and brought the riding habit to her. "I'm glad to hear it, my lady. We've all been wishing for Lord Dunsford to have a happy marriage, seeing as his last one...." She bit her lip, looking as though she'd gone too far.

"I know it wasn't happy," Mariah admitted, stepping into the skirt of her riding habit as Ginny held it for her.

The two of them were silent for a moment as Mariah dressed. "I'm under the impression that Lord William owes a lot of money."

Ginny hummed, one of her brows arching.

Mariah was on the right track. "I take it those debts are owed to unsavory sorts."

Ginny met Mariah's questioning look with silent confirmation, then shifted behind her to do up the buttons of her bodice.

"Does Lord William interfere with the servants?" Mariah asked on. She'd heard horrible stories of maids who had been compromised by gentlemen, and how those maids had been forced into lives of prostitution, or worse, when the blame for that abuse fell on their shoulders.

Behind her, Ginny hummed in a way that confirmed Mariah's suspicion and sent a chill down her spine.

Mariah glanced over her shoulder. "Has he attempted anything with you?"

"Once," she answered with a firmness that brought a proud smile to Mariah's face. Ginny had obviously stood up to the man.

"Does Peter know about Lord William's behavior?" Mariah asked.

Ginny let out a breath then moved to stand in front of Mariah, glancing over her to make sure the riding habit was in order. "His lordship has done everything he can to stop Lord William, my lady, but we all know that he can't toss the blackguard out on his ear, begging your pardon."

"Because of Peter's agreement with his brother," Mariah said.

Ginny sighed. "I don't think Lord Dunsford could possibly have known what he was getting into with that deal, but it's too late now. And bless him, he's had so many other things to worry about that Mrs. Wilson is loath to tell him about every offence his nephew commits." As soon as the words were out, Ginny snapped her mouth shut and met Mariah's eyes warily. "I shouldn't have said that."

"I'm glad you did." Mariah reassured her. "Perhaps,

in the future, Mrs. Wilson could come to me with these things."

"That would be nice, my lady." Ginny hesitated. "But if I were you, I would urge Lord Dunsford to keep Lord William under lock and key until he agrees to leave on his own accord."

"I wonder if he could actually do that." Mariah headed into her bedroom, but Ginny chased after her.

"Lock the blackguard up, my lady?" she asked.

"Yes."

Ginny grinned. "If he doesn't, downstairs, we all have bets that the law will someday."

Mariah stopped, eyes going wide. "Is Lord William that much of a criminal?"

Ginny made a scoffing sound. "He has been seen keeping company with a rough sort at the pubs in Truro."

"You've seen him?"

"Not me, my lady." Ginny shook her head. "But Davy says he's witnessed things that would make my hair curl. Although to be honest, I suspect young Davy says half the things he does in an attempt to impress the ladies."

Mariah laughed. "Young men are all the same. It makes me glad I've married one who is past all that nonsense." Although after the morning she'd had, she was beginning to think that nonsense never truly went away, it just changed forms.

"Lord Dunsford is a catch, my lady," Ginny assured

her. "And we're all certain he'll find a way to rid us of his nephew."

"I certainly hope so," Mariah said as they made their way to the hall. "Even so, I fear Starcross Castle won't be completely safe until...." She let her words trail off and pressed a hand to her belly.

"Don't worry, my lady." Ginny grinned. "I'm sure that blessed day is right around the corner."

Mariah wanted to hug her maid, but propriety stopped her. "Thank you, Ginny."

Perhaps with friends like Ginny in her corner, there was hope for her new life being a smooth one after all.

Peter paced the courtyard in front of the stables, wondering what was taking Mariah so long. He'd never minded when Anne took hours to dress for the simplest things, but with Mariah, every moment they spent apart seemed too long. That, and the longer she was out of his sight, the greater the chance that William might find her and cause damage he couldn't fix.

His conversation with William continued to irritate him. Try as Peter did to measure his responses to William's manipulative tactics, his nephew had hit the sorest spot possible by suggesting he had put his own pleasure ahead of Anne's wellbeing. Not because mating with Anne had been pleasurable. Exactly the opposite. But he could have tried harder to stop her. And now here he was, hanging his hopes on having a child with

Mariah. But at what cost to her? If he truly cared about her, he would send her away until he could figure out how to neutralize William. And William knew it. Peter had left their conversation with the feeling that William was about to try something outlandish to get what he wanted.

"My lord." Harry, the head stableman, cleared his throat. "Perhaps you'd like me to saddle one of the horses with a calmer temperament than Charger?"

Peter shook himself out of his dark thoughts and turned to Harry with a puzzled frown. "Why? Is something wrong with Charger?" He glanced to his tall, black steed. Charger was perhaps his favorite of every horse he'd ever owned, and he was currently pawing at the cobblestones as if ready to run.

Harry cleared his throat again. "Only, my lord, you know how he tends to feel the mood of whoever's riding him."

Peter loosened his shoulders as Harry's observation hit him. The black mood that William had left him with was that obvious. He scolded himself, walking over to Charger and stroking his nose. "I'm sorry, old boy. Too much to think about these days."

Charger blew out a breath and bobbed his head, as if telling Peter to come to his senses or else. Peter couldn't help but grin.

"There's a reason I like you best," he murmured to the horse, patting his neck.

The door to the house opened, and Mariah entered

the courtyard dressed in a fashionable, grey riding habit. Even at a distance, she was beautiful.

"Except her," he said to Charger. "I like her best of all."

Beside him, Harry hid a wide grin by coughing into his hand. Peter raised an eyebrow at the man, then headed across the courtyard to meet Mariah.

"You made it," he said, reaching for her, but pulling back. He glanced at the windows of the house that faced the courtyard, anxious over whether William was spying on him from above. It was a paranoia that he had to get rid of as soon as possible.

"I wouldn't have been able to find my way without Mr. Snyder's help," she said, smiling at the butler.

"Thank you, Snyder." Peter nodded at him. Snyder bowed in return, then headed back into the house. Peter offered his arm to Mariah, and was relieved when she took it. If he had his way, the rest of the world would disappear, leaving them to enjoy each other's company worry-free. "This is Harry, our stableman." He walked Mariah over to where Harry was bringing a gray mare out of the stable.

"How do you do?" Mariah greeted the man.

"Very well, my lady." Harry bowed in return. "I've got Lady Jane saddled and ready for you."

Mariah smiled at both Harry and the mare. Peter stood back and watched as Harry helped her to mount. She seemed to know what she was doing, which was a blessing. He liked to ride, though he had little time for it.

But if it were a pastime that Mariah enjoyed, maybe he'd do more of it. Once she was secure in her sidesaddle, he strode over to Charger and mounted in one, swift movement.

"Oh my." Mariah's eyes were wide and her cheeks were pink when he wheeled Charger around to face her.

"Is there a problem?" Peter asked, using his legs to guide Charger closer to her as he settled in his seat.

Mariah raked him with a glance, her eyes sparkling. "I didn't realize you were such an accomplished horseman."

Peter grinned, trying not to feel too full of himself. All things considered, after the morning they'd had, it was impossible not to gloat at being noticed for physical prowess. "I was an officer in the army," he reminded her, nudging Charger into a walk and making sure Mariah kept up by his side. He headed to the gate that led out of the courtyard and into the castle's front garden. "Horsemanship was a necessity."

"It looks like you've stayed in practice," she said, her smile growing.

Peter chuckled, turning down a path that would lead them around the immediate property of the castle. The farther they got from the castle and any possibility of William's prying eyes, the easier he felt. "I may be a scholar by nature, but I'm a soldier by training."

"And is horsemanship the only military skill you've maintained?" Mariah asked. She too seemed easier as they rode.

"No, I have a few other martial skills up my sleeves," he said.

"Like what?"

His grin turned downright wicked. "You'll have to wait until the time is right, then I'll show you."

The way she laughed and sent him a sultry look made him wish they were miles away from everything. "I suppose that explains a few things," she said.

"Such as?"

Her lips twitched in a coy smile. "Such as how a desiccated mummy can have such a powerful physique."

It was as perfect a compliment as he'd ever received, and it made the effort he'd put into staying healthy worth it. But Mariah's admiring gaze was captured by something else entirely as they turned a corner, rode out from behind one of the hedge-lined gardens and onto an open lawn. The castle loomed to one side in all its sunlit glory.

"It really is a castle," Mariah gasped, her eyes wide.

She pulled Lady Jane to a halt, and Peter stopped beside her. He'd grown up in Starcross Castle, but it wasn't hard to imagine what the first sight of the place could do to people. It had been too dark for Mariah to see it properly when they arrived the day before, but now there it was, the original keep with its crenelated towers, the Georgian extension that blended so well with the rest of it, and the modern wing that made it look like something out of a storybook. It was magnificent, if he did say so himself.

"Behold, my lady. Your castle."

Mariah swallowed, and her dazzled smile became overwhelmed. "I don't know if I'm ready to be mistress of all this."

"Of course you are," he said, nudging Charger to walk on and Lady Jane to follow. "Your father assures me you are not only competent, but that you need something to keep you occupied and useful."

Mariah shook herself out of her trance and laughed. "Dear Papa. He's right about that." She sent him a fetching grin.

Peter was surprised at how quickly the world set itself to right without the threat of William looming over him. He took Mariah around the castle itself, then picked up their pace to venture farther afield, toward the mines and some of the tenant villages. Charger was in a mood to gallop, so he let him, only to find Mariah doing an admirable job of keeping up. It was enough to make him consider taking her somewhere other than Starcross Castle for their honeymoon period after all.

And yet, there was so much to do in Cornwall.

"Is this the mine?" Mariah asked as they rounded the crest of a hill and looked down to a valley that was built up with purposeful, stone buildings.

"One of them," Peter answered. "This is Carleen."

She blinked at him. "You have more than one mine?"

A twist of pride filled him. "Yes, the estate has had quite a few mines over the years. This area of Cornwall is rich in ore."

She continued to look as though pieces were falling

into place in her mind. "But that must mean...that must mean that you have quite a bit of money."

"*We* have more than enough to suit our needs," he told her, downplaying the extent of his wealth. Riches had never mattered to him apart from what they could do for those who depended on him. He'd been more concerned about who he would leave them to than enjoying them himself.

Mariah frowned. "If you have so much money, why not pay off William's debts so that he'll go away?"

The cheer that Peter had been feeling flattened. Charger danced sideways at his change in mood, which gave Peter the blessed seconds he needed to gather his thoughts. "I have paid off some of them, but for men like William, all the money in the world still wouldn't be enough," he said, meeting and holding Mariah's gaze. "I've seen men my age take a prosperous estate that is hundreds of years old and squander every last farthing. Money is challenging to earn, but far too easy to waste."

Mariah hummed in agreement and nodded. "I think I know what you mean. Like the man in Parliament who my father is always butting heads with, Mr. Turpin. Papa says he squandered a large fortune on cards and horses."

"And bad investments," Peter added. He hoped Edmund had been wise enough not to tell someone as innocent as Mariah how else Turpin had lost everything he'd inherited. To explain would mean talking about Theodore Shayles, and no one as pure and innocent as Mariah should know anything about Shayles and his world. "Which is why I refuse to give William the money he says he needs."

"Because it would be opening the floodgates," Mariah said.

Peter nodded. "I'm glad you understand and that you don't think I'm some sort of horrible, old skinflint."

A grin tweaked the corner of Mariah's mouth. "I think we've established that you're not as old as others seem to think you are."

He laughed, wishing they were closer to home and his bedroom.

Mariah grew more serious. "And I think I understand what you mean about William. Would it hurt you if I were to say I don't like him?"

Strangely enough, it did fill Peter with a sense of disappointment. Not because Mariah didn't give her approval, but because he hadn't been able to make William into someone likable. He shook his head. "I only regret that I didn't have time to explain the situation more fully or to prepare before he descended on Starcross Castle. Believe me when I say I didn't think he'd be here to greet you."

"I believe you." Mariah sent him a smile that was far kinder than he deserved. "And anyhow, I'm not sure any amount of time would have prepared me for William." Before he could reply, she went on with, "Why don't you show me your mine so that I can get an idea of where our wealth and opulence comes from?"

She was back to flirting, for which Peter was

grateful. "Right this way, my lady," he said, nudging Charger to start down into the valley. He could forget about the looming problem of William for a moment. The way things were, with William stubbornly refusing to leave, the best he could do was to spend as much time with Mariah in his sight as possible.

※

THE BACK ROOM OF THE COUNTY ARMS IN TRURO wasn't crowded in the middle of the afternoon, which was just what William needed. Most of the regulars wouldn't arrive at the inn and its pub until after dark, meaning no one who counted would see him slip into the smoky room to sit at one of its three small tables with two strangers.

"Do you have the money?" the shorter of the two men asked.

"Now, now, Poole." William's casual smile hid the panicked drumming of his heart against his ribs. "I told you these things take time."

"Shayles doesn't have time," the other man, taller with reddish hair, growled.

"Robinson." William shook his head and clucked his tongue. "Lord Shayles has faith in me, and so should you."

"Shayles's faith has its limits," Poole went on. "He wants his money."

"I'm still the heir to the Dunsford title and fortune," William reminded them with feigned casualness.

"Not for long," Robinson snarled.

William shook his head, leaning forward, elbows on the table. "Listen. You tell Lord Shayles that he has nothing to worry about. The chit my uncle married is as weak as milk toast. There isn't enough of a spark between the two of them to light a match." Although, after what he'd witnessed in Peter's study, he wasn't as confident of that as he'd been upon first meeting his new aunt. He was risking everything on the bet that the new wife was just for show and that his uncle was well past breeding. "Even if there was," he went on with a shrug, "I've got my contingency plan primed and ready to go."

Poole and Robinson exchanged flat looks. "You mean the nonsense in your father's will about you getting half the estate if your uncle gives you the boot?"

William swallowed hard, shifting in his chair as though it were covered with tacks, pointy side up. "You know about that?"

"Shayles knows about it, and that's all that matters," Robinson said.

Poole leaned across the table in imitation of William's posture. "Shayles doesn't put much stock in your so-called contingency plan. He wanted us to tell you that your uncle has ten times the backbone you have."

"Lord Shayles is wrong," William snapped.

Poole and Robinson laughed as though William had shared a bawdy joke. Poole shook his head. "Look. It's simple. Shayles wants his money back, and he doesn't care how you get it. You can try to get Dunsford to kick you out, but the boss won't wait forever."

"What do you mean?" William asked, squirming even harder.

"Shayles wants to be paid in full by June first."

"June first? He said I had all summer."

"June first," Poole repeated.

"That's less than a fortnight away." Panic squeezed at William's throat, turning his stomach and his blood to ice.

Robinson shrugged as though he didn't care. Poole shook his head. "It didn't take you more than a fortnight to spend five hundred thousand pounds, so it stands to reason that it shouldn't take you that long to raise it, right?"

William wanted to argue that it'd taken him years to sink five hundred thousand pounds into the hole, but his protest would have fallen on deaf ears. "What if I get my uncle to declare me his heir regardless of any child this new wife of his might have?"

Poole and Robinson snorted and rolled their eyes.

"What earl in his right mind would declare someone other than his own son to be his heir?" Robinson said. "Even if the law would let him."

"All right, what if I have him declare me heir until whatever phantom child of his comes of age?" William scrambled for another way out. "My uncle is ancient already. Even if he does have a son—which is doubtful, given that he couldn't get his seed to grow in Anne's garden for twenty years—Uncle is sure to die years before the brat comes of age."

"Shayles wants his money now," Poole insisted, growing visibly impatient.

"And...and what if I can't get it?" Sweat dripped down William's back and began to bead on his brow.

"Your money or your life," Poole said with a smile. Robinson underscored the point by leaning back in his chair, brushing his coat aside, and revealing a shiny revolver in his belt.

"This isn't the Wild West of America," William said with a snort, hoping he came off as dismissive and not ready to soil himself.

"It doesn't have to be," Poole went on. "Shayles wants his money. If he can't get it, he'll use you to send a message to others who try to default on their loans."

William swallowed the rush of bile in his throat. Words failed him. All he could do was stare at the gun. Damn Peter for marrying that young bitch. Damn him for not accepting the way things should have been. If he thought he could get away with cutting him out of the inheritance that was rightfully his, he had another thing coming.

"June first?" William repeated, forcing himself to look calm, even though he raged and quailed in equal measure on the inside.

"June first." Poole nodded. "Or else."

"Not a problem." William knocked on the table and stood. "Shayles will have proof that my uncle still considers me his heir or a note from his solicitor stating that he has defaulted on the terms of my father's will by throwing me out by the end of the month."

"You really think you can get your uncle to turn on you now when he hasn't after all these years?" Robinson asked.

William grinned. "He hasn't exposed his flank as egregiously in all these years. The old cheat might think he's thwarted me by taking a young wife, but all it's done is shown me how to strike him where it hurts. And I intend to strike hard."

CHAPTER 11

*B*y the time they returned to the castle, the sun was beginning to set, and Mariah was starving. Not just for supper either. Seeing Peter astride a horse, in command of all he surveyed, had fired Mariah's blood. As Ginny helped her to change out of her riding habit and into supper clothes, she had half a mind to slip through the dressing rooms into Peter's room.

"You should, my lady," Ginny whispered, winking.

"You don't think he'd mind?" Mariah asked, hesitating to step into the dress that Ginny held out for her.

Ginny clutched the dress to her chest. "Mind? My lady, he's probably waiting with his ear pressed to the door for you to go to him."

Mariah raised a hand to her mouth to hide her giggle, glanced from Ginny to the door leading to Peter's dressing room, then tip-toed over to it.

But when she tried the handle, it was locked.

"That's odd," she said, trying not to feel disappointed. She walked slowly back to Ginny, glancing over her shoulder at the door.

"Perhaps Mr. Wright locked it accidentally," Ginny said. "He's not used to anyone using these rooms."

"You're probably right."

She finished dressing and had Ginny fix her hair before she went downstairs for supper. She intended to ask Peter about the locked door before they ate, but as it turned out, he'd never made it back to his room. One of the men from the mine had been waiting in his office when they returned. They were still engaged in conversation, which meant Mariah had to continue on to the dining room alone.

"Well, if it isn't the Countess of Dunsford." William was seated at the table, already being served by a footman. He looked worse for wear, as though he'd been outside but the sunny May weather hadn't agreed with him.

"Lord William." Mariah nodded to him, then glanced over her shoulder and into the hall, hoping Peter would finish with his business soon, before going in to take her seat.

"Abandoned, are we?" William asked with a lascivious flicker of his eyebrow as Mariah sat across from him.

"Peter is attending to business." Mariah focused on Davy as the young footman served her, not on William.

"Such is the life of a countess, I suppose," William said, starting on his soup.

"I beg your pardon." Mariah was already losing her appetite.

William shrugged. "You can expect to spend a lot of nights alone where my uncle is concerned. He has so much *business* to take care of."

"Yes, I'm sure he does."

They ate in silence. Mariah was halfway through the main course before Peter joined them.

"I'm sorry I'm late," he said with an irritated frown, taking his place at the head of the table between the two of them. "I'm afraid the business with the mine couldn't wait."

"Perfectly understandable," William said before Mariah could open her mouth. "As long as you're with us now."

"Yes, well." Peter nodded to Davy as he served supper, then sent an apologetic look to Mariah as he picked up his fork.

He hadn't taken three bites when Mr. Snyder appeared in the doorway and cleared his throat. "My lord, it seems there is a matter of utmost urgency that needs your attention."

"Now?" Peter's frustration was palpable.

"Yes, my lord," Mr. Snyder said, looking as apologetic as the man could. "It is in regards to a delicate situation involving one of the tenants."

Peter let out a breath and stood. "I'll be back as soon as possible," he told Mariah.

She gave him a smile of encouragement as he left, but

that vanished as soon as she saw the smug look on William's face.

"Like I said, Uncle has ever so much business."

Peter didn't return to dinner, though Mariah waited for him. William gave up and left, but it was little relief. Eventually she gave up too. She headed to Peter's library, but the door was closed. There didn't seem to be anything else to do but go up to bed.

Ginny had a bath waiting and her nightgown laid out, but even that couldn't soothe Mariah's irritation with the way the day had gone. Worse still, after she finished bathing and donned her nightgown, the door to Peter's dressing room was still locked. So was the door to his room from the hall. It couldn't possibly be on purpose, not after the afternoon they'd had. But there was nothing Mariah could do but climb into her own bed to wait until Peter came for her.

Whether he did or not, she never found out. She fell asleep.

In the morning, she tried the door to Peter's dressing room again, but it was still locked. She told herself that he must have finished with his business late at night and let her sleep out of respect. She planned to ask him about the lock at breakfast, only William was in rare form as the three of them sat around the table. His bitterness and insults were so off-putting that when Mrs. Wilson interrupted to ask if she might have a word with Mariah about the running of the house, Mariah was only too glad to flee.

Not that it did much good. She could run away from William, but the gnawing hollowness of being apart from Peter for so long followed her. She missed him, and she wasn't ashamed to say so. She missed the heat of his body and the heady pleasure of making love, but more than that, she missed talking to him. There was so much she still had to learn about her new husband. How was she supposed to learn it all when responsibility kept them apart?

It was one thing to be a new wife missing her husband, but it was an entirely different thing to be a new countess.

"Here are the menus for the week." Mrs. Wilson handed over a set of cards as the two of them sat at a small table in a room that had been allocated as Mariah's office. "I'm a bit concerned about Thursday's tea, if you must know, my lady," Mrs. Wilson went on. "It's Mrs. Harmon's first attempt at salmagundi, and her results with new dishes are inconsistent."

"I'm sure it'll be fine." Mariah smiled, wriggling restlessly in her seat. "Especially since it will just be the three of us for tea."

Mrs. Wilson gave her look that said she wished it were only two before going on with, "I should mention that Mrs. Harmon has been dreaming of the day when you entertain, my lady."

"Oh?" The very idea of having people over to Starcross Castle when things were so new and unsettled sent a quiver through her gut.

"Yes, my lady. Mrs. Harmon prides herself on some of the more elaborate dishes in her arsenal, and she is most eager to impress you."

"I see. Well, I wouldn't mind if she felt like impressing me regardless of how many people we have to dine." She grinned.

Mrs. Wilson met the look of friendship with the warm sort of respect that Mariah had come to expect from her. Ginny might have been willing to lower the boundaries of hierarchy a little, but Mrs. Wilson was a stickler for propriety.

"Now, my lady, about the situation in the dairy," Mrs. Wilson went on.

Mariah blinked. "We have a dairy?"

"Yes, my lady," Mrs. Wilson said with utmost patience. "And it seems that we need to hire a new milkmaid, since the last one left to marry."

A dizzying rush of embarrassment at the memory of Robert running off with a milkmaid heated Mariah's face. She didn't suppose she would ever get over the shock of Robert's betrayal, as happy as she was with Peter.

"Just make sure she's a good, honest girl," she said, a catch in her throat.

Mrs. Wilson looked at her oddly. It was Mariah's luck that Mr. Snyder passed by the open door of her office at that moment.

"Excuse me, Mrs. Wilson," she said leaping out of her seat. "I see Mr. Snyder with the mail, and I'm...I'm expecting a letter from my mother. Everything here looks satisfactory."

She rushed out of the room, leaving Mrs. Wilson bewildered in her wake. It wasn't the most dignified thing she'd ever done, but the past had a way of causing embarrassment far longer than it should, and she wasn't up to dealing with it at the moment.

"Is that the mail, Mr. Snyder?" She caught the butler several yards down the hall.

Mr. Snyder turned to her, his brow raised. "Yes, my lady. I was just taking it to his lordship."

A thrill zipped through Mariah's chest. "Would you mind if I took it?" she asked. Not only would the errand give her a chance to forget about milkmaids, it would further her efforts to keep a close eye on Peter and to make sure William didn't bother him.

"Yes, my lady." Mr. Snyder nodded, then handed the mail over. He continued on to some other task as Mariah carried the mail across the hall to Peter.

Peter was in his office, at his desk, frowning away at a pile of letters and papers. Mariah paused in the doorway to study him, quivering with relief at the sight of him. His face was as expressive as a canvas and ever-changing. That morning, it was careworn and lined with concern. And yet, in spite of what Victoria would say if she were looking at him, Mariah no longer thought of Peter's serious expressions as old. Responsible, yes. Duty-bound, definitely. But not old.

Proving her point, he glanced up and smiled when he

saw her in the doorway. Years and cares rolled off him, leaving the man she was quickly coming to love.

"This is a surprise," he said, standing and coming around his desk to meet her.

Mariah walked all the way into the room. When they met, Peter glanced cautiously to the door, and when it was clear they were alone, he rested a hand on her hip and leaned in for a kiss. Mariah could ignore every other care pressing down on her for kisses like that. His arms were warm and firm around her, and the scent of him made her blush with memories of their bodies joined together.

"I missed you last night," she said with a heavy sigh, unwilling to leave the sanctuary of his arms just yet.

"And I missed you," he said, stealing another kiss. "I suppose you needed your rest, though."

"And I guess your business was pressing."

He arched an eyebrow. "Not as much as it could have been. I did my best to wrap it up, but Mr. Palmer went on and on. I didn't want to be rude." He let her go and took a step back. "What do you have here?"

"I brought your mail," she said with an appreciative grin.

"Excellent." Peter kept a hand on her waist as he escorted her to the desk. He seemed to like staying in contact with her when they were together, something she never would have imagined she'd like so much.

He took the mail when they reached the desk and sat

to shuffle through it. Mariah perched on the side of his desk, glancing at the papers that covered it.

"Is this about the mine?" she asked.

Peter's brow lifted first, then he dragged his eyes away from the mail to look at her. "Yes. It's the report Owen Llewellyn put together after his initial survey of the estate."

"What does it say?"

He blinked. "You really want to know?"

"Of course," she laughed, then stood and pivoted to stand beside his chair, where she could have a better view of the papers. "They're *our* mines, after all."

His answering smile was both endearing and perplexing. "That's true, they are."

"Then what's that look for?"

He chuckled. "I never would have expected my wife to be interested in mines and ore and surveyor's reports."

Her mouth twitched, and she wasn't sure whether it was with amusement or offense. "You mean Anne was never interested."

He lost some of his amusement and nodded. "No, she wasn't. But neither was my mother."

Mariah rested a hand on her hip and stared at him. "You know I'm not Anne, right?"

"I know." He turned his gaze back to the papers, picking one up uselessly and putting it down again.

Mariah put a hand on his shoulder. "I'm not, Peter."

"I never said you were." He glanced up and met her eyes.

Mariah had the impression he was trying to prove the sincerity of his words with the look, but she saw more vulnerability in their blue depths than he probably intended.

She cleared her throat and turned back to the desk. "So what do these reports say?"

A ghost of a grin twitched at the corner of Peter's lips, and he shifted to sit straight in his chair. Clearly, he knew she was changing the subject. "There are two reports. One is an assessment of how much copper is left in the Carleen mine. Short answer, not enough to justify the expense of keeping it open. The other is an initial report of possible locations of ore deposits across the estate, though it is only an amateur assessment done by one of my newer mine foremen."

Mariah wasn't sure what she was looking at, but she'd been paying attention enough in the past few weeks to interpret the low numbers on the report about the Carleen mine. "That doesn't look good."

"No," Peter said, rubbing the bottom half of his face. "It's not."

"But this one...." She picked up the letter from the surveyor. "So there are potential copper deposits on your property?"

"There are," Peter sighed. "But none of them look to be substantial enough to keep production at the level it is now."

"And that's important." Mariah looked for a place to sit down so that she could study the information in front of her.

Peter must have understood what she was looking for. He hooked an arm around her waist and drew her to sit on the chair between his legs. Mariah couldn't help but giggle at the gesture, or at the way he breathed in as if smelling her hair. Any minute, she expected to feel the stir of something hard against her backside, given the way she was wedged against him.

To her surprise, Peter cleared his throat and picked up a ledger from the side of the desk. "These are reports of production from Carleen and all of the other, smaller mines on the property for the past few years. But they also show the amounts that have been paid out in wages to the men who work the mines."

He spread the ledger open on top of the rest of the papers and let Mariah leaf through it. His hand rested on her waist, but the excitement that had her heart beating faster wasn't for their physical closeness. He was trusting her with the business of the estate. As far as she was concerned, that was as intimate as burying himself within her.

"Good gracious. You employ more than a hundred men?" She twisted to look at him.

"Far more," he said. "This is only part of what makes up the estate. Aside from the mines, we have quite a few tenant farmers."

"And they're your responsibility." She nodded, glancing back to the ledgers. "Do you pay them a fixed wage or is it dependent on production from the mines?"

"It's a fixed wage, but I try to increase it from year-to-year." He paused, leaning to the side to get a better look at her. "Are you certain you want to know about all this?"

"Yes," she answered emphatically. "This is what you care about. I want to be a part of all of this."

The smile that lit his face was deeper than anything Mariah could have expected. "No one, not even William, has been interested in poring over all this with me before."

"What about your brother, William's father?"

Peter shrugged. "He was as involved as he needed to be when he thought there was a chance he might inherit. He didn't enjoy it, though."

"And do you?"

His smile grew. "I enjoy knowing that the land that has been in my family for generations provides for the families who depend on it. And I worry for their welfare, if the mines should be forced to close permanently or...."

"Or if William inherits," she finished for him.

He nodded, resting his forehead against the side of her head with a sigh.

"Don't worry." She squeezed his thigh. "We're not about to let that happen."

As expected, she felt the stir of his arousal against her backside. How she'd missed him the night before! She giggled and made a show of turning back to the ledgers, and wriggling against him.

"Now." She cleared her throat. "Explain to me everything about how mines work. I want to know it all."

"Yes, my lady," he said, resting a hand over her belly.

The gesture was both teasing and heartbreaking, considering what he could be thinking by holding her that way. Mariah did her best to focus as Peter launched into an explanation of the basics of finding and extracting copper ore, how it was brought to market, and what prices had been recently. Mariah was highly conscious of the heat and power of his body around hers, but as his explanation continued, they both became more interested in the lesson than in dallying. It was as much of a surprise to Mariah as it was a delight. She already knew they were compatible on a sensual level. It was wonderful to discover that they also got along when business was on the table.

"So the estate isn't precisely in danger if more copper is not found," she concluded half an hour later, skimming through a page of the ledger, "but it would mean completely changing the economic focus of everyone who depends on us."

"Yes." Peter nodded, then kissed her shoulder. Mariah grinned. "And the way grand estates like this one have been faring recently, I'm afraid it would only be a matter of time before we would have to stop employing so many people and start turning over the land for public use."

"Selling, you mean."

He shrugged. "It's been happening all across the nation."

"But you wouldn't let Starcross Castle and its estate be broken up."

"Not if I can help it, but—"

"Uncle, I've had an idea."

Mariah felt as though ice water had been dumped over her as Lord William strode into the room without warning, a ledger of some sort in his hands. There wasn't enough time for her to extract herself from Peter's embrace or his chair, and as soon as William spotted them sitting together, his eyes flashed with fury.

"What is she doing here?"

Mariah rose as fast as she could and stepped to the side. She tried not to look at Peter, but wondered if they'd blundered too badly to recover the illusion of indifference to each other.

"Mariah brought me the day's mail," Peter said, his voice clipped. He stood as well. "What do you want?"

Mariah peeked at William, assessing whether she needed to find a way to deflect his suspicions. There didn't seem to be anything to do, though, especially when William glanced at the front of Peter's trousers and narrowed his eyes.

Peter cleared his throat, color splashing his face. "What do you want, William?" he repeated.

"I've been looking at the reports from the tenant farms," William said, approaching the desk with a look of calculation. "I think I've discovered a way to make them more productive."

"Why?" Peter asked.

William studied him for a few more seconds, sending an assessing glance to Mariah, then relaxed into a wry smirk. "You told me to solve my problems on my own, so I am."

"I don't understand," Peter said.

Mariah stepped to the side, glancing to the door and wondering if she should leave. She caught a quick glance from Peter that told her to stay where she was.

"I'm still the heir," William said, glancing suspiciously between Peter and Mariah. "For the time being," he muttered. "And in that capacity, I have decided that I should take more of an active role in running the estate."

Peter squared his shoulders, an expression of grave severity turning his face to stone. "Running the estate or finding ways to skim off the top to pay your debts?"

"Uncle, how could you suggest that I would do such a thing?" William balked, but he wasn't quick enough to hide his frustration. That told Mariah that Peter's guess had been correct. "Now," he went on, "tell your pretty little wife to go play with her dolls somewhere so that the grown-ups can talk business."

Anger rose up in Mariah so fast that she grew dizzy. "How dare you?" she demanded.

Peter raised a hand to her, warning her to keep calm. "Mariah stays if she wants to," he said.

William's whole body tensed, and his frown turned bitter. "So that's the way it is, is it? You're tossing me over for a bit of skirt?"

"I am not now, nor will I ever toss you over, out, or under anything, William." Peter took a small step toward her. "Mariah has every right to have a say in the running of the estate. It is her home now."

William gaped in outrage. He recovered quickly, though, huffing in indignation and rolling his eyes. "I see. *Her* house and not mine. Not your own flesh and blood, to whom you made a promise."

Peter sighed. "I did make a promise, William, and I will keep it. You would do well to start some sort of enterprise on your own to pay your creditors."

"I don't have time—" William paused, face red, then let out a breath. His expression shifted quickly from anger to calculation. "Fine, then. You force my hand." He cleared his throat. "Is this what you promised her in order to get her into your bed? A piece of the pie?"

"How dare you insinuate that Peter has to coerce me into intimacy," Mariah snapped. It would have been wiser to bite her tongue, seeing as William's attempt to bait her was so obvious, but she was tired of the young man's implications, tired of pretending her marriage was a sham, and tired of not knowing what was really going on. "Why don't you just say what you're after so that we can all move on with our lives?"

"Mariah." Peter frowned, warning more than scolding.

William let his arms drop, closing the farm ledger with a snap as he did. "You want to know what I'm after?" He paced toward Mariah, his eyes narrowed, his grin vicious. "I'm after what is mine and not yours.

Where were you last year, or last month, for that matter? Did you even know this place existed? I grew up here."

"You grew up at Mulberry Court." Peter countered him, moving to stand between William and Mariah. "Which you were forced to sell to pay off debts."

William sent a look of pure murder at Peter then turned it on Mariah with so much threat that it made her shiver. "You, my lady, have taken everything from me. Don't make me return the favor."

"That's enough," Peter said. He turned to William. "You will—"

"Leave this house?" William asked, too much eagerness in his eyes. "Was that enough to convince you to throw me out?"

"Stay away from my wife," Peter growled with an air of finality.

"Only if you do as well." William took a step toward him.

The two men glared at each other, toe to toe. Peter was a good three inches taller than William, but it was clear to Mariah that William had a will of iron and that he wouldn't back down.

"Mrs. Wilson implied that we should host a dinner party," Mariah said, desperate to break up the impending fight.

Both men blinked and stared at her in confusion.

Mariah licked her lips and clasped her hands in front of her. The ploy had worked, but she had no idea where she should go from there. "Perhaps you could both recommend some neighbors that I could invite."

William looked at her as though she'd gone mad. Peter's look wasn't all that different to start, but it quickly flashed with inspiration. "Captain Tennant and his new wife are still in the area." He stared at William. "I'm sure they would love to see you again."

"Oh no." William laughed, shifting his weight from one foot to the other, a manic look in his eyes. "I'm not going to turn tail and run. I'm not afraid of Tennant."

"Fine." A tight smile made Peter seem even more dangerous. "Then stay and explain yourself to Albert."

"I will." William crossed his arms, holding the ledger under his arm. "And I recommend, my lady, that you invite Lord Barkley."

Peter sucked in a breath, but was quick to hide the intensity of his reaction.

Mariah frowned. "Who is Lord Barkley?"

"Anne's brother," Peter answered with a deep frown.

"I'm sure he'd like to meet the woman who took his sister's place," William said with a triumphant grin.

Mariah bit the inside of her lip, trying not to let either man see what she was thinking. She was eager to meet Captain Tennant, especially if it meant she could ask about the sinking of his ship. And if she were honest, she wanted to meet Anne's brother as well. While she couldn't ask him anything outright, perhaps speaking with him over supper would untangle some of the mystery that still hung over Anne.

"All right," she said, shrugging to make it look as though she didn't care one way or another. "I'll have Mrs. Wilson put together invitations right away. Anyone else I should consider inviting?"

Peter and William were still staring daggers at each other, wrapped up in their own tug-o-war. "The Goodmans and the St. Aubyns should be invited as well, seeing as they're our closest neighbors," Peter said.

"Very well." Mariah took a hesitant step toward the door. She hated to leave Peter alone, but the sooner she brought in reinforcements the better. "Is there anything else you need me for?" she asked.

Peter pulled his gaze away from William and met her eyes with frustration and apology. "We'll speak later."

"Yes, dearest," William added with a mocking sneer. "We'll speak later."

Mariah nodded to Peter, hoping he could see how worried she was for him, then turned to go. There had to be a way to get William out of their lives. Every moment that he remained at the center of her marriage made her wonder how she and Peter would ever be truly happy.

CHAPTER 12

She was locking her door. Peter couldn't figure out why. He paced his bedroom, wondering if he'd said something to upset her. But of course he had. Everything was upsetting when William was around. If he could have thrown his nephew out without risking half his family's heritage, he would have. But every time he considered whether it might just be worth the price to be rid of the whelp, Will's voice popped into his head, scolding him for turning his back on the only family he had left.

Only family except Mariah. And, God willing, their children. Which they were never going to have if he didn't resolve whatever mystery was keeping them apart.

He sighed and rubbed a hand over his face. His pacing took him to the head of his bed, and he snatched up a pillow, throwing it across the room in frustration. He could march through his dressing room and pound on

Mariah's door until she let him in, but he remembered too well the sinking dread in his gut on the nights when Anne pounded on his door, demanding that he perform. He remembered the guilt that clung to him like stale sweat, knowing their nights together would only lead to more pain.

In the end, he gritted his teeth, ignored what his heart was screaming at him, and left Mariah alone. If she didn't want him to pleasure her, the least he could do was respect her. But it made for a restless night, and landed him in a foul temper the next day.

"What's wrong, Uncle?" William asked him with a taunting smile halfway through the morning.

Peter paced the courtyard in front of the stables as Harry saddled Charger. His already sour mood worsened at the sight of William. "What do you want?" he asked.

"Nothing." William blinked with feigned innocence. "I was simply coming to have Harry saddle Lightning so that I could ride out to the tenant farms."

Peter narrowed his eyes. William's newfound interest in the tenants worried him. But then, everything worried him where William was concerned. He nodded, then ignored his nephew, staring into the stable and willing Harry to hurry up.

"Trouble in bed?" William asked with a sneer.

Peter glared at him, half because of the impertinence of the question, and half because his nephew had hit the nail on the head far too quickly. "What would you know of it?" he snapped.

William's grin widened. "You were always in a wretched mood on the days after you failed with Anne too."

Teeth clenched, Peter growled, "You'd do better to keep your assumptions to yourself, since they are, and always have been, wrong."

William's grin dropped. "He said he locked—" His mouth clamped shut and he rubbed a hand over the lower half of his face, muttering.

But he didn't have a chance to say or do anything more. Harry led Charger out of the stable and, as fast as he could, Peter mounted and rode off.

It wasn't until he was halfway to the mines that the oddness of William's comment struck him. Who said what? Had someone other than Mariah locked her door? He had half a mind to head back to the castle, find her, and ask her himself. What if the last two nights were simply a misunderstanding born of a nasty trick on William's part? The more he thought about it, the more certain he was that William was responsible for everything.

But the business of the mines kept him occupied for the better part of the day, and by the time he made it back to the castle, Mariah was nowhere to be found.

"She's downstairs with Mrs. Wilson, my lord," Ginny informed him when he went to check on the locks in their dressing rooms.

The faithful maid was hard at work sewing a rip in the hem of Mariah's riding habit. Peter had never had cause to doubt Ginny. Indeed, he considered her to be one of his most valuable and industrious servants, but his entire life was on edge.

"Ginny, you don't know anything about the doors between my and Mariah's dressing rooms being locked, do you?"

Ginny blushed, keeping her eyes on her work. "Her ladyship was disappointed."

Peter blew out a breath of relief, which was quickly followed by frustration. "I'm going to wring William's neck," he muttered, marching out of the room.

The rest of the day passed like a snail moving through treacle. Peter resisted the urge to find Mariah and take her up to bed, but only barely. He hadn't been so worked up and eager to slide between the sheets with a woman since he'd been a young university student who had just discovered the sensation of a woman's body pressed to his.

"Did you have a productive day?" he asked Mariah over supper, barely able to sit still long enough to finish the meal. He moved his foot under the table until he found her leg.

"Productive and exhausting," Mariah replied with a tired smile.

Peter tried not to be disappointed by her less than enthusiastic reaction to his flirtation. "I suppose Mrs. Wilson kept you busy."

"Yes, we have a great deal to plan for supper on

Friday." Mariah took a bite of beef, chewed for a moment, then set her fork down.

"Do you think you're ready to play the grand hostess?" William asked. He leaned forward in his seat, watching her with far too much interest for Peter's liking. "Or is being a countess too much for you?"

"Everything will be fine," Mariah replied, her voice a bit weak. Her complexion had gone a tad...green as well. "Mrs. Wilson is a great help."

"If this is all too much for you, you could always go home, you know," William went on, an intense light in his eyes. "I'm sure your parents would welcome you back into the bosom of your family. And don't you miss your sister? Victoria, I think her name was."

Mariah touched her fingers to her lips. Peter frowned, realizing she hadn't looked well since the soup course.

"Mariah, is something wrong?" he asked.

"I...." She rose suddenly. "Please excuse me, I think I'm going to be sick."

Peter was helpless to do anything but watch as Mariah rushed out of the room. The sound of retching followed as she turned the corner. He jumped to his feet, burning with concern. And though his first instinct was to wonder if she could be pregnant, sense told him it was far too soon. Sense and the triumphant smirk William wore as he sawed away at his roast.

"What did you do to her?" he demanded, already starting out of the room.

William shrugged. "It must have been something she ate."

It must have been, and Peter was willing to bet that whatever it was, William had been responsible.

Mariah was sick for days, and for days Peter stayed by her side as much as he could, caught between heartbreak over how miserable she felt and fury at the thought that William had deliberately poisoned her. He was ready to fire someone in the kitchens, especially when it was discovered that somehow a prawn that had spoiled had fallen into Mariah's soup before it was served.

"It's obvious what's going on here," Peter said Friday morning, pacing in front of Mariah's bed as she sat up, sipping tea and eating toast. "William is trying to get me to throw him out so that he wins half the estate. And barring that, he's trying to keep us from...." He flushed and glanced her way. "Producing an heir."

"He can't keep us away from each other forever," Mariah sighed.

Peter huffed a laugh. "Logic and reason were never William's strong points. He thinks from one moment to the next. It's how he wastes so much money and lands in so much trouble. And he knows he has nothing to lose by being transparent in his scheming."

"Should we employ someone to taste our food before we eat it, then?" Mariah asked.

Peter stopped pacing and marched to the side of her bed, sitting beside her. The color was back in her cheeks, and if her humor had returned as well, she was definitely on the mend. "I would hire an army to protect you if I thought it would help." He kissed her forehead. It was no longer hot and clammy as it'd been for the past few days.

She laughed and set her tea and toast aside, snuggling against him. "You know that I wouldn't last one day with an army tailing me."

The sweet heat of her body and the softness of her curves pressed against him sent fire through Peter's blood. He pulled her across his lap and slid a hand up her side to cradle her breast. "He can't keep us apart forever," he said before kissing her. He didn't even mind that her breath wasn't as fresh as it could have been or that she hadn't bathed in days.

She, however, did. "Peter." She pushed him back with a laugh. "I'm hardly in any state for intimacy right now."

"I don't care," he said, brushing a thumb across her nipple over the fabric of her nightgown. "You're beautiful to me in any condition."

She rested a hand on his face, smiling at him with a burst of affection that tied his heart in knots. "You're wonderful, you know."

He shook his head. "Not really."

"I think you are." She kissed his lips lightly.

Sickbed or not, he'd waited long enough to be with her again. He kissed her back, harder, slipping a hand under the covers, under her nightgown, and up her thigh. He wanted to feel her heat and wetness, to hear her sigh with pleasure. His cock was rigid with need and growing harder by the second.

And then Ginny threw open the door.

The poor maid stopped short when she saw Peter and Mariah together, her mouth dropping open. "I'm so sorry, my lord." She rushed out of the room, shutting the door behind her.

Peter blew out a breath, resting his forehead against the side of Mariah's head as she burst into laughter.

"This really isn't the time," she giggled. "And to be honest, I'd prefer to be clean and to be in your bed, not this musty thing."

"Tonight, then," he murmured, kissing the side of her neck.

"We have the supper tonight," Mariah reminded him.

"When they leave," he said. "I don't care how late it is. I don't care if we're both too tired to do anything but grab hold of each other and wiggle."

Mariah laughed louder. It was the most wonderful sound he'd ever heard.

"All right," she said, kissing him one last time, then crawling out of bed.

Peter winced at the signs that she was still weak. He promised himself he would be as gentle with her as possible that night. If only he didn't have to wait.

MARIAH WASN'T SURE IF SHE WAS HAVING A RELAPSE of the food poisoning that had taken her down for nearly a week or if it was simply nerves that tied her stomach in knots as she and Peter greeted their noble and notable guests for supper. She certainly didn't feel like a countess, in spite of the way Ginny had spruced up her nicest dress for the occasion.

"Good evening, my lady." Captain Albert Tennant cut quite an imposing figure as he took Mariah's hand and bowed over it in the front hall. "It is indeed a pleasure to meet you at last."

"Peter told us so much about you," Mrs. Domenica Tennant added, taking Mariah's hand when her husband let it go. Mariah was startled by her Spanish-American accent and her darkly exotic looks.

"Did he?" she asked with a smile, glancing to Peter.

"Albert is one of my closest friends," Peter answered, his eyes shining as he looked at her. "I mentioned to him that we would be marrying when he was staying here this past January."

A few feet to Peter's other side, William snorted and muttered, "You could have mentioned it to me."

Mariah flushed with anger and embarrassment, working to ignore William. "I hope I meet with your approval," she said to Captain Tennant.

Again, William snorted and shook his head. Captain Tennant's jaw clenched in disapproval. "I'm sure you will exceed expectations, my lady." He glared at William, then thumped Peter on the back, returning to a smile. "She's lovely, my friend. Remind me to write to Edmund to congratulate him on a match well made."

"I hear he has another daughter that he could foist off on some old man," William said with a tight smile. "Oh, but you've already tied the knot. Too bad."

Mariah's cheeks burned. "Can't you do something about him?" she whispered to Peter as Captain and Mrs. Tennant moved on into the salon to wait for supper with the other guests.

"I had hoped that seeing Albert again would shut him up," Peter answered, clearly bristling with frustration. "I forgot that William has no shame."

"William lacks several things," Mariah said. She could have gone on, but another, older couple arrived, and she was forced to turn to greet them.

"Ah ha! Peter." The gentleman, greying and paunchy with a ruddy complexion, stepped forward to shake Peter's hand and thump him on the arm. "So this is the fresh young filly we've been hearing about."

Peter nodded to the man with a wariness that Mariah could almost feel. "Barkley."

One word, and Mariah's heart rate doubled. Lord Barkley. Anne's brother. "My lord." She gave him what she hoped was her most respectful curtsey.

"This is her?" Lord Barkley leaned back and squinted at her. His gaze dropped straight to her chest. "Well, well. I can see the appeal." He laughed and smacked Peter's arm again. "I suppose a man with your appetites would need a spritely young thing to keep up with you. My poor sister wasn't up to the task," he confided in Mariah behind one hand.

Prickles raced across Mariah's skin. Lord Barkley was only pretending to joke. There was an angry light in his eyes that had Mariah pressing a hand to her stomach to keep it from lurching.

"Lady Barkley." Peter nodded to the tight-faced woman holding Lord Barkley's arm. "It is a pleasure to see you again."

Lady Barkley nodded to him, but didn't say a word.

"It is a pleasure to meet you, my lady," Mariah said, smiling and sinking into a curtsey.

The woman tilted her chin up and dragged her husband on to greet William.

"How nice of you to come tonight." William smiled as he took Lord Barkley's hand, sending a smarmy look Mariah's way. "Sorry about the replacement bride. I didn't know about her either until it was too late."

"Ah well," Lord Barkley laughed. "We can't always have things the way we want them. If we could, my dear sister would be here with us tonight instead of cold in her grave. But such is life." His words sounded cheerful, but not a soul in the room mistook them for anything other than the jab that they were.

"How long do these suppers last?" Mariah asked Peter in a whisper as the couple moved on.

"Too long by far," he answered. "Ah, St. Aubyn. Welcome to our home."

Mariah did her best to smile and greet the rest of her guests as graciously as possible, in spite of feeling out of her depth. Whenever her parents had entertained, she and Victoria had faded into the background, Victoria because of her age and Mariah because of the debacle with Robert. She'd never expected to find herself in a position as hostess anywhere, let alone as a countess in a castle. She wasn't ready, and everyone would know. But there was little that could be done but to soldier on.

"I will help in any way I can," Domenica Tennant whispered to her as the complement of guests made their way from the salon to the dining room when Mr. Snyder announced they were ready. "But I don't have much experience with this sort of thing myself."

"Thank you," Mariah whispered back, grateful for the woman's presence. "William is the problem. I hate to ask you to engage him in conversation, but—"

"Consider it done." Domenica smiled grimly and squeezed her hand before Captain Tennant fetched her to lead her into dinner.

Things started out easily enough. The guests found seats at the table with relative ease. Peter sat at the head of the table with Captain Tennant to his left. But as Mariah started to sit on Peter's right, Lord Barkley hooked a hand under her elbow and whisked her to the far end of the table.

"Oh no," he said with a falsely jovial laugh. "I can't have you taking poor Anne's place. You must sit in a seat of honor, being the new breeding stock—I mean, countess and all."

A shiver of dread shot down Mariah's spine. She

turned anxiously to Peter, only to find him rising from his chair with a look of fury.

"I'll join Lady Dunsford at this end of the table," Domenica said, leaping out of the seat she'd taken beside her husband and rushing to sit on Mariah's right.

"I was going to sit there," William protested, leaning toward Domenica with a look that was so lascivious Mariah felt embarrassed for him.

"You'll have to sit somewhere else," Domenica fired back, scooting her chair toward the table.

William sniffed. "I'm not sure the countess wants a whore sitting by her side."

Lady St. Aubyn and Mrs. Goodman—who had arrived with her husband just as the party was moving into the dining room—gasped. Mariah's eyes went wide, more in shock that William could be so crude than because she believed him.

"I beg your pardon," she said.

"What, you didn't know?" William chuckled, glancing around the table, then taking a seat by Domenica's side. "Captain Tennant's new bride worked in a brothel in the American West before nabbing him."

Lord Barkley burst into laughter. Mrs. Goodman commenced fanning herself as Lady Barkley gestured for Davy to pour wine into the glass at her place. The other guests gaped and blushed, or pretended not to have heard the comment as their faces reddened.

Mariah sent a desperate look down the long table to Peter. He seemed miles away with so many places between them. The look of stone that frightened her was back on his face as he glared at William. He turned that look on her, but he seemed too angry for concern to soften it. The effect withered Mariah's confidence.

"Mrs. Harmon, our cook, has gone out of her way to display her skills tonight," she said, feeling weak and shaky. "I hope you all enjoy her efforts."

"I'm sure we will," Lady St. Aubyn said, raising her voice as if to take command of the conversation. "We recently hired a French chef for our kitchens, and he has produced the most astounding dishes."

Mariah could have kissed the woman for taking charge of the conversation. As soup was served—Mariah could barely look at it, much less taste it after what her last bowl of soup had done to her—and for five entire minutes, things looked as though they would proceed smoothly.

Until Lord Barkley asked, "So, Dunsford, have you worn this one out yet?" He gestured to Mariah with his thumb. The motion was all the more pointed as he sat directly to her left.

The table went silent.

"Lord Barkley, have some respect," Captain Tennant growled when the tension became too much.

"I expect he has," William went on as though Captain Tennant had never spoken. "They've been locked away in the countess's room for days now."

Mrs. Goodman dropped her spoon, which clattered against the side of her soup bowl.

"Beware, my dear." Lord Barkley leaned close to Mariah, placing his hand over hers. "He rode my poor sister into her grave. Don't let him do the same to you."

"I—" Tears of embarrassment stung at Mariah's eyes. She pleaded with Peter for help across the table.

"Lord Barkley, there are ladies present," Peter said, fiery warning in his eyes. He gestured for the footmen to take away the soup and bring on the next course.

"Yes, yes, of course." Lord Barkley pretended to be chastised. "We wouldn't want to offend the *ladies*."

"Of course, Lady Dunsford has only been a lady for a fortnight or so now," William went on, not letting the conversation drop. "Three weeks ago, she was nothing more than Miss Travers, rejected spinster."

Mariah's stomach turned. When Davy stepped forward to take away her untouched soup, she pushed all the way to the back of her chair. She would have sunk under the table entirely if Domenica hadn't reached out to take her hand.

"Yes, I heard something about that," Lord Barkley continued the wretched conversation. "Some rumor about the new countess's former fiancé dying in an effort to flee the altar?"

"Really, gentlemen," Lord St. Aubyn scolded. "Is this a proper conversation for supper?"

"We're simply trying to get to know the new countess better," William said. "I certainly haven't had a chance to converse with her. Not with the way my uncle has been keeping her locked away. But then, I suppose if one wants to get an heir...."

"I'm warning you, William," Peter said in a dark, dangerous voice, his eyes glaring.

"Warning me of what?" William shrugged. "There's nothing left that you can do to me now that you're working so very hard to replace me."

"Didn't work with Anne, won't work with this one," Lord Barkley said, digging into the salmon mousse Davy placed in front of him.

"You haven't seen the way he runs panting after her, Lord Barkley," William shot back. His brow shot up and he turned to Domenica. "I know. Why don't you teach my new aunt all the tricks you learned to keep a man satisfied? I'm sure it'd be quite the lesson. I'd even attend those classes myself." He winked at Mariah, his grin wolfish.

It was the last straw. Mariah shot to her feet. Her head spun with so much anger that she had to grip the table to keep from keeling over. "If you will excuse me," she said in a thin, shaky voice. "I haven't been well this week, and I'm afraid I'm not up to entertaining tonight."

She pushed her chair back and stepped around the corner of the table to flee for the door. More chairs scraped as Peter, Captain Tennant, and Domenica stood as well.

"Delicate little thing, isn't she?" Lord Barkley said as Mariah pressed a hand to her mouth in her flight. "She'll be dead within a year, if you ask me."

CHAPTER 13

Tears burst from Mariah's eyes as she ran into the hall. She didn't know where she was going, only that she had to get away before she crumbled into dust. Mr. Snyder stood in the dining room doorway and gestured to someone across the hall.

"This way, my lady," Ginny said from the far end of the vast room.

Mariah fled to her, weeping when Ginny slipped an arm around her shoulders and led her toward the morning parlor at the far end of the hall.

"Mariah," Peter called after her before they reached the room.

Mariah glanced over her shoulder, not sure if she wanted to run to Peter and collapse into his arms or rail at him for exposing her to a monster like William. She did neither when she saw Captain Tennant and Domenica following him, and let Ginny nudge her on.

Within moments of reaching the parlor, Ginny had Mariah seated on one of the sofas, before she broke away to light the lamps. Peter dashed into the room and came to sit by Mariah's side, taking her hands. Captain Tennant and Domenica paused just inside the doorway.

"I'll wring his neck," Peter growled, pulling Mariah into his arms. "I won't let him get away with this."

"How could he say such horrible things?" Mariah cried, planting her forehead on Peter's shoulder. "And in front of company. How could both of them say such disgusting things?"

"I'll have Barkley sent away at once," Peter said.

Mariah felt him nod, then raised her head in time to see Captain Tennant nod back then leave the room.

"And William too," she said, gripping Peter's arms. Hot tears rolled down her cheeks. "Send William away too."

Instead of rushing to make it so, Peter winced, lowering his head. "You know I would if I could."

Mariah's throat squeezed tight with anger. "You can and you should."

He let out a breath and looked up at her. He raised a hand to her cheek, wiping away her tears with his thumb. "Mariah, you know I can't simply hand half of Starcross Castle to him because of one disgraceful night."

"Then lock him in a tower." It seemed so obvious to her. Why couldn't Peter see it? "Chain him in the dungeon. Just get him away from me."

"Give it time," Peter said. "If he sees that he can't break you, then he'll get bored and go back to London."

Mariah wrenched herself away from Peter and stood. She balled her fists at her sides. "I know we haven't known each other as long as most married couples, but I have a very hard time believing that you would put that bastard of a nephew before our marriage."

Peter stood, letting out a frustrated breath, and rested his hands on Mariah's arms. "I'm not putting William before us, believe me."

"Then *do something*." Mariah stomped. She didn't want to throw a fit, but every moment that ticked by with William still in the house made her feel more and more helpless. "Peter, he is clearly bent on destroying the two of us. How can you not see that?"

"I can see it, I assure you," he said, his voice deceptively calm.

"Then why aren't you doing something?"

"I'm doing everything I can," he argued.

"Were you doing everything you could when he poisoned me?"

"What?" Domenica interjected from the doorway.

Bristling with misery, Mariah glanced past Peter to her. "I became ill last week after eating tainted soup. William was almost certainly responsible."

"And you have proof of this?" Domenica asked, looking at Peter as though she would start railing at him any moment.

"No," Peter replied, miserable. "No more than we have proof that William set the fire on Albert's ship."

"But we *know* he set the fire," Domenica said taking a step toward them.

"And we know William is hell-bent on keeping his status as my heir," Peter went on. "But we can't *prove* that he's the sole person responsible for the soup. Or the locked doors."

"We know he is," Mariah argued. "How long before you end up risking my life for his sake?"

"William doesn't have it in him to murder you outright," Peter said.

Domenica huffed as though she disagreed.

Peter frowned at her, then turned back to Mariah with a plea for patience in his eyes. "William wasn't solely responsible for the fire on Albert's ship, and if he isn't acting alone in his attempts to keep the two of us apart, then locking him up will leave an unknown accomplice in the house. An accomplice who would be able to cause mischief whether William was free or shackled to a grate."

Mariah snapped her mouth shut over the protest she wanted to shout. She spun away from Peter, pacing toward the table where Ginny was lighting the last of the lamps.

"I would do anything to keep you safe, Mariah," Peter called after her, "but I honestly believe we have no choice but to wait this out and to keep a sharp eye on him."

Mariah squeezed her eyes shut over the tears that threatened to spill again.

"Is there anything I can do for you, my lady?" Ginny whispered.

Mariah shook her head. "No, there isn't." Her voice rose through the sentence, until she turned to glare at Peter. "Apparently there's nothing that anyone can do." She marched toward him, unable to fight down the beast of anger that raged within her. "I wasn't happy in Aylesbury, but I wasn't being poisoned either."

"Mariah, please." Peter reached for her, the lines of his face deep with pain.

The pull to slip into his arms and let him comfort her was almost too strong to resist, but it solved nothing. She shook her head. "He humiliated me in there." She pointed toward the dining room. "I have been insulted and mortified in front of your friends and neighbors. I can never regain that first impression."

"If it helps...." Domenica stepped forward. "William and that Lord Barkley are the ones who came off as the fools, not you."

"William brought up my past," Mariah went on, blinking to hide the sting in her eyes and appealing to Peter. "And Lord Barkley couldn't have been more obvious in the way he lay blame for his sister's death at your feet than if he'd thrown down a gauntlet."

"Barkley has always been an ass," Peter said.

"That doesn't make me feel better," Mariah shouted at him.

He winced. "I know. But if you could just trust me to know how to manage my nephew, I—"

"Trust you?" Mariah gaped at him. "Since marrying you, I have been laughed at, humiliated in public, and poisoned. How can I trust that if William remains under this roof with me, I won't meet a worse fate?"

"I would give my life to—"

"How can I believe that?" Mariah cried, pulling away from him. "How can I believe that a man I didn't know existed a month ago would sacrifice everything for me? And why should I be forced to sacrifice everything for you when you can't even stop me from being humiliated at a supper party?"

She shook her head and walked away from Peter. The wildness of her emotions overwhelmed her, making her dizzy. She hadn't recovered from being sick enough to handle the hopeless, miserable situation, and she hadn't settled into her new life comfortably enough to be confident that all would turn out for the best in the end.

"Perhaps William is right," she said, her voice shaking, as she turned back to Peter. It broke her heart to see the misery that surrounded him, but at the end of the day, he was still a stranger to her. "Perhaps I should just go home."

"Please don't," Peter said, misery personified. "I will make this right."

"How?"

He opened his mouth, but no words came out. "I

don't know yet," he said, squaring his shoulders. "But I will think of something. Just please, don't go."

Mariah's heart felt as though it were being run through a wringer. She knew that Peter was good and kind and passionate, but at that moment, it didn't feel like enough to build a marriage on.

"William goes," she said, taking a breath and pressing her hands to her stomach. "Or I do."

She met his eyes and held them. She wouldn't be the perpetual child, subject to the whims of the men who controlled her life, anymore. Even if it meant losing the most beautiful surprise she'd ever had. It would have been so easy to give her full heart to Peter, but not if it meant surrendering her pride along with it.

With one last, pleading look, she turned to go.

Peter's heart shattered as Mariah turned her back on him and marched out of the room. Not once in more than twenty years had Anne bruised him the way that Mariah did. Worst of all, it was entirely his own fault.

"Mariah."

He started after her, but only made it two steps. Albert crossed paths with Mariah as he strode back into the room, his face as grim as death. "Barkley is gone," he announced.

"Good." Peter launched into motion again. "I have to go after her." His gaze remained fixed on Mariah's retreating form as she crossed the hall and ran up the stairs.

His focus was so honed in that it was a surprise when Domenica stepped into his path. "Perhaps, my lord, you should let her go for now."

Peter glared at her, but before he could do something he would regret and raise his voice to a woman, Ginny jumped in with, "I'll go after her, my lord." She scurried across the room, wringing her hands in front of her. "Sometimes a woman needs a good cry and another woman to listen to her before she's in the right spot to see the truth of things."

The loyal maid's words brought two kinds of solace to Peter. Mariah was lucky to have Ginny to stand up for her, but more than that, Ginny had heard everything he'd said, and from the sound of things, she agreed with him. But it only went so far to easing the pain that pounded through every part of him.

"Go," he said, voice hoarse, and nodded.

Ginny curtsied and rushed from the room. Peter was left with an aching sense of emptiness. He pivoted and marched toward the fireplace, rubbing a hand over his face.

"I've failed," he said, leaning against the mantel. "Again, I've failed."

"Don't say that, my lord." Domenica crossed the room to his side. "It's just a fight. Albert and I fight over the silliest things, and we make up the next day."

Peter gave her a wary smile of thanks, then stood straighter as Albert joined them by the fire.

"She's right, old friend." Albert patted his back. "And making up is the best part. I'm sure you and Mariah will be sighing in each other's arms in no time."

"Yes," Peter said with a scowl, pushing away from the fireplace. "Because after Barkley's display, all of Cornwall will know my maniacal penchant for bedding women half my age."

"As you said, Barkley is an ass, and everyone knows it." Albert followed Peter as he returned to the sofa and flopped to sit. "St. Aubyn and Goodman know your true character. They thanked me for sending the lout on his way."

It was a small consolation, but Peter took no comfort in it. His mind was already churning away at the inescapable problem of William. "Mariah is right," he said pressing a hand to his temples. "I have to banish William. Our marriage can't thrive or survive with him here."

"True." Albert crossed his arms where he stood beside the sofa as Domenica took a seat on the far end. "But you were absolutely correct when you said that you can't send him away."

Peter huffed a humorless laugh. "So that's it, then. To keep Mariah I have to let her go."

"He has to," Domenica argued. "You know what William is capable of. Or do you not remember the way he treated me aboard the *Kestrel*?"

"That was different," Albert said. "Peter has everything at stake here, his home, his livelihood, his reputation. Surely, Mariah will see that."

Peter shook his head. "She shouldn't have to see anything. She deserves a carefree and happy life. She deserves a husband who makes her happy and a passel of children to make her laugh." The intensity of the vision his words brought to mind made his heart ache beyond measure. Those were all the things he wanted too, all the things he had dreamed of his entire life. They seemed further out of his reach now than they ever had.

"All right, then let's approach this one bit at a time. It seems to me that William is the crux of your problems," Albert said, pacing in front of the sofa while scratching his chin.

Peter came dangerously close to rolling his eyes at his friend. "Tell me something I don't know."

Albert ignored his snide tone. "You can't get rid of him, and yet you can't keep him here. At least not unless you discover who his agent in the house is."

"I can have Snyder interview the staff to discover the mole," Peter said, growing more exhausted by the moment. He wanted to drag himself up to bed, but seeing as there was little chance that Mariah would be there now—or any time in the near future—it hardly seemed worth it.

"Snyder is a good man, and I'm sure he'll ferret out whoever it is." Albert nodded.

Peter sighed. "And in the meantime, the longer

William stays under this roof, the angrier Mariah will be."

"She will be furious," Domenica agreed. She tilted her head to the side as if listening to an idea. "If you are unwilling to take her away from William, you will need to guard her with your life. Be with her as much as possible so that William and his mole don't have a chance to strike. But that could solve more problems than it creates."

"How so?"

"Perhaps you should take this opportunity to woo your wife. Your courtship was fast, was it not?"

"It was non-existent," Peter confessed. "Edmund failed to mention to her that he'd promised her hand to me until the day before I arrived in Aylesbury."

Albert barked a laugh, then shook his head. "Sorry. It's just so typically Edmund." He chuckled.

Having his friend there eased a fraction of the gloom creeping through him, but it couldn't change his outlook of the situation. "I'm no good at wooing," he said. "I didn't have to woo Anne either. My father chose her for me."

"You've never courted a woman?" Domenica asked.

"No."

"And you're how old?" Albert asked.

"Don't you start," Peter said with a frown.

"It's clear what you have to do then," Domenica said. She glanced to Albert, who nodded as though the two of them had discussed the problem at length.

Peter raised his eyebrows in question.

Albert stopped his pacing and stood at attention, as though he were on the prow of a ship. "Keep your friends close and your enemies closer, yes?"

"Yes?" Peter narrowed his eyes in suspicion.

"So let William continue to think he's winning his reprehensible little game."

"Why?" Peter asked through clenched teeth.

"People who think they're winning let their guard down."

"How will that help? William won't stop threatening Mariah unless I flee everything that is rightfully ours, like a dog with its tail tucked between its legs."

Albert held up a hand as if to soothe Peter's growing frustration. "Let William think he's winning," he repeated, "but bring in reinforcements."

"Define reinforcements."

Albert glanced to Domenica. "We'll stay."

Domenica smiled. "We will."

"What, here?" Peter asked.

"That's the keeping your friends close part," Albert said with a grim smile. "And if I were you, I'd write to Malcolm and get him involved."

"Malcolm Campbell?" Peter blinked, then frowned. "Why should I interrupt whatever Malcolm is doing to drag him all the way out here to Cornwall?"

"Because no one is better at rooting out moles than Malcolm," Albert said. "And besides, isn't William terrified of him?"

Peter let out a breath and lowered his shoulders. "He is." A thought struck him, and he smirked. "I can't throw William out, but Malcolm's presence might be enough to get him to leave on his own, voluntarily. And if I had witnesses to the fact that he left of his own free will and not because I banished him, even if he did sue for half the estate, he would lose."

"There you go." Albert nodded.

"And does Mariah have anyone she might want near her at a time like this? Her mother? A sister?"

"Victoria," Peter said, a ripple of unease traveling down his spine. "She's close with her sister Victoria. She's close to her entire family, if truth be told. I wouldn't say no to having Edmund on hand right now."

"Then tell her to write to her family and have them come to stay for a while," Domenica said, resting a hand on Peter's knee. "We'll call it a house party."

"It sounds like a lark." Albert smiled as though his wife had suggested they go on safari in Africa.

"I'll send the invitations right away," Peter said, starting for the door.

"Before or after your dinner party finishes?" Albert asked, his mouth twitching.

Peter nearly groaned. The idea of entertaining what remained of his guests, baffled as they must be by the way the evening had gone, was torture. But if he was going to save even a little bit of face, for Mariah's sake, he had to march back into battle. Sebastopol hadn't been as daunting as his dining room was that evening.

"After supper," he said, starting toward the door, Albert and Domenica in tow. "And starting tomorrow, if there's any way to make things right with Mariah short of cutting off my arm, I'll find it."

CHAPTER 14

Mariah fully expected to be up all night, tossing and turning. Even after Ginny sent another maid, Poppy, to the kitchen for warm milk and biscuits. Ginny was so compassionate, rubbing Mariah's back and listening to her rehash the fiasco of supper that Mariah wasn't sure she'd ever be able to repay the woman. She'd sipped her warm milk, nibbled on a biscuit, and let Ginny tuck her into bed, where she promptly fell asleep.

In the morning light, a different kind of embarrassment swept in on Mariah. She was convinced she'd behaved like a child. And that after complaining about being trapped in the role of child as a spinster. The thought made her wince as she climbed out of bed and went to her dressing room to use the chamber pot. Granted, she had every reason to be upset over William's behavior and Peter's refusal to banish him, but she wasn't proud of the way her emotions had spun out of control. It wasn't like her at all. She wasn't herself.

"Feeling better this morning, my lady?" Ginny asked when she came to help Mariah dress.

Mariah heaved a sigh. "If by 'better' you mean no longer furious, but equally melancholy, then yes."

Ginny gave her a sympathetic smile as she shook out the day dress Mariah had chosen to wear. "All will be well," she said, her optimism humbling to Mariah. "You'll see."

"I hope so," Mariah replied, staring at herself in the mirror. She didn't look like the woman who had left Aylesbury more than a fortnight ago. Gone was the determined innocence of the woman who had demanded to be sold a book of poetry. She wasn't sure who was staring back at her now or what that woman's place in the world was.

A thump sounded on the other side of the dressing room door. Mariah's heart leapt to her throat, and she glanced over her shoulder, wishing and praying that Peter would come through and…and what? Apologize? Yes. Wrap his arms around her and tell her she was more important to him than his villainous nephew? Absolutely. Let her beg his forgiveness for behaving like a wild gypsy in a temper? That too.

But the thumping gradually subsided without so much as a knock, and Mariah's hopes sunk with it.

"I'm sure that was just Mr. Wright," Ginny said. "I believe Lord Dunsford went downstairs an hour ago."

"So early?" Mariah bit her lip, continuing to stare at the door until Ginny held out her petticoats for her to step into.

"Yes, my lady. Considering the guests and all."

Mariah blinked and glanced to Ginny. "Don't tell me the supper guests are still here."

Ginny lifted the top of Mariah's petticoats to her waist, then tied them at her back. "Captain Tennant and his wife have decided to stay for a while."

"Oh." Mariah's shoulders dropped.

Ginny frowned as she went to fetch Mariah's skirt. "I thought you'd be pleased, my lady. You seemed to like the Tennants last night."

"They were wonderful," Mariah said. "I can see that they are true friends to Peter, but…." She glanced down. If Peter was inviting his friends to stay, did that mean he'd given up on what was supposed to be a honeymoon, given up on building their marriage?

Ginny helped Mariah into her skirt and bodice, then squeezed Mariah's arm. "Cheer up, my lady. It might never happen. The bad things, that is. You'll see."

Mariah wished she could share her maid's confidence. Nothing seemed right as she made her way down to the breakfast room. Both Peter and his guests had already eaten, and not even William was there to watch her pick at cold eggs and sausages. Only Davy witnessed her coming close to tears again, and he said nothing.

But whether it was the cup of tea she choked down or impatience with her moodiness, by the time Mariah finished breakfast, a new determination had filled her. She may have been broken and humiliated, her husband might have given up on her, but she was still a countess. The house had guests, and she would take her responsibilities as hostess seriously. She sought out Mrs. Wilson to check on the menus for the coming week, made sure that Captain and Mrs. Tennant had all the help they needed from the staff, then headed out to the gardens to choose blooms for bouquets to be placed in all of the public rooms. She might have been miserable, but she would do her best to make sure the house was cheery.

"If it's cheer you want," Nick, the gardener, told her as they stood in the center of a vast spread of carefully-tended flowerbeds, "delphiniums and freesia can't be beat." He walked her to a particularly colorful flower bed set up so that the blooms formed cascades of beauty and scent. "Although if you ask me, it's not truly June without lilies." He crossed to another bed where a wide variety of lilies grew.

"June?" Mariah blinked at him.

"As of today, yes, my lady."

"Where did the time go?" Mariah sighed, shaking her head.

"I believe they say it flies, my lady."

Nick's friendly smile went a long way toward putting Mariah back in at least halfway decent spirits. The staff of Starcross Castle was so wonderful that she had a hard time believing someone amongst them was working with

William against her and Peter. But she needed to think of other things for a change to preserve her sanity.

"These are all so beautiful," Mariah said, overwhelmed by sight and scent. "And you grew them all?"

"Yes, my lady," Nick answered with a proud nod.

"You're awfully young to be a head gardener, aren't you?"

Nick laughed. "My father was the head gardener here before me, my lady. I may only be thirty, but I've had my hands in the dirt here since I knew how to walk."

"I see." Mariah smiled. "Would you mind cutting a few stems for me so that I can take them inside?"

"Certainly, my lady."

Mariah's soul began to settle itself as she walked through the garden a few steps behind Nick. She held her arms out as he piled blooms into them, and before long her arms were full of flowers. The flowers, the sunshine, and the fresh air were a balm, but she would have enjoyed them all much more if Peter were by her side. She found herself looking for him every time they turned a corner or walked into a new part of the garden. At one point, she spotted Captain Tennant sitting very close to Domenica in the rose garden. Close enough that she blushed and turned to immediately walk in the other direction. Seeing them like that only drove home how alone she was.

"There you go, my lady," Nick said as he added one final stem of freesia to the enormous bouquet Mariah carried. "That should be enough for Poppy to make a dozen arrangements for the castle."

"Is Poppy the one who does the arrangements?"

Nick grinned, a distinct twinkle in his eyes. "She's just recently come up from being a kitchen maid, my lady, but she has a way with flowers."

Mariah returned his smile. She suspected Poppy had a way with the man who grew flowers as well. On her way back to the house, she made a note to keep an eye out for the young maid to gauge whether she returned Nick's interest. If she couldn't look forward to her own romance, at least she could live vicariously through the servants.

"Isn't this lovely." William stepped out from one of the arched doorways leading from the garden into the castle as Mariah approached, scaring her out of her wits. "You're the prettiest bloom of them all."

Mariah's steps faltered as she gaped at William. "*Now* you compliment me?" she snapped. "After humiliating me last night?"

"Who humiliated whom?" William shrugged. "I simply made observations, most of which are true."

"You're a vile snake," Mariah hissed, her stomach turning all over again. "Get out of my way."

Rather than stepping aside, William widened his stance, blocking the door. "Good choice," he said.

Mariah huffed. "I don't have time for your games. Move."

"I assumed you'd choose someone like Davy for your

dalliances," William went on, unmoving, "but Nick is a fine, strapping man."

"What are you talking about?" she asked through clenched teeth.

"Personally, I think he's a little hulking for you. With a physique like that, Nick's likely to split you in two when you're rutting."

Mariah was offended to the point of speechlessness. She glared at William, working enough moisture into her mouth for the put-down he deserved. "I would never be unfaithful to Peter," she hissed at last. "How dare you suggest otherwise?"

"Come now," William went on, crossing his arms and leaning against one side of the doorway. "I've never known a countess yet who hasn't taken a string of lovers. And believe me, I'd know."

"I'm sure you would." Mariah pushed forward, hoping to wedge past him, but the flowers in her arms made it difficult.

"Of course, if it's pleasure you're after, you should come to me." He looked at his nails, dripping cockiness. "I'd have you screaming with ecstasy in no time. And I don't think I'd mind if Uncle's heir was mine, after all."

"You disgust me," Mariah growled. "I want nothing more than for you to leave at once. Just get out. Go away."

William's brow went up, and he straightened. "You want to get rid of me?"

"Yes," she said with so much passion she nearly shouted.

"Fine. Then tell my dear uncle to throw me out."

Mariah winced, defeat slithering down her spine. "You know I can't do that," she said rather than admitting she'd already made the demand.

"Because of some little agreement?" William snorted.

"I know what you win if Peter throws you out," Mariah said, facing him.

"And I know that all I have to do is push you too far and you'll break."

They stared at each other, and Mariah had the sinking feeling he was right. She would break long before he did.

"But I'll make a deal with you. I'll leave," William went on, leaning toward her, "if you convince my uncle to give me the money I've asked for."

"No," Mariah snapped.

She tried to walk on, but William caught her arm, yanking her back. "I don't have time to mess about. Convince him to give me what I want and I'll be out of your life forever," he said. There was too much seriousness in his eyes for Mariah to doubt his sincerity, but she doubted his true motives down to her core. "Convince him to name me as his heir, regardless of how many brats the two of you have, and I'll promise to name whomever you want as my heir."

Mariah's eyes widened. "How dare you try to make a bargain with me?"

"I dare because I know how desperate you are to be rid of me," William said, eyes narrowed. "And believe me, auntie dear, I can make you so much more desperate than you already are. So what do you say? Can we strike a bargain?" He held out his hand as if expecting Mariah to take it.

She was glad for the pile of flowers in her arms, not because she was tempted to shake on the deal, but because it kept her from slapping him across the face with all her might. Without a word, she pushed past him and stomped into the house.

Two steps in, she stopped with a gasp. Peter stood at the far end of the room, a few letters in his hands, watching the two of them. He wore the look that made her gut tremble, and thanked heaven that it was directed at William and not her.

She forced herself to recover and walked on, intending to march right past Peter and on to the servant's stairs.

"William, you have a letter," Peter said. When Mariah was within feet of him, he added in a soft voice, "I'd like to talk to you."

She stopped, trying not to let herself meet his eyes but failing. The tenderness and regret that radiated from him turned her heart to jelly in an instant.

"What letter?" William marched into the room, full of swagger. He gave Peter a smarmy grin as he held up the envelope. William snatched it from his hand and read the return address. His face instantly went pale, and all signs of arrogance vanished. Without a word, he rushed from the room.

Mariah watched him go, more anxious than she'd been before, though it made no sense. "Who was the letter from?" she whispered.

"I'm not certain," Peter replied, letting his imposing demeanor melt away. "There was no name on the return address, only a street number. In London."

"One of his creditors?"

"Or worse."

The two of them stood silently, staring at the door William had disappeared through for a moment. Mariah could feel the heat of Peter's body as he inched closer to her. She fancied she could smell the heady, masculine scent of him as well, although the flowers were powerful.

At last, she peeked at him. "What did you want to talk to me about?" She prayed he wanted to reconcile, that he would forgive her for her outburst and beg forgiveness in turn.

"You look beautiful with those flowers," he said instead. He raised a hand as if to touch her, but pulled back. Mariah's heart ached for the touch he withheld. "I have something for you."

"For me?" She blinked, the ache spinning into something quivering.

"Yes." He smiled awkwardly and reached into the pocket of his jacket. A flush spread across his face, and for a moment Mariah had the strange feeling that he was talking himself through the steps of whatever gesture he was making, as though it didn't come naturally to him. He drew a beautiful, enameled hairpin set with pearls from his pocket and presented it to her. "For you."

"I...." Mariah stared at the pin, heart fluttering, words escaping her.

Peter's flush deepened. "I understand it's customary, when couples are courting, to exchange gifts."

"But we're not courting. We're already married." Although the giddy feeling that swirled around her reminded her very much of the first flush of infatuation she'd felt for Robert. Heavens, she couldn't remember the last time she'd thought about Robert. How could she when she had Peter.

He didn't seem to know what to say. Instead, he stepped forward, tucking the hairpin into the braided chignon Ginny had styled that morning. "There," he said.

Mariah's heart thumped against her ribs, but she had never been more at a loss for words. "I...I hear we have houseguests," she said, swallowing the lump that had formed in her throat. How could she love Peter so tenderly and be so frustrated with him simultaneously? "I asked Nick to pick out some blooms so that we could have fresh flowers throughout the house for their enjoyment."

"Yes." Peter shifted to hold his hands behind his back. "After you retired last night, Albert and Domenica convinced me that it would be a good idea for them to stay for a while."

"So that you don't have to put up with me alone?" Mariah fought not to let her voice crack.

"No." Peter's voice remained even, but she could see in his eyes that her words hurt him...which only made her ache more. "I would banish the entire world to be alone with you," he added in a tender voice. Before she could remind him that William was part of the entire world, he went on. "Albert thinks, and I agree, that in order to foil whatever plan William has, we will need reinforcements."

"Reinforcements?" The soft feelings his gift had left her with solidified into determination. "Why? He's a man. A bitter, nasty, evil man. He's not an invading army."

"In a way, he is an army. Especially since he has help in the house."

Mariah pressed her lips together without answering. "I still can't believe any of the servants would help him."

"I know." Peter sighed. "Albert suggested inviting a mutual friend of ours, Lord Malcolm Campbell, to the house to serve as a spy."

Mariah arched a brow. "*Is* he a spy?"

Peter didn't answer.

"Oh." The ice in Mariah's stomach turned to snakes. She was in much further over her head than she'd imagined.

Peter glanced up at her again. "From there, the idea grew to that of hosting a house party."

"A house party? Here? *Now?*"

"The more people William has around him, many of them people he doesn't like, the greater the possibility that he will either slip up and expose himself and his accomplices or that he will leave of his own volition."

"But with that many people in the house, how will we—" Mariah clamped her mouth shut and looked down.

Peter rested a hand on her cheek. "We'll find a way," he said. "It won't be like this between us forever."

She wanted to believe him with all her heart, but her thoughts and emotions were so jumbled up that she didn't know what to believe.

"I thought you might want to invite your parents and Victoria," he went on.

Mariah frowned. "William's antics have grown so bad that you're importing a spy to thwart him, we are on rocky ground with each other, and you want me to invite my family for a visit?"

Peter let out a breath, rubbing a hand over his face. "I thought you would feel more secure with them here," he said. "Considering that you're thinking of going back to them."

Mariah's throat closed up. She was embarrassed that she'd made that threat the night before. The last thing she wanted to do was give up and run home to Mama. But she couldn't quite bring herself to say as much aloud.

"What if William lashes out at them?" she asked.

"I believe it's me he's after," Peter said. "Well, he's after what he thinks I owe him."

Mariah shifted the flowers in her arms, which were beginning to ache as much as the rest of her. "He tried to enlist me to convince you to give him the money he wants and to make him your heir with the understanding that he would name any son of ours his heir."

"And did you believe him?"

"No," Mariah answered without hesitation. "He's a liar and a rogue."

Peter's answering grin held no warmth. "Then you're every bit as intelligent as I knew you to be." He stepped closer, his hand brushing her waist and sending shivers through her. "And I hope—"

"Peter, there you are. And Mariah too."

The moment Captain Tennant strode through the door from the garden, holding Domenica's hand as she walked beside him, Peter took a step back. Mariah turned away to hide the blush that heated her cheeks.

"Domenica and I were wondering if the two of you wanted to go for a picnic with us," Captain Tennant went on.

"Yes," Domenica added. "It's a beautiful day."

Mariah glanced sideways at Peter, only to find him looking at her. "I need to take these to Poppy downstairs," she said. "Perhaps tomorrow, when I'm feeling a bit better."

"Do you need help?" Domenica asked.

Mariah hesitated. She peeked at Peter again, but his expression had clouded over. All she wanted was to figure out how to be with him, but with more people in the house, she didn't see how that would be possible.

"I have to write a letter to my mother," she answered Domenica. "But perhaps later I could show you through the gardens. I've just learned a great many things about them, and I would appreciate the chance to practice sharing that with guests."

"Of course, my lady," Domenica said with a friendly and open smile.

The four of them were silent. Mariah waited for Peter to ask her to stay, to go with him instead of facing her responsibilities, but he did nothing other than frown at a spot on the floor, as though his thoughts were a million miles away.

"Well, I'd best be going then," she said at last, smiling at Captain Tennant and Domenica, sending Peter one last, wistful look, then turning to go. It would take far more than she felt capable of to fix the broken situation she'd landed in.

IN THE CONFINES OF HIS ROOM, WILLIAM TORE OPEN the letter from London. The return address was nonsense, designed to frighten him. Unfortunately, it did exactly that.

What was more frightening was the single sheet of paper the envelope contained. On it, one sentence was printed in the distinct, looping handwriting used by Theodore Shayles: "Your time is up."

Shaking, heart pounding, William rushed to his fireplace. It was too warm to have the fire lit, but using the matches on the mantel, he ignited the letter and threw it into the empty hearth. He then stood back and watched the paper burn. Not that it would do any good.

They were coming for him. He could run, hide, even leave the country, but it wouldn't do any good. If Shayles wanted him dead, he was dead.

Unless he played his cards right. He was clever enough to get out of the noose around his neck, he was sure. All he had to do was wait for the assassins, then make them an offer better than whatever Shayles had promised them.

And in the meantime, he could still get what he was owed from his uncle. The game wasn't over yet.

CHAPTER 15

The invitations went out the next day. Mariah wrote to her parents, filled with doubt about whether more people at Starcross Castle was truly the solution to the problem of William. If he did have someone in the castle working for his interests, she was convinced it would be smarter to isolate him so that he couldn't communicate with that person.

"You'd be surprised, my lady," Ginny said when Mariah expressed those concerns to her as Ginny styled her hair for the day. "There's no limit to what a bad man will do when he feels cornered."

"But surely if William was confined to a few rooms, he wouldn't be able to order his mole to do things like poison my soup or...or whatever other dastardly things he has planned." She shuddered to think what they could be. Locked doors could be the least of her problems.

Ginny hummed around the hairpins she'd put in her

mouth as she worked. As soon as they were all in place, she said, "He could make even more trouble if he believed he was imprisoned."

Mariah sighed. "There is that. And in truth, I hate the idea of being anyone's jailor."

"Anyone's?" Ginny asked with one brow raised.

Mariah met her eyes in the mirror and gave her a guilty look. "I don't suppose I'd mind it if someone else took responsibility."

The two of them shared a laugh. But there really didn't seem to be a good way to keep William under close supervision.

The situation was frustratingly impossible, and every day that passed saw Mariah's mood sour even more. The worst bit was that a large part of her knew that if she could just let go of her anger and steal through the dressing room doors at night to slip into Peter's bed, even if just to sleep in his arms, she would feel better. But the stubborn part of her was waiting for him to come to her first.

The first guest to arrive at the castle was Lord Malcolm Campbell, a mere two days after his invitation was sent.

"I came as soon as I could," he said without greeting as Mr. Snyder showed him into the front parlor.

It was a grey, wet day, and Mariah, Peter, Captain Tennant, and Domenica were passing the time in the only room in the house that didn't seem to have a damp chill in the air. Each of them was absorbed reading their own book in silence, and they all glanced up when Lord Malcolm strode into the room.

"Malcolm." Peter jumped to his feet from the other side of the sofa he'd been sharing with Mariah. He tossed his book aside without marking the page, as if he hadn't been reading at all, and crossed to shake his friend's hand. "I'm so glad you could come."

"Your letter sounded serious." Lord Malcolm frowned as he shook Peter's hand, then walked on to greet Captain Tennant. He nodded to Domenica, then turned his scrutinizing gaze to Mariah as she stood. "So this is the new countess," he said.

"Mariah," Peter confirmed, moving to stand by Mariah's side. His smile was full of hope.

"My lady." Lord Malcolm snapped his heels together and bowed with military precision. "You look just like your mother. I always liked her. It's a pleasure to meet a woman who makes my old friend as happy as his letters indicate."

A burst of emotion swelled in Mariah's chest. Had she spent the last week being too hard on Peter by waiting for an apology before mending fences?

"The pleasure is all mine, Lord Malcolm," she replied with a polite nod of her head. "Peter has told me so much about you." If hinting that Lord Malcolm was some sort of spy was telling her about him.

"Don't listen to a word he says." Lord Malcolm grinned. He was average height and build, with more grey in his hair than brown, but he had a wicked flash of mischief in his brown eyes, and energy rippled off him. Mariah couldn't help but like him instantly, and be glad that he'd come. He clapped his hands together. "So, where is that reprehensible nephew of yours? I've been dreaming up ways to set him in his place since I left London."

"Heaven knows," Peter answered with a roll of his eyes. "He's been unreliable this past week. He spends half his time taunting my guests—" He glanced warily to Domenica. "—and half the time off in town or some such."

"And has he tried to harm your bride again since the soup incident?"

Mariah's brow flew up. So Peter had explained everything after all. "Not that I know of," she answered. "But I will admit, I haven't felt quite right since learning how William resents me."

"Of course not." Malcolm shrugged. "Half of London wants William's head on a platter for the pile of unpaid bills he left there, and if he thinks he can extort money and more from Peter here by making you miserable, well, I'd feel as though I were walking on eggshells too."

Mariah blinked. She glanced to Peter, wondering if his friend was always so blunt. The look Peter sent her in return—half apologetic, half relieved that someone else would back what he'd been saying all along—confirmed her suspicions.

"We just need to keep him from turning the place

upside down until he gives up his schemes as a hopeless cause," Peter said.

"Easy enough." Malcolm nodded. "And you suspect there's someone in the house doing his bidding?"

"Possibly," Peter answered.

Malcolm shrugged. "It's usually a servant with a lower position in situations like this. And money is usually the motivator. All you have to do is figure out which of your staff has new acquisitions or trinkets that they couldn't afford on what you pay them and you'll have your mole."

Mariah was impressed, and for the first time since arriving at Starcross Castle, she had hope that something could be done.

It kept her spirits lifted enough through the next three days to prepare a truly grand welcome for her parents. She was eager for them to see that she was a success as a countess after all, even if everything in the more intimate parts of her life was a mess.

So it was with an excited knot in her stomach that she stood on the front steps of Starcross Castle, Peter by her side, the staff lined up like a regiment waiting to be inspected, on a sunny June afternoon, watching a hired carriage roll up the drive.

"I think this will help," Peter said, stepping closer to her.

Mariah peeked up at him. "Do you think?"

He sent her a tender smile. "I want you to be happy, Mariah. And even though no new groom in their right mind would want their in-laws hovering around while he's trying to pitch woo to his new wife, if it makes you feel more secure, I'll make the sacrifice."

Mariah laughed in spite of herself. "You've been trying to pitch woo to me?"

He turned fully toward her, no longer pretending to be watching the carriage approach. "Am I that bad at it?"

Her stubborn heart melted a little at his genuine wince. "When did you try to woo me?"

"I read that book you recommended the other day when we were stuck inside," he said.

Mariah's lips twitched.

"And I let you have the last of the clotted cream at tea yesterday," he went on.

"That's pitching woo?"

"I gave you that hairpin."

Mariah's hand flew instantly to the precious gift, nestled carefully in her hairstyle. "You don't have to buy me things to woo me."

He let out a sigh, but his face was more relaxed than it had been. "I told you, I'm not very good at it. I never had to court a woman before."

"You don't have to court me now," Mariah said as the carriage rounded the top of the drive and pulled to a stop. Davy jumped forward to open the door.

"Oh, but I do," Peter said with mock seriousness, straightening and clasping his hands behind his back in preparation to meet her parents. "I've made a terrible mess of things between us, and the only way for me to set things right is to start over and court you properly."

A flutter passed through Mariah's heart, but she didn't have time to dwell on it, or any of the lovely things Peter had just said. If he truly was trying to start over with her, there had to be a way she could help.

"I do love the hairpin," she whispered, her cheeks pinking.

He had no time to reply. Victoria hopped down from the carriage a moment later. "Heavens above, Mariah," she gasped, pressing a hand to her chest and looking up at the castle. "I take back everything I said about the horror of marrying your fossil. This is so magnificent that even I would marry him."

Heat stained Mariah's cheeks, and she glanced to Peter, hoping he wouldn't be too offended. But paradoxically, Peter looked happier than he had all week. He looked as though he were about to laugh.

"Victoria." Mariah stepped forward, arms outstretched to greet her sister. "I'm so happy to see you."

"And I'm thrilled to see you." She leapt forward, throwing herself into Mariah's arms so hard that the two of them almost spilled to the ground. "You look magnificent," Victoria said with a squeal. "Very countess-like. Mama and Papa are going to be so sad to have missed this."

Mariah blinked. "What?" She glanced past Victoria to the carriage, but Davy was already shutting the door as the other footmen took two trunks down from the back. "Where are they?"

"Mama and Papa?" Victoria glanced to the carriage, then back to Mariah. "They decided to stay home. Mama was curious about the castle, of course, but then Papa reminded her that they hadn't had the house to themselves, just the two of them, in decades." She made a disgusted sound. "You would have been sick if you'd heard the two of them talking about it and cooing at each other over tea."

"Oh?" Mariah was beginning to feel sick at the thought of Victoria being at Starcross Castle alone. Without supervision. With William on the loose.

"What a large staff you have," Victoria said, rushing past Mariah to inspect the line of Starcross servants. "And they're all so fetching." Her gaze lingered on the footmen as they carried her trunks inside. Davy had the audacity to grin back at her.

Out of the corner of her eye, Mariah caught a half snort from Ginny as she clapped a hand over her mouth. That was enough to send giggles bubbling up in her throat. She just hoped Ginny would be willing to help babysit her sister.

The strained, wary looks on Mrs. Wilson and Mr. Snyder's face made Mariah lose her smile, though. "Victoria, you remember Peter, don't you?" She did her best to steer her sister away from ogling the footmen and on to proper things.

"Of course I do," Victoria said, stepping over to Peter

with a suspicious look. "You look younger than the last time I saw you."

"It's probably the castle," Peter said. Mariah stifled a giggle with her hand. "It's a pleasure to see you again, Victoria. Please come inside."

Whether it was the sunshine or Victoria's vivacity, for a moment, Mariah felt as though everything would be all right after all. She needed the infusion of light that her sister would provide, and she couldn't wait for Victoria to meet Domenica. The three of them might actually have fun together.

But not more than three steps into the castle, her hopes were dashed.

"Well, well. Is this the sister I've heard so much about?" William asked as he descended the grand staircase in the front hall.

"Oh my," Victoria said, pressing a hand to her stomach. Her eyes shone as she glanced up at William, as though she were seeing an apparition.

"Uncle, why don't you introduce me to your new guest?" William picked up his pace, marching toward them with a wolfish smile.

"This was a bad idea," Peter mumbled.

"Keep William away from my sister at all costs," Mariah agreed.

"Indeed." Peter cleared his throat and moved to stand between Victoria and William. "William, this is Mariah's sister, Victoria. Show her the respect she's due."

"Absolutely," William replied in a tone that showed everything but respect.

Unfortunately, Victoria burst into a laugh, her cheeks going pink. "I'm ever so happy to meet you," she said, extending her hand.

William took it, bowing and bringing her hand to his lips. His eyes traveled to Victoria's chest. "I think we will be the best of friends."

"I think not," Mariah said, louder than she intended to. "Come, Victoria. Let me show you to your room."

"Oh," Victoria said as Mariah hooked her arm and pulled her across the front hall. "I should really stay and be sociable." She grinned at William.

"You can see the Channel from your window," Mariah went on through clenched teeth. She shot Peter a warning look as she went.

Peter nodded to her, then leaned in close to William and murmured something that Mariah couldn't hear.

"I'll pursue whomever I want, Uncle," William answered, loud enough for Mariah—and worse, Victoria —to hear.

Victoria sighed. "He's so handsome," she said as Mariah pulled her up the stairs.

"You need to stay away from him," Mariah said. "He's a rogue and a criminal."

"A criminal?" Victoria sounded a little too excited by the prospect.

Mariah sighed and shook her head. "I have so much to tell you, my dear. I just hope you'll listen."

. . .

Peter was convinced that few men in England had a greater propensity than he did to take his troubles and make them worse. Of course Victoria would take to William right away. She was just the kind of inexperienced girl who would see a handsome face and charming manners and nothing else about a man's character. And William had made clear in the last two days that he would pursue Mariah's sister with single-minded focus.

"And I thought the biggest problem we'd have would be catching the rebel servant," he grumbled as his sword clashed against Malcolm's.

"You should have called me in a lot sooner," Malcolm said, parrying Peter's thrust with speed and precision.

The two of them sparred in the French garden at the back of the castle. It had been a relief when Malcolm suggested they practice that morning. No one fought with swords anymore, but for those of them who had learned how in the dawn of their youth, there was no more satisfying means of exercise. And if clashing with Malcolm helped him to hone the sort of skills he would need to spear William through the heart if he interfered with Mariah's sister, then all the better.

"I didn't know he would be a problem earlier," Peter went on with a grunt, pivoting so that he could bring his sword around to attempt an attack at Malcolm's thigh. They both wore padding, and the blades were blunted, but the strength behind his attempt was all that mattered.

"I thought William was always a thorn in your side." Malcolm underscored his comment by slashing at Peter's side.

Reflexes saved him, and he wheeled around with deft precision to ward off the blow. Sweat dripped down his back and wet his hair. His body was hot and alive with activity. It was a blessed relief from the tension that had been steadily growing through all the nights he'd spent alone in bed. His arms burned as he brought his sword up one more time, and his thighs were on fire as he maintained his attack stance.

At last, he struck a blow that caused Malcolm to lose his grip on his sword. It clattered to the ground, and Malcolm took a step back, hands raised, chuckling. "Someone's not spending enough time in bed with his wife."

If it were any other man, Peter would have slapped him with the flat of his sword, but since it was Malcolm, he laughed along with him, although without much humor. "Someone isn't spending any time in bed with his wife, and hasn't for weeks, thanks to the situation at hand."

Malcolm hummed and nodded, bending to retrieve his sword. "At least Mariah isn't as predatory as Anne."

Peter winced. "Don't use that word. Anne was sick. She couldn't help herself."

Malcolm sent him a doubtful look as he straightened and wiped his blade with his gloved hand. "Sick or not, Anne drove herself to destruction." He pointed his sword at Peter. "You were too lenient with her, and you're too lenient with William."

The irritation of Malcolm's statement had Peter buzzing with energy and ready for another round of sparring as Malcolm made an initial thrust. He was so frustrated with the whole thing that he danced his way through a quick series of thrusts, slashes, and parries and smacked his sword against Malcolm's arm within seconds.

"I just cut your arm off," he said through panting breaths. "That will teach you to dredge up Anne, like everyone else keeps doing, when the poor woman deserves to rest in peace."

Malcolm shot him a look that was half grimace, half sympathy as he rubbed his arm. "You deserve peace too, my friend." He nodded at something past Peter's shoulder. "I hope you find it with her."

Peter's chest squeezed as he turned, knowing what he'd see. Sure enough, Mariah was watching him from the top of the stairs that led from the house to the garden. Victoria stood by her side, whispering something to her. Domenica was at her other side, one hand on her hip, wearing a grin.

"I'm supposed to be wooing her," Peter told Malcolm in a grim voice.

Malcolm laughed. "You? Wooing a woman?"

"Your confidence in me is astounding." He fixed Malcolm with a flat stare.

"Well, here. I'll help you."

He raised his sword and attacked before Peter was ready. His senses were still heightened enough that he was able to fend off the attack with relative ease before launching into one of his own. It was as though Malcolm had only been playing with him before. His friend threw his full effort into sparring, forcing Peter to hone in his attention, parrying and moving with every bit of skill and agility he had. He went on the offensive, swinging his sword around to clash loudly with Malcolm's. The effort of battle had him sweating and his blood pounding again in no time.

At last, Malcolm's strength flagged, and Peter was able to strike a winning blow to his padded side. Malcolm reeled back, holding up his hands in surrender. "All right. All right, my friend. You win." His eyes flashed with mischief as he glanced past Peter. "You definitely win."

Peter turned, still panting from the fight. He wiped the sweat from his brow with his sleeve, blinking as he watched Mariah walking toward him. She was lit up with excitement, and, if he could believe what he was seeing, lust.

"This must be one of those other martial skills you told me you have," she said, a little breathless.

Heaven help him, Peter felt like a cocky young lad impressing the ladies for the first time. "You never know when you'll need to defeat Saladin's armies single-handedly," he said, resting the point of his sword in the dirt and leaning on it.

Mariah raised a hand to her mouth to hide a giggle.

He wanted to sweep her into his arms then and there and kiss her until every misunderstanding and frustration between them was cleared up.

"Where did you learn these knightly skills, my lord?" she asked, playing along.

Peter softened his stance. "When I was young. Sword-fighting was outdated even then, but a group of my school friends who shared a fascination with history convinced one of the old teachers at our school who had fought against Napoleon to teach us what he knew." He shrugged. "I kept up with it over the years as a means of exercise."

"You could have taken up cricket or tennis, you know," Victoria said, crossing her arms.

"Where's the fun in that?" Malcolm asked, stepping forward. Before Victoria could answer, he went on with, "Where were you after supper last night, Miss Victoria?"

The arousal in Mariah's expression dampened, and she flushed as she turned to her sister. "She went to bed early."

"I went to bed early," Victoria repeated, turning bright pink.

Dread filled Peter's gut. Victoria was as transparent as a window. At least William had been out, at the pub in Truro, no doubt.

"We should organize some sort of group activity for this evening," Malcolm went on, the light of calculation in his eyes. "And for tomorrow, and the next day and the next."

The thought of so much time in company exhausted Peter. He glanced to Mariah. "I hope we are all given some leave to spend our time in more intimate groups."

Mariah bit her lip to hide a smile and seemed to notice something in one of the nearby flower beds that was fascinating.

The only bed Peter was interested in was the one up in his room. It wouldn't take much to convince Mariah to break down the wall between them and take up her rightful place by his side in that bed. And under him as well. He was so close to resolving things with her that he could feel it in every fiber of his body.

"If you'd like," he started, hesitant, hoping what he was about to suggest wouldn't backfire on him, "I could teach you the basics of swordplay."

Mariah glanced back to him with a smile. "I think I'd like that."

Relief rushed through Peter. "It's very simple." He handed her his sword. Malcolm and the other women faded to the edges of his awareness. All that existed for him was Mariah. "Hold the hilt like this."

He stepped behind her, wrapping his arms around her and closing his hands over hers to show her the correct grip. It was so intoxicating to have her close that his body reacted in far stronger ways than it should have with the others standing right there.

"Like this?" Mariah asked softly, glancing up at him.

Their faces were only inches away. It would only take a small movement and he could kiss her. Everything about the look she gave him and the way she leaned toward him hinted that she wanted to be kissed. Malcolm would forgive him if he kissed his wife and ignored him. He could just—

"My lord." Snyder's anxious call threw cold water over everything Peter was trying to enjoy. He was forced to take a step back so that he could deal with his butler. "My lord, I think you should come at once."

"What is it, Snyder?" he growled, frustration closing its iron grip around him once more.

Snyder closed the distance, nodding to the ladies and to Malcolm, then turning to him. "My lord, more guests have arrived."

Peter frowned. "I didn't invite any more guests."

"I know, my lord. But they're here regardless."

CHAPTER 16

*P*eter clenched his jaw, wondering what new mayhem was about to befall. "Who are they?" he asked Snyder, pushing himself into motion.

Snyder turned to walk with him back toward the castle. Behind them, Mariah handed her sword off to Malcolm, then picked up her skirts and hurried to Peter's side.

"They gave their names as Mr. Poole and Mr. Robinson, my lord," Snyder said.

"Poole and Robinson?" Peter ran a hand over his face to clear the last of his sweat from practice away. He should have gone up to his room to bathe and change before meeting the unexpected guests, but since he doubted they had invitations, he didn't feel it was necessary. "Did they say anything else?" he asked as they stepped into the house through the morning parlor and headed toward the front hall.

"Only that they have been invited by Lord William to attend the house party, my lord."

Understanding mingled with dread in Peter's gut. "I see."

He wore a deep frown by the time he strode into the front hall. A pair of men were waiting by the front door, hats in their hands, looking around as if they'd never been in a country estate before. They weren't the brash, smirking sort of men that Peter had expected William to have as friends, so rather than going on the attack from the first, he proceeded with caution.

"Gentlemen," he said, greeting them with the air of command he'd honed in the military. "What can I do for you?"

One of the men stepped forward. He was short, with thinning hair, but his suit was finely tailored enough to mark him as a member of the upper classes, or at least the upper middle class.

"Benjamin Poole, my lord," he said, holding out his hand with a hesitant smile. "And this is my friend Dick Robinson." He gestured to the other man, tall with reddish hair, with his thumb.

"My lord," Robinson said, bobbing awkwardly as he came forward.

Peter worked to remain expressionless as he shook each man's hand. They weren't upper class. Their accents gave them away. That and the way they seemed out of their depth. So why were they pretending to be something they weren't?

"Are you friends of William's?" Peter asked. He was highly aware of Mariah coming to stand by his side, as if she wanted to be introduced. But the thought of letting two strange men have anything to do with Mariah made his blood run cold.

Poole and Robinson exchanged looks. A flash of something that seemed to confirm Peter's darkest suspicions passed between the two of them. It was gone as soon as it appeared, though, leaving Peter wondering what exactly he'd seen.

"William told us we'd be expected," Poole went on. "And...and welcomed."

"We wouldn't have come otherwise," Robinson added. "Only, he said there was a house party and all."

"Is this the missus?" Poole asked, sending a toothy smile Mariah's way.

Mariah started to smile in greeting, but Peter cut her off with, "This is the Countess of Dunsford."

Poole pulled back the hand he had begun to extend to Mariah.

Mariah flushed, suddenly glaring at Peter.

Peter sighed inwardly. He would catch hell for coming between Mariah and the guests later, but until he was certain they were harmless, he didn't want her to risk falling into whatever trap William had set.

He was spared having to confront Mariah then and there—or having to send her away—as Malcolm strode into the hall from the morning parlor. "These are the new guests?" he asked without preamble.

Poole and Robinson tried to hide their flinches, but they weren't fast enough. And any man who flinched at the sight of Malcolm Campbell wasn't a man he wanted in his house.

"Mr. Benjamin Poole and Mr. Dick Robinson," Peter introduced them.

Malcolm hummed as he came to a stop by Peter's side. He glanced across to Mariah. "Domenica was hoping you'd join her in the garden, my lady."

Mariah's cheeks flushed a darker shade of rose. "I'm fine here for the time being, Lord Malcolm."

Poole and Robinson glanced between the two, and Peter suddenly felt as though he were playing umpire in a particularly contentious cricket match.

"Mariah." He turned to her, lowering and softening his voice. "I think it would be best if you join Domenica until we can figure out who these gentlemen are and why they're here."

Mariah's back went straight and her eyes opened wide with offense, but before she could say anything, Poole said, "We're friends of William, like you said. He invited us to stay for a while, as long as you were having guests."

"He did, did he?" Malcolm crossed his arms, studying the men while stroking his chin.

"Yeah," Robinson said, mirroring the gesture with a hint of hostility. "We go way back, William and us. We're thick as thieves."

"I don't doubt that last part," Malcolm muttered.

The need to do something about the new arrivals made it hard for Peter to stand still. He was on the verge of telling the pair there had been some mistake and that they wouldn't be able to stay, when a peal of laughter announced Victoria and William as they strolled into the front hall, arm in arm. Peter's frown darkened.

William saw Poole and Robinson and nearly missed a step. The color drained from his face, but before Victoria had finished laughing at whatever joke they had between them, William had recovered.

"Gentlemen," he said, letting go of Victoria's arm and striding to meet the new arrivals. "You're here." His voice cracked.

"William, who are these men?" Peter asked.

"They're, ah, friends of mine, of course," William said, maneuvering between the two and draping his arms over their shoulders. "I invited them, but I didn't think they'd actually come." He said the last bit through clenched teeth.

"Not come?" Poole chuckled. "And miss a chance for a relaxing vacation in Cornwall?"

"Yeah, we couldn't do that," Robinson said.

"Of course not." William's smile was entirely too large. "Well, let's get you gents settled, and we'll talk about all the fun we can have during my uncle's party. Besides which, I have a proposition for the two of you. About that matter we discussed last month. Snyder?"

William pushed his friends toward the stairs. Snyder

glanced questioningly at Peter instead of following after them.

Peter blew out a breath and rubbed a hand over his face. "What is it Albert says? Keep your friends close and your enemies closer?"

"That's fine for him," Malcolm said, heading for the stairs as well. "He lives on a boat."

Peter watched as his wily friend followed Snyder up the stairs. Heaven only knew what he hoped to learn about the men by tailing them.

He was ready to escape to the garden to find Albert and apprise him of the new development when Mariah wheeled on him and hissed, "How could you embarrass me like that?"

Peter was so taken by surprise that he stepped back, blinking. "I beg your pardon?"

"They are our guests. It was my duty to greet them," Mariah seethed.

"Neither of them was particularly handsome," Victoria—who had inched forward during the conversation—added as if trying to console her sister.

Mariah pursed her lips and shot Victoria a sharp, sideways look. Her inexplicable wrath was mostly for Peter, though. "How am I supposed to find my way as mistress of this house if you keep throwing house parties without informing me and telling me to be silent while you're greeting our guests, as though I'm some sort of child?"

"I wouldn't exactly classify William's friends as

houseguests," Peter said, knowing that whatever came out of his mouth was going to be the wrong thing to say. Like anything he had tried to say to console Anne when she was in a mood. Since he was doomed to failure, the least he could do was voice his concerns about the men. "Any friend of William's is someone who both of you should stay away from," he said.

Mariah's jaw hardened, and she balled her hands into fists at her sides. "So now you're forbidding me to talk to our guests? Should I simply stay in my room for the next few weeks, until everyone leaves?"

Peter's jaw fell open. Not more than fifteen minutes ago, Mariah was looking at him with a smile that whispered of reconciliation and the potential for ending his lonely nights. Now she glared at him as though he were the devil. And it felt too familiar. He'd traveled this path before, and it had brought him nothing but misery.

"My dear," he said, trying to keep the weariness he felt out of his voice. "It was never my intention to drop you into the pit of vipers that is William and his friends. I would grab each one of them by the collar and toss them out the nearest window if I thought it would keep you safe. I would carry you off to the Orient if doing so would eliminate the dangers we're facing right now. And yes, if it stops you from being poisoned again or worse, I would wrap you up in cotton-wool and keep you in a tower. But it's not because I think of you as a child or incapable. It is because I fear what I might be capable of if William brings this whole debacle to a head. I would rather not have to snap my brother's son's neck. Forgive me for seeking out a way to protect you without violence."

Mariah studied him, tension and emotion radiating from her in the silence. Peter couldn't tell if she wanted to slap him or fall into his arms. He wanted to give her the world and all it contained, but for the moment the only thing he felt like he could give her was time to think.

"Excuse me," he said with a short bow. "I need to wash up before supper."

With a stab of guilt sharper than any sword, he walked past Mariah and mounted the stairs two at a time. Once again, he'd been a fool to hope that his life would be settled and happy at last. There didn't seem to be a thing he could do that would make a wife happy.

Mariah watched Peter retreat, wanting to scream at him...and wanting to cry out for him to stay. She wasn't sure where her burst of temper had come from, other than the feeling of being treated like a child. But his words were so beautiful they'd stunned her. It hadn't dawned on her that his efforts to protect her could come from fear. Nothing frightened Peter. Or so she'd thought. Now she wasn't so sure.

"William would never be so rude," Victoria said, gloating.

Mariah glared at her in disgust, but misery quickly overtook that emotion. She snapped away from Victoria and rushed through the hall and the morning parlor and back out into the garden.

"My lady, what happened?" Domenica asked as Mariah fled past her.

Mariah paused in her flight, biting her lip. Part of her wanted to be alone in her misery, but her new American friend was marching toward her as if she wouldn't stop until she discovered what was wrong. So Mariah smoothed her hands over her skirts, sniffed, wiped her eyes...and burst into fresh tears.

"*Mi amiga.*" Domenica picked up her speed, closing her arms around Mariah and hugging her like a sister. "Tell me what's wrong."

"I'm being silly," Mariah wailed as Domenica walked her over to a bench in the shade of a wisteria-covered arch. She growled at herself, then wiped her tears away with her sleeve. "Peter is probably right to forbid Victoria and I from speaking to the new guests."

"Who are they?" Domenica asked, rubbing her back.

Mariah shrugged. The gesture turned into an uncomfortable roll of her shoulders. "I'm still not quite certain. Friends of William's?"

"Lord William has friends?" Domenica's voice was thick with sarcasm.

It was almost enough to make Mariah laugh. "I know that Peter is only trying to protect me, but why does it make me feel like I'm being treated like a child?"

"How does it make you feel that way?" Domenica continued to rub her back.

"Not letting me speak. Attempting to send me away. Behaving as though I'm incapable of handling the trouble William has caused. It all reminds me of the way people have pitied me and tried to shelter me since Robert jilted me."

Domenica arched a brow. "Your husband is not coddling you, *mi amiga*. He is protecting you. He doesn't want you to be hurt."

"I know," Mariah sighed, picking at her skirt. "And part of me thinks I'm overreacting. But I'm just so...so angry. And so sad. And a thousand other emotions I can't keep straight."

"Truly?" Domenica shifted to face her more fully, a curious look on her face. "Are you usually emotional?"

"No," Mariah cried, throwing out her hands in a helpless gesture. "That's what frustrates me. I'm not like this, Domenica, I swear. But ever since marrying Peter. Ever since having my life turned upside down, I don't know who I am anymore. Did you know that my father failed to mention he'd promised me to Peter until the day before he arrived at our house?"

"Albert told me." Domenica nodded, then frowned. "Were you forced to go through with the marriage?"

"No." Mariah's shoulders slumped, and she went back to picking at her skirt. "Peter and I talked. He was more than willing to let me call it off."

"But you agreed to marry him. Why?"

Mariah bit her lip. "Because he seemed so kind and... and sad. Like he needed someone in his life. He talked about his first wife, how she died childless after several heartbreaking miscarriages."

Domenica hummed, nodding.

"And as my mother said, Peter was my last chance of ever marrying."

"Why?" Domenica shrugged. "You're still young and pretty, not to mention intelligent. Men should be lining up for your hand."

Mariah sent her a watery smile. "None of that was likely, thanks to the rumors my former fiancé spread before he died."

"Rumors?"

Mariah glanced down. "That I was cold, uninterested in intimacy."

"But you're not." Domenica spoke as though she were certain and not just guessing.

Mariah's cheeks heated. "No, I'm not. In fact, in spite of the fact that Peter was willing to give me time before...." She nodded, hoping Domenica would understand without her having to say it.

A knowing grin spread across her friend's face. "Then I was right." Her smile grew.

"Well, you were. Those first few days of our marriage...." Again, she let her sentence drift off with a sigh. "But then everything turned sour once we arrived here."

"Once William came between you?"

Mariah nodded. "To tell you the truth, I miss the way things were between Peter and I at first."

"You miss the joy of being one with a man who loves and cares for you," Domenica said, a wicked flash in her eyes.

Mariah bit her lip. "I wouldn't say that Peter loves me."

"You wouldn't? He looks besotted to me."

"We've only known each other for a month or so."

"Is that how long you've been married?"

Mariah counted the days in her head. It felt as though she'd been at Starcross Castle for years, but between the turmoil of their arrival, the days she lost in bed with food poisoning, and the business of having houseguests, it had been a month.

Something else about the time that had passed struck her as strange, but she couldn't think what.

She sighed. "This will all be a distant memory if we can convince William to leave," she went on. "If I can make it that long."

"You will, *mi amiga*." Domenica took her hand and squeezed it.

"I just wish that I could believe we really will have seen the last of William once he's given up," Mariah went on. "But if the man can bribe one of the servants to taint my food and make me sick, there's no end to what he could do to me. Especially if he's still Peter's heir."

"Well, now, I don't think he will be for much longer," Domenica said with a grin.

Mariah shook her head. "If Peter and I don't find a

way to reconcile, if he doesn't stop treating me like a child who can't manage my own affairs—"

"And if you can't find it in your heart to forgive him for wanting to keep you safe?" Domenica added, her expression downright mothering. "Don't forget that his first wife was of a fragile and unpredictable character. Chances are, he's not used to women who can stand up for themselves."

"I hadn't thought of that," Mariah said, feeling worse than ever.

"Give him time."

Mariah let out a weary breath and nodded. "It would be so much easier if William were gone, or if the house weren't crawling with people, or if I felt right in my own skin." When Domenica tilted her head in question, Mariah went on with, "I just want to feel like myself again."

"And you say this odd feeling has been with you since marrying Peter?"

"Yes." Mariah sighed. "At first I thought it was because my monthly was coming, but—"

She stopped, a wild idea taking hold in her mind. She glanced to Domenica, only to find her grinning as if she knew the answer to a riddle that Mariah didn't.

"You don't think...." she began, but was too overwhelmed to finish the thought. Domenica's smile widened. "But that's far too soon, isn't it? I mean, we've only known each other for a month."

"*Chiquita*, it only takes one time." She squeezed

Mariah's hands. "I've spent most of my life around women who lay with men, enough to know the signs. For some, it never happens, no matter how often they're with a man. For others, God help them, the first night they spend with a man leaves them with a child."

Mariah swallowed hard. The idea of being pregnant was one thing, but hearing Domenica speak about such things so openly made her tremble. "It doesn't seem possible."

"Believe me. It is possible. And it seems it is more than that now. How late are you?"

Mariah closed her eyes and counted. "More than a fortnight."

"And are you reliable?"

A sudden ache filled Mariah's heart as all of the pieces came together. It wasn't just time. She hadn't felt right for weeks. She'd blamed it on starting a new life, food poisoning, and stress. But it was all suddenly clear to her.

"I'm pregnant," she whispered. A moment of terror made her feel hollow, but before she could grab hold of that, a deeper joy filled her. "Peter will have his child so much sooner than he anticipated." She managed a smile. "William won't have any sort of hold on him, or Starcross Castle. All we have to do is make it through the mess in front of us."

"And you will make it, *mi amiga*," Domenica said, hugging her tightly. "I will be here with you to make certain you do."

"Thank you, Domenica. Thank you so much." She hugged Domenica back, unendingly grateful to have such a good friend.

"So, are you going to tell your husband?" Domenica asked.

A cold shiver curled down Mariah's spine. "I suppose I have to," she said. "But I don't know how I can."

"You will know when the time is right," Domenica assured her. "And when you do, I'm certain whatever other troubles you have, especially those caused by Lord William, will vanish."

CHAPTER 17

There was a reason that courting was a young man's game. Desperate though he was to chase after Mariah so that he could simply be with her and talk through the muddle between them, Peter found himself tossed from one responsibility to another in the next few days.

"Poole and Robinson are definitely up to something," Malcolm reported several hours after William's guests had arrived helping himself to a tumbler of Peter's finest scotch. Although, it was probably scotch that Malcolm had given him years ago, that he hadn't gotten around to drinking yet. "The puzzling thing is that I'm not sure William knows what it is."

"Oh?" Peter asked, pouring himself a fraction of the drink Malcolm was swirling in his glass as he stood by the fireplace in the library.

"William didn't have the look of a man who was about to launch a nefarious plot as he escorted his friends to their room. If I had to put money on it, I'd say they pose more of a danger to him than to anyone else in the house."

"Should I send the ladies away after all then?" Peter asked, ready to do anything to keep Mariah out of harm's way. Even if she would never forgive him for it. He needed to find a way to make her see that what she interpreted as treating her like a child was, in fact, desperation to keep her from another food poisoning incident, or worse.

But Malcolm shook his head. "You, Albert, and I are here, and I suspect that your Snyder would be willing to don battle armor to keep the ladies out of harm's way as well."

"But is it enough?" He'd thought so at first, but now he wasn't so sure.

"I think so," Malcolm said with an uninspiring nod, narrowing his eyes. "Does Snyder have any idea who William's helper in the house is?"

Malcolm winced and took a drink before answering, "He's convinced it could be any of the footmen. Aside from Davy, they're all new within the last year."

It was true. Owen Llewellyn had gone to work at the mines, making way for Davy to be promoted, and of the other two footmen whom he'd employed a year ago, Clarence had gone back to work on his father's farm and John had moved on to his London townhouse. But

Snyder had hired the new lads, and Peter had always found his butler to be a good judge of character.

The problems of William's mole and his guests were only part of what kept Peter from approaching Mariah the next day. He had everything planned, had even asked Nick to pick a bouquet of Mariah's favorite blooms for him to give to her, but just as he was working up the nerve to ask his wife to accompany him on a ride around the estate, Sinclair showed up at the house.

"Mr. Adler, the surveyor you hired, thinks he's found something, my lord," Sinclair explained before Peter could take the man into the library. "It's not copper, but he thinks you'll want to see it right away."

"Not copper?" Peter followed the man as he gestured toward the door and led him outside. "What is it then?"

"He can explain, my lord."

Those simple words ended with Peter mounting Charger and, instead of spending his day on a pleasurable ride intended to smooth over his troubles with Mariah, it took him from one end of the estate to the other, looking at hillocks and vales while the surveyor explained in painful detail what the presence of certain plants or the colors of rocks meant, and how a large tin deposit was very likely waiting under their feet.

He'd been so weary when he arrived home, late for supper but just in time for a scolding frown from Mariah, that he gave up any hope of wooing his wife in favor of going to bed. After all, the one thing the army had taught him was the importance of a good night's sleep before charging into battle.

By the third day, Peter was convinced that there was a reason men went courting before the responsibilities of life piled on their shoulders.

"I always thought that people played games at house parties," Victoria said at breakfast, more of a pout to her words than Peter wanted to think about.

Mariah must have felt the same way. She rolled her eyes at her sister, then glanced in Peter's direction. Peter had been so distracted by the letter he'd received from his man of business in London first thing that morning that he grinned back at her, forgetting that she was angry with him. He blinked when, instead of frowning, she answered his look with a pink-cheeked smile, lowering her head as if suddenly bashful. But coyness was the last thing he expected from a woman who had argued with him so pointedly just days before. He couldn't keep up.

"What kind of games did you have in mind, my dear?" William asked. He sat next to Mariah at the other end of the table. The edginess that had rippled off him on the day his friends had arrived was gone, though Peter wasn't sure he liked the feigned casualness he sported now.

"Like charades or cards, or even sardines," Victoria went on.

"Sardines?" Malcolm asked with a frown. He sat directly across the table from William. The way he constantly glared at William would have put Peter off his eggs.

"It's such a jolly game," Victoria said, bursting with enthusiasm. "It starts with one person who dashes off to find a hiding place. Then, everyone else in the party searches around the estate to find them. Once they do, they join that person in hiding. Every subsequent person who finds them hides with them, and so on and so on, until everyone is crammed into a single hiding place, like sardines."

"Hide-and-seek?" Domenica asked, looking surprised and amused.

"Yes," Victoria said. "But the other way around."

"Aren't we a little too old to be playing hide-and-seek?" Albert asked.

"You're never too old for fun," William answered. "Well, unless you're my uncle here." He nodded in Peter's direction without looking at him. "He's too old for much of anything."

Robinson snorted, but the others at the table had the good sense to look uncomfortable.

"He's not too old." Mariah defended him, but her comment wasn't loud enough for William to hear. Peter noticed, though, and once again, the light of hope flared within him.

"I think we should play this jolly game of Victoria's," William went on.

"Yes, we should." Victoria clapped her hands, nearly upsetting her tea as she did.

"No." Malcolm shook his head. "It's not a good idea."

"Why?" William sneered at him. "Because it won't give you the chance to spy on me, like you've been doing since you darkened the castle's doorstep?"

Everyone at the table dropped what they were doing to look up, suddenly tense.

"Don't think I haven't noticed," William went on. "That's obviously what my dear uncle brought you here for." He snorted and busied himself slicing the sausages on his plate. "As if you think I'm stupid."

"Oh, I don't think you're stupid at all," Malcolm said, far grimmer than Peter would have preferred.

"No?" William speared a piece of sausage and bit it off his fork. He chewed for a few seconds, pointing his fork at Malcolm. "I know what those two have been up to." He glanced between Peter and Mariah. "Do you really think I'm foolish enough not to see the writing on the wall?"

The table remained silent. Peter exchanged a puzzled glance with Malcolm, then frowned at William. "I've always been willing to give you a chance to improve yourself," he said, wondering if it would be wiser to keep his mouth shut.

William let out an exasperated sigh. "In no time at all, I will be thoroughly replaced. What else am I to do but endear myself to you, dear uncle, so that I might remain in your good graces?" He glanced up the table to Mariah.

Mariah's cheeks turned an even darker shade of pink,

and she stared at her plate. But it was the way William sent a challenging look to his friend Poole that had Peter's mind buzzing. As if William were trying to make the point that he might still stay in favor, not to him or to Mariah, but to his friends.

Friends indeed. If Peter's guess was right, Poole and Robinson were William's creditors. The whole thing made sense now. He turned to Malcolm, wondering if his friend had put the pieces together.

"All right," Malcolm said with a shift in his posture that told Peter yes, he had figured it out. "We'll play sardines, then."

Peter blinked. "We will?"

Malcolm glanced to him, warning in his eyes. "We'll do what young Victoria here wants and play sardines. It should be fun."

It would be a disaster. Everyone in the house party scattering across the grounds, hiding from each other?

Unless Malcolm used it as a way to get to the bottom of the mysteries that were mounting up like William's debts.

"I'll tell Snyder to prepare for a game this afternoon," Peter said, unable to believe he was going along with the plan.

"Huzzah," Victoria said, clapping again. She finished by clasping her hands in front of her and gazing longingly at William. Poole and Robinson also exchanged victorious glances.

Peter clenched his jaw and hoped that Malcolm

knew what he was doing. But when he caught the suddenly expectant look in Mariah's eyes, his attitude changed. Perhaps he could find the chance to speak to Mariah alone at last while everyone was out searching the castle for the sardines.

"Keep the guests outside," Malcolm murmured to Peter as they left the breakfast room later.

"I thought you had something up your sleeve," Peter said with a grim smile.

"If you can clear the house, I should be able to get an idea of what Poole and Robinson are here for," Malcolm confirmed. "At the very least, I can sniff out your traitorous servant."

Peter arched a brow at him. "You make it sound like some sort of gothic novel."

"I'm trying to prevent the gothic part." Malcolm thumped him on the back before marching out into the hall to have a word with Snyder.

Peter had half a mind to speak to Snyder himself, but before he could join Malcolm, Mariah stepped out of the breakfast room. She came to an abrupt stop when she saw him. Peter's heart turned a cartwheel in his chest. He started toward her.

"My lady."

It was his turn to be brought up short when Ginny dashed across the front hall. She saw him, then stopped with an, "Oh!"

Mariah glanced anxiously between him and her maid. "Is something the matter?"

Peter couldn't tell whether she was asking Ginny or him.

"It's your closet, my lady," Ginny started slowly, glancing to Peter to see if she had permission to continue.

Peter nodded to her as Mariah asked, "What about my closet?" with a frown.

"I've discovered some...damage to a few of your dresses, my lady."

Mariah blinked. "Damage? What kind of damage?"

Peter was equally confused, but figured it was of a delicate nature when Ginny sent a furtive look his way before saying, "I think you should come see for yourself."

Mariah let out a breath and dropped her shoulders. "I hope you don't mind," she told him. "I...I was hoping to speak with you."

A quick grin pulled at Peter's lips. "I was hoping to speak to you."

Her brow lifted slightly with hope and regret. She glanced to Ginny, then back to him. "We'll talk later."

With that, she walked off, Ginny at her side. Peter watched the two of them mount the stairs, and rubbed a hand over his face. He should be used to his plans being thwarted by now. With a shrug, he turned to seek out Albert, his one last hope for friendly conversation that morning.

• • •

As it happened, Peter didn't have a chance to be alone with Mariah again before the game of sardines began after lunch.

"This is how we play," Victoria instructed them all, a child teaching adults. "I'll start the game by finding a place in the garden to hide."

Peter was relieved that he didn't have to step in and declare the house off-limits. Victoria had come up with that all on her own.

"I will have ten minutes to find a suitable hiding place," Victoria went on. "After that time has passed, Davy here, who has so kindly offered to assist us—" She gestured to the footman, who looked more than a little put out. "—will give each of you a different door to exit the castle through."

"We're leaving through different doors?" Mariah asked, glancing to Peter.

"Yes, silly," Victoria laughed. "That way there will be no cheating. You can't look for me in groups, you know. Everyone must fend for themselves."

"I see," Mariah said, frowning.

Peter was equally disappointed. So much for whisking her off so they could chat. He attempted to step over to her side to whisper a rendezvous point, but Victoria caught him and said, "No cheating. Davy, make sure the players don't whisper to each other while I'm hiding."

"Yes, miss," Davy said, looking bored.

"All right, then. Here I go."

With a giggle and a swish of her skirts, Victoria dashed out to the garden through the French doors. As soon as she left, Peter continued toward Mariah.

"Ah-ah, Uncle." William stopped him. "You heard what Victoria said. No cheating. And that includes giving your wife clues about the best hiding places in the garden."

Peter blew out an exasperated breath. "I simply wanted to tell her—"

"No." William crossed his arms.

Peter turned and marched over to the unlit fireplace, sending Mariah a look of exasperation. He was beginning to think she'd been right and that he shouldn't have invited so many people to the house. Malcolm's plan to bring the mysteries hanging over them to an end had better work, and William had better be serious about knowing he didn't have enough time to trick him into giving up half the estate. At least Mariah seemed content to wait.

Ten minutes passed, then Davy began leading the guests out of the parlor one by one. William was allowed to slip out through the same exit Victoria had taken, which didn't seem entirely fair. But Peter was beyond the point of caring. He was escorted to the rarely-used ballroom on the far side of the house and turned loose in an old hedge maze that Nick had been working on recovering. Where Mariah would be let out of the house was anyone's guess, so Peter began a long, irritated walk to the first stretch of flat, open land he could think of.

It happened that along the way he passed a small, pretty garden, surrounded on three sides by a wall—a garden he hadn't visited for years. He slowed his steps, a wave of guilt overcoming him. In the center of the garden was a slender slab of rose-colored marble that bore the words "Anne Barkley deVere, loving wife. September 12, 1832 – March 5, 1874."

Peter let out a long breath, shook his head, then changed directions. He walked slowly until he stood at the foot of Anne's tomb. The overwhelming sense of failure that the memory of Anne brought him pushed down on his shoulders, no matter how lovely the memorial garden he'd had made for her was. He should have been able to give her what she wanted, or else he should have helped her to find something besides a baby to make her life complete. All she'd wanted was something to care for, something of herself to leave behind in the world. She'd been denied that, and he couldn't help but feel like it was his fault.

"I'm sorry," he said with a weary sigh. "I should have been a better man for you. I couldn't give you what you wanted."

He pressed his mouth shut, fighting the overwhelming grief that welled up inside him. He looked up at the sky, blinking away twenty wasted years.

"Give me the chance to do better this time," he pleaded...not sure with whom. "I know I've made mistakes, but I can do better. And Mariah...." He swallowed, lowering his gaze to Anne's grave once more. "I'm sorry, Anne, but I feel a connection with her that we never had. She has such strength in her. If I hadn't made such a mess of things, our life together would have started out so much better than this."

"It isn't your fault."

Peter sucked in a breath and whipped around to find Mariah standing at the entrance to the garden, her hands clasped in front of her. She wore a sober look as she stepped into the garden, meeting and holding his gaze.

"None of this is your fault, Peter. And I know—" She rolled her eyes to the side, cheeks going pink. "I know that I have been too hard on you. William is the problem, not you, but I haven't been in my right mind since arriving at Starcross."

"Don't say that," he said, more serious than he intended to be. He glanced at Anne's tomb, then moved to meet Mariah. "You are more in your right mind than anyone here."

"No, I'm not," she said with one brow arched and a twitch of her lips. Instead of explaining her answer, she approached Anne's tombstone, glancing solemnly down at it. "Why do you think you failed her?"

"I don't think it, I know it." He stood by Mariah's side, staring at the grave. "All Anne ever wanted was a child."

"But she miscarried over and over instead," Mariah said. She put a hand on his arm. Glancing up at him. "It seems to me as though you did everything right and the failing, if there is such a thing, was God's will."

Peter shook his head, pulling away and pacing around the tomb. He didn't deserve Mariah's touch. "It was more than that. We were told by multiple doctors that a healthy pregnancy would be unlikely, and that for Anne's sake, we should stop trying."

He reached the far end of the slab of marble and risked a glance at Mariah. She watched him with a compassion in her eyes that tied his stomach in knots.

"Barkley accuses me of killing Anne at every opportunity, and he's not far off the mark." He couldn't bear to look at Mariah as he confessed, so he studied the cold letters of Anne's name instead. "I knew it was hopeless, but I couldn't say no to her when she came to my bed."

"You cared for her," Mariah said. "It's only natural when a husband cares for his wife to want to be with her."

"But I didn't love her. Not like I should have."

Mariah shook her head in confusion. "There are many kinds of love. It sounds to me like you did love her in your own way."

"But I should have been able to resist her." He raised his voice in spite of himself looking up at her. "To keep her safe, to save her life. I should have been able to keep her out of my bed." He lowered his head again. "But I suppose on some level I truly am the kind of man who puts my own pleasure ahead of others' wellbeing."

Mariah was silent, and when he peeked up at her, she wore a look as though something suddenly made sense to her. "You don't sound as though you took pleasure in any of it."

Prickles like a jolt of electricity raced down Peter's spine. "No," he breathed out. "I didn't. With Anne—" He swallowed, his mouth going dry and his pulse kicking up with anxiety. And yet, he felt as though he could say these things to Mariah without the risk that she would judge or laugh at him. "It wasn't an equal exchange. She took what she wanted from me without mercy, and her purpose had nothing to do with me. It was all about getting with child."

"She hurt you," Mariah said, as soft as a summer breeze.

"No." He denied it as fast as he could, but his heart knew otherwise.

"You need to be loved, Peter." Mariah started around the tomb, her eyes never leaving him. "That was one of the first things I noticed about you. It was the reason I knew I should marry you."

He watched her approach with wary confusion. "It was?"

She nodded, reaching for his hands when she came close. "I'm sorry I lost sight of what I knew from the moment we had our first conversation."

His confusion doubled, but so did the ache in his chest and the longing to take her into his arms. "I must seem pitiful to you."

"No." She shook her head, squeezing his hands. "You seem like a man who has tried very hard to be a good husband for a very long time. You seem like a man who takes responsibility for other people's shortcomings, even when they are not your fault." He tried to deny it, but she went on before he could find his voice. "You seem like a man who has worked thanklessly to keep the people close to him from harm. It's not just Anne, it's William too."

Peter let out a wry huff and shook his head. "I was a fool to think I could guide him to be a better person."

"You were an optimist," she corrected him. "But William is his own man. You didn't make him who he is. Just as I expect Anne was determined to destroy herself no matter how hard you tried to save her."

His breath caught in his chest, and he stared at Mariah with a frown.

"Did you ever stop to think that Anne knew she would never have a child? That she knew further attempts would kill her?"

"I—" A burst of wind swirled through the trees around them. It felt as icy as December, not the pleasant June breeze that had been there only a moment before.

"You say that many doctors told you what would happen if the two of you continued to try for a child. Surely Anne listened to them. Perhaps she would rather have died trying than live without what she longed for. And if that was her aim, then nothing you could have done would have stopped her."

Peter began to shake as Mariah's words burrowed into him. Could Anne really have known what she was doing? And if he had shut her out of his bed, would she have found some other way to kill herself? He wasn't sure if the prospect was comforting or horrifying. But for the first time, a tiny part of him considered just how powerless he had been in the situation, and with that came a dizzying sense of freedom.

It was short-lived, though.

"I haven't been able to keep you safe from William's machinations," he said.

A wry grin tweaked the corner of her lips. "No, you haven't. But William's machinations will come to an end soon."

"I don't want to underestimate my nephew's desperation," Peter said with a shake of his head. "If he feels he's cornered, he'll still do whatever it takes to claim his place as my heir."

"He can try," Mariah went on, a mischievous light glittering in her eyes, "but he'll have some fierce competition."

"Competition never deterred William. He'll drive the two of us to insanity in his efforts to keep us from conceiving. He's already proven how low he'll stoop to set us at odds with each other."

"He can try whatever he wants," she said, her grin inexplicably triumphant. "But he's already too late."

"Don't tell that to William. He'll never give up, even if—"

He stopped. The whole world seemed to stop. Mariah smiled brighter, even as a tidal wave of emotions slammed into Peter. His chest squeezed so hard that he couldn't breathe.

At last, he managed to ask in a hoarse voice, "Are you?"

Mariah nodded, her eyes shining with what he could only hope were happy tears. "At least, I think so. It's still quite early, but when I told you I wasn't in my right mind and that I haven't felt like myself since arriving at Starcross, I was serious. I haven't felt like myself because it's extremely likely that I am two people at the moment."

"Mariah," he breathed out her name as though it were a prayer, then swept her into his arms.

The whole world seemed to blossom into a safe and beautiful haven as he hugged her close. It couldn't possibly be true. It was too wonderful. And so soon. But there was something in the glow that radiated from her, something in the sensation that expanded quickly through him, telling him that all was right with the world, that made it undeniable.

"This is wonderful," he said, unable to catch his breath as he loosened his hold on her. "But we have to be careful. So careful. Perhaps you should stay in bed."

"For nine months?" she laughed.

"I'll send the guests away. I'll be with you every moment of every day. I'll have Ginny stay with you whenever I can't be there."

"You can't send William away," Mariah said, her arms around his waist like she would never let go.

"Then *we'll* go away," he said. "Today. Right now.

We'll pack our things and leave. We should have left as soon as we returned home to find William here. We'll go to the continent, to your parent's house, to—"

"No." She pressed her fingers to her lips. "I'm not going anywhere."

"But it isn't safe here. Not with William—"

"This is my home now, Peter," she said, half laughing, half scolding him. "This is where our child, our children, will be born. This is where they will grow up. I won't let William chase me out of my own home, and now I understand why you have held your ground this whole time."

"I held my ground because I was too foolish not to plan a strategic retreat," he argued.

She shook her head. "You stayed here with me, in spite of William, because Starcross Castle is as much a part of you as your beautiful, white hair."

She raised a hand to thread her fingers through it. Peter was reminded of how it felt to have her tug his hair when they were in the throes of passion. His body responded instantly, and he tightened his hold on her.

"The only home I know is wherever I'm with you," he said, his voice filled with longing. "And I am willing to fight for this home with everything I have within me."

Before she could protest, he slanted his mouth over hers in a kiss. It felt as though an eternity had passed since their last kiss, and every fiber of his being rejoiced. She gave into him with a sigh, wrapping her arms around him and kissing him back with equal passion. How could he have let the everyday cares of the world intrude on the magic that existed between the two of them? His weary, old, December heart had found its home in her. For the first time in his long life, he knew what true, deep love felt like.

"You know," he said, his voice deep and rumbling as he broke their kiss and rested his forehead against hers. "With everyone dashing about the garden playing hide-and-seek, we could slip upstairs and make up for the time we've lost."

"What an intriguing idea, my lord," Mariah hummed in return. "I can't tell you how much I've missed sharing your bed."

"You could show me," he suggested in a tone so sultry he was certain she would laugh at him.

"I could." She moved a hand to his chest, sliding it slowly downward.

Peter couldn't help but kiss her again, reveling in the taste of her, the way her body fit so well against his. He had half a mind to take her right there in the garden, if he could just—

"There you are." Domenica flounced around the corner, out of breath. As soon as she saw Peter and Mariah's passionate embrace, she gasped, "Oh. I'm so sorry." She started to leave, but bit her lip and turned back with a wince. "It's just that you might like to know that no one has been able to find Victoria."

"No one?" Mariah pulled back, not quite leaving his embrace. Her cheeks were pink, which made Peter's blood pump harder.

"No one," Domenica repeated. "And William is missing too." She hesitated, then added, "So are his friends."

Peter let out a frustrated growl, taking Mariah's hands and starting for the path. "I knew this silly game was an excuse for William to get up to no good."

"We'd better find Victoria before she gets into more trouble than she can handle," Mariah agreed.

They raced off with Domenica to solve yet another problem. The way things were going, William's efforts to keep Peter and Mariah apart might end up being more effective than he anticipated.

CHAPTER 18

Mariah was ready to murder her sister. Or at least lock her in the tower of the medieval part of Starcross Castle. It took the better part of an hour to find Victoria. An hour that she could have spent in Peter's arms. Because, at last, she felt as though she and Peter had found the solid ground they needed to build their marriage on. Her heart had nearly broken when she'd put two and two together while listening to his sad tale. But not only had she suddenly understood what Anne's motivation to pursue a child at all costs could be, she remembered the afternoon she and Peter had first met, their conversation by the river. She remembered all the reasons she had chosen to marry him when he had given her the chance to back out.

She loved him. There was no telling when it had happened, but seeing the suffering in his eyes had made her problems seem trivial. And feeling the way he responded to the simplest show of affection filled her with a power that no one, not even William, could vanquish. She would give Peter the happiness he deserved.

Just as soon as she wrung her sister's neck.

"We've looked all over the gardens, my lord," Nick reported as the house party guests gathered in the French garden at the back of the house. "Miss Victoria isn't anywhere to be found."

"Do you think she's trying to fool us all by hiding in the house?" Captain Tennant asked, staring up at the windows of Starcross Castle.

"For two hours?" Peter asked, frowning.

"Victoria could get into a lot of trouble in two hours," Mariah sighed, rubbing her stomach.

She had just decided to march into the house, intent on turning every room inside out, when Malcolm strode out through the French doors, holding a struggling Davy by the collar.

"Get off me, let go!" Davy protested, but Malcolm held him tight.

Peter rolled his eyes before settling into a look of righteous fury and striding across the garden to meet them. "What's going on here?" he demanded.

Mariah rushed to his side as Malcolm said, "Schoolboy pranks multiplied to the point where they become dangerous." He held up a large envelope.

Peter took the envelope and opened it, flinching at the powdery contents. "What's this?"

He started to sniff it, but Malcolm threw out a hand to stop him. "It's a mixture of ground rose hip, stinging nettles, and velvet beans." When both the deVeres and the Tennants stared at him in confusion, Malcolm went on with, "Commonly known as itching powder."

"Itching powder?" Mariah blinked and shook her head.

"Like I said, a schoolboy prank," Malcolm went on. "But not at this potency, and not when sprinkled through bed linens."

"Whose bed linens?" Peter asked, scowling at Davy.

"Yours, of course," Malcolm said. "And Mariah's."

Mariah's eyes went wide, and she glared at Davy. "You? You're William's accomplice?"

"I didn't," Davy sputtered. "I never."

She didn't believe him. Innocent men didn't squirm and look at their master with terror in their eyes.

"Take him to Snyder," Peter said in a low voice. "Have his room searched. And ask Mrs. Harmon if Davy had access to Mariah's tainted soup."

"Of course he did," Mariah said. "He served it. He serves all our food."

"There's one mystery solved," Domenica murmured from a few steps behind Mariah.

"Get rid of him," Peter repeated.

Malcolm nodded, dragging the protesting footman off.

"It's a good thing Malcolm caught the bastard,"

Captain Tennant said, thumping Peter's shoulder. "Aren't you allergic to nettles?"

"Very," Peter growled. "And William knows it."

"I know what?" William bounded onto the scene with a bright smile and red cheeks, as though he'd run up from the village.

Mariah was ready to give him the slap he deserved, but Peter held up a hand to stop her. He wore his look of stony fury, but did little more than narrow his eyes.

"Your mole has been caught," he said. "Itching powder?" He took a step toward William, shaking his head as though William were twelve. "What kind of juvenile prank are you planning next? Will you dip Mariah's pigtails in ink to try to upset her into leaving?"

"Actually," Mariah admitted, stepping forward. "He may have already tried that. Or something similar. It seems as though half my dresses were—" She cleared her throat, suddenly embarrassed about what Ginny had showed her the day before. "—urinated on. The stains may not come out."

Peter's jaw clenched. "Explain yourself."

William wasn't moved at all. He shrugged. "Sounds like someone with an infantile mind has been tweaking your nose, Uncle."

"I believe I know exactly who that mind belongs to," Peter seethed.

"Davy, apparently," William went on, breaking into a lop-sided grin. "He fits the bill, after all. Barely twenty, overworked, resentful after you promoted

Llewellyn to the position of mine foreman instead of him."

"Davy never expressed any interest in working at the mines," Peter said.

"Or perhaps you never cared to listen to him." William clicked his tongue and shook his head. "I think it's a clear-cut case of lower-class jealousy, don't you think?"

"It's jealousy, all right," Captain Tennant said, crossing his arms.

"I've always known what you were capable of." Peter shook his head. "But I never realized how low you would stoop."

"Me?" William pretended to be affronted. "What do I have to do with any of this?"

"There's no point in pretending innocence anymore." Mariah stepped forward. She couldn't remember the last time she'd been so furious. "Whatever ploys you have to trick Peter into kicking you out, whatever plans you have to keep the two of us apart or to drive me away so that Peter never has an heir, they're all for naught."

"You think so?" William crossed his arms, looking down his nose at her.

"I know so. All we have to do is wait."

"Auntie dear, perhaps your mummy failed to mention these things to you, but you'll have to do a great deal more before the stork will flutter down to your doorstep."

It was Mariah's turn to grin in triumph. She placed a

hand on her stomach. "Yes. I know. And Mama was absolutely right when she said that older men make the best lovers."

It was crude and far more personal than she ever would have dreamed of being in any other circumstance, but her announcement hit its mark. William's smug expression froze, then gradually soured until he was grimacing at Mariah. At her hand on her stomach.

"No." He shook his head. "It's too soon. And you couldn't have. I made sure of it."

"We married several days before returning to Starcross Castle," Peter said, his voice grim, his smile victorious.

"But this is preposterous," William sputtered on. "An old relic like you? You couldn't possibly."

"What's ridiculous is the assumption that a woman would only want a short-sighted young whelp like you," Domenica said, planting her hands on her hips. "But then, I saw how blinded you are by your own self-importance the first time I met you."

William sneered at her, but stayed focused on Mariah. "You think you're clever, do you?"

"I don't think I'm clever," she answered. "But I am Peter's wife, and soon I will be the mother of his child and heir. Where will that leave you?"

"Look who I found on my way back from handing Davy over to Snyder?" Lord Malcolm stepped out into the tension of the garden stand-off once more, this time leading Victoria.

"Look at this," Victoria said with a nervous laugh. "I brought you all together in the same place like sardines after all."

Mariah took a step toward her sister, ready to give her a stern lecture. Until she noticed that Victoria's hair was tousled, her skirt was badly wrinkled, and her bodice was buttoned wrong. She sent a furious look to William instead. "How could you?"

"With pleasure," William drawled. He turned his sickening grin to Peter. "Ready to throw me out yet?"

Peter bared his teeth, balled a fist, and lunged at William, but Captain Tennant reached out to catch him before he could land any blows. Victoria screamed, and Mariah stood frozen between wanting to punch William herself and cry out for it all to stop.

It was Lord Malcolm who reached William first. He grabbed the younger man's arm and twisted it behind William's back with so much force that William pitched forward, his face hitting the grass. Lord Malcolm planted a foot on the small of William's back and bent to whisper, "Peter might not be able to throw you out without losing half his estate, but if you stay, there's nothing to keep me from slicing you from throat to balls while you sleep."

William let out an unmanly whimper, but Lord Malcolm only pulled his arm tighter. Peter gestured to Captain Tennant to let him go, and as soon as he was free, he shook his arms out and straightened his jacket. "I refuse to banish you from Starcross Castle," he said loud enough for everyone to hear. "And I refuse to allow you to lock your bedroom doors as well." He glanced to Lord Malcolm.

"Oh, he can lock his doors all he wants," Lord Malcolm said. "I have ways of getting around that."

"I'll go, I'll go," William wept.

"I'll have Snyder help you pack at once," Peter said. His voice was as cold as stone, but his eyes flashed with victory.

"One more thing," Lord Malcolm said, letting William's arm go, but continuing to stand on his back. "Where are your friends, Poole and Robinson?"

"I don't know," William stammered. "Truly, I don't know." Malcolm must have pressed down with his foot, because William yelped in pain. "I'm telling the truth. I haven't spoken to them since this morning."

"Are you sure he's not lying?" Mariah asked.

"I'm not lying. Ask Victoria. I've been with her since I left the parlor to search for her."

Dreading what she would see, Mariah turned to her sister. "Is he telling the truth?"

Victoria looked guiltier than Mariah had ever seen her. "Yes, it's true. We...we had an arrangement. I didn't really hide. I went straight back into the house, to...to my bedroom. William met me there." She lowered her head, her cheeks blazing.

"Victoria, for shame." Mariah marched up to her, wanting to take her by the arms and shake her senseless for ruining herself the way she had. "What would Mama and Papa say?"

Victoria met her eyes with a peevish pout. "We didn't *do* anything. William was a perfect gentleman. He read me poetry." She sent a moony look to William, who crossed his arms in smug satisfaction.

"Oh, Victoria." Mariah pressed a hand to her eyes, wanting to weep over her sister's stupidity.

"Don't 'oh, Victoria' me." Victoria stomped. "William is handsome and dashing, and he has a beautiful townhouse in London and a fancy carriage and a great many friends. And nothing untoward happened."

Mariah's eyes snapped wide. "What do you know about his London townhouse?"

"Only that he promised to take me there once we're married." Victoria tilted her chin up in defiance.

"My foolish dear," Mariah groaned. "The house in question likely belongs to Peter. And I doubt very much that William ever intended to marry you."

"He did," Victoria insisted. "He does. Otherwise I would never have let him kiss me." She gasped, clapping a hand to her mouth.

"I think we've had just about enough of this," Peter said. "Malcolm, take William up to his room. If he chooses to stay there, then so be it. But I'll send Snyder around to see if he'd like help with anything. Such as packing." He turned away from William as though he never wanted to see him again. "Victoria, I am deeply sorry for allowing you to fall into this unfortunate position, and I promise you that whatever help you may need in the future, should your reputation suffer because of my nephew, I will give it."

"Reputation?" Victoria laughed, but there was a nervous quickness to the way she looked at everyone who was watching her. "Suffer? What do you mean? Nothing happened. No one will know anything. Unless you tell them." She gasped. "You wouldn't be so cruel as to make one little kiss a cause for public scandal, would you?"

Mariah took her hand with a sigh. "No one is going to say anything, but still. Come into the house. I'll have tea brought up, and you can tell me the full extent of the damage."

With a longing look at Peter, Mariah led Victoria toward the door to the morning parlor. Domenica whispered something to her husband, then hurried after them. "I thought you could use some support," she told Mariah.

After the excitement of the morning, the afternoon turned suddenly anticlimactic. Listening to Victoria confess to what she considered much ado about nothing was as far from the euphoria she'd felt with Peter's arms around her in Anne's garden.

"I should have kept a closer eye on her," Mariah confessed after supper, after an exhausted evening of conversation with the guests, and after donning her nightgown and heading straight to Peter's room once everyone went to bed for the evening. "With everything else going on, I simply lost track of what was most important."

Peter laughed as he shrugged out of his jacket and

tossed it into his dressing room. "Now you know how I've felt every moment since bringing you home."

Mariah grinned and crossed the room to slide her arms around his waist. He closed her in a hug that infused her, body and soul, with warmth. It had been far too long since she'd held him, since she'd breathed in his scent and felt his heart beat next to hers.

But before she could get too comfortable, she leaned back. "Did you ever find Poole and Robinson?"

Peter huffed a wry laugh. "They were at the pub in Truro."

"Really?"

"Oddly enough, yes. The way they tell it, as soon as they met up in the garden after searching for Victoria, they decided the game was ridiculous and opted for a pint instead."

Mariah frowned. "And you believe them?"

Peter tightened his arms around her, resting his cheek against the side of her head. "I want to believe them. I want to believe that they really are just friends that William decided to invite to the house to spite me."

"But you don't think that's true?"

He let out a breath, shifting so that he cupped her face with both hands. "Could we put off thinking about it until tomorrow? I have much nicer things I'd like to think about at the moment."

Poole and Robinson were instantly forgotten, and Mariah smiled. She lifted to her toes and kissed Peter lightly, then with more insistence. He brushed his thumbs over her cheeks and kissed her back with all the lingering tenderness of a man who was sipping chocolate for the first time. His lips caressed hers, and his tongue brushed along the seam of her mouth. She opened to him at once, drinking him in and sliding her tongue along his.

"I missed this," she sighed.

"You did?" He quirked an eyebrow at her. "I thought you were cross with me."

Mariah laughed. "I was just cross, and out of sorts, and, if what Domenica tells me is true, suffering from early signs of pregnancy."

Peter shook his head, sliding his hands down her arms to rest at her sides. "It's too early, isn't it?"

"To feel as if my body is going through some kind of momentous change?" She grinned as his hands brushed across her stomach. "I don't think so."

A hint of worry pinched Peter's face. "You don't think we should...abstain, do you? To keep the baby safe?"

Mariah giggled, stroking his worried face. She hardly saw the lines left by decades of trouble and laughter now. All she saw was the tenderness that radiated from him. "I'm no expert," she said, "but somehow I don't think we could do anything but good by loving each other."

His eyes snapped up to meet hers. "I do love you, Mariah. I love you so much."

She held her breath, mouth open, heart overflowing. "I can't see why. I've been nothing but trouble for you since we married."

"You've become everything to me," he said, closing his arms around her fully. "You've been such a useful sounding board with the mines."

She smirked. "The mines have been doing quite well on their own, and the surveyor's full report is due any day now."

"And I don't know how I would have handled William without you there to support me."

Her brow flew up. "I've caused more problems where William is concerned than I've solved. Without me around, William would have stayed in London."

"But he still would have been my heir."

She smiled. "Now you don't have to worry about that."

He stroked her back, letting his hand settle on the curve of her backside. "What if this one is a girl?"

"Then we'll just have to keep trying."

His mischievous grin faltered. "What if something happens."

"What if I miscarry?"

He nodded, lowering his eyes.

"I won't." She rested her hands on his face and lifted onto her toes to kiss him. "I'm not Anne."

"No, you're not," he said with growing confidence. But the pinch of worry was still in his eyes. "I don't want to leave you, not when I'm finally happy."

She blinked, leaning back. "Who said you're going to leave me?"

He shrugged. "I'm not a young man."

Her lips twitched into a wry grin. "Peter, we've discussed this before."

"I know, I know." He kissed her lightly. "But chances are I'll die long before you do and leave you alone."

"But I won't be alone," she said, stroking his face. "I'll have this little one, and hopefully plenty more with me."

"But—"

"And youth didn't stop Robert from dying before his time."

He stilled, regret filling his eyes. "I forgot about Robert."

"So did I," she smiled. "Probably for the first time in five years. It's rather nice, actually."

His smile returned. "Yes, it is nice to forget the past when it has finished being useful."

"The point is, we don't know how long we'll have together. For all we know, you'll live to be a spritely one hundred, and our children and grandchildren will roll their eyes at us as we hold hands and steal kisses while tucked up on the sofa together, covered in blankets."

"I like the sound of that." He brushed his fingers through her hair and kissed her with a sudden burst of passion. "We'd better get started on those grandchildren right away."

Mariah laughed out loud. "We've already taken care of that, remember?"

Peter shrugged, taking a half step back to work loose the buttons of his vest. "We'll have to start practicing for next time, then."

Mariah bit her lip. "I agree." She reached to help him with his buttons.

Within seconds, their fingers had tangled as they worked to free him from his clothes. Mariah eventually gave up and let him continue on his own while she shimmied out of her nightgown and climbed into his bed. And even though she had spent almost every night at Starcross Castle in the other room, it felt as though she were in her own bed at last. Peter's scent enveloped her, and the excitement of what was to come had fire racing through her veins.

When Peter returned from his dressing room naked and started putting out the lanterns around the room, Mariah didn't know whether she wanted to watch him or to urge him to hurry up. She understood now where his powerful physique came from. Memories of him with sword in hand and his shirt sticking to his sweating back returned to her, making her wriggle in anticipation.

"At last," she sighed when he doused the final lamp and climbed into bed with her. Their bodies molded together, his hardness a perfect match to her softness. The thickness of his erection pressed against her thigh, taking her breath away.

"Why did we stay apart so long?" he asked as he kissed her cheeks, her lips, her neck.

"I can't remember," she said, arching into him. "Something silly."

His only response was a hum as he kissed and licked his way down her neck to her shoulder. "You're the most delicious thing I've ever tasted," he said, continuing along her collarbone and the top of her chest toward her breast.

"And you are very good at tasting."

He laughed, the vibrations filling her. He reached her breast and took his time as he stroked a hand up her side and lifted her breast to meet his mouth. Mariah gasped at the heavenly sensation, better even than she remembered it. He drew her nipple into his mouth and suckled it, circling his tongue around and around until she was tight and aching. She threaded her hands through his hair, pressing her fingertips into his scalp.

"At the risk of embarrassing myself," he said suddenly, glancing up to meet her eyes with a look of fire. "I should tell you that it drives me wild when you tug on my hair like that."

"Really?" She wasn't sure whether she wanted to laugh or hum with pleasure at his confession.

"Particularly when I am in a certain position, engaged in a particular activity." His cheeks were bright red, even as his eyes shone with desire. The juxtaposition of boldness and bashfulness left Mariah tingling and aching.

"Which activity is that?"

"I'll show you."

He lowered to kiss her breast tenderly once more. Mariah caught her breath at the sensation. And then he began to move lower. Not only that, but he drew his arm down her side, over her hip, and across her thigh to hook around her knee. The simple gesture carried with it a world of pleasures that Mariah had yet to explore, but it was the way he drew her knee up and to the side that brought a host of recent memories rushing in on her. She remembered this. She remembered the way he had touched her and kissed her in her most intimate spots when they were newly married. The memory of everything they had done before swirled with the gentle kisses he laid on her stomach now, doubling the ache of expectation building inside of her.

When he shifted to draw her other leg up, exposing her center fully, she could barely breathe with anticipation. He inched lower, out of her reach, as he planted kisses along her inner thighs, but it was the waiting, burning part of her that longed to feel him.

He kissed his way higher and higher up the inside of her thighs until he was so close to her that she cried out in frustration.

"Patience," he whispered, his breath sending shivers through her.

She laughed at his ridiculous command and caught her hands in his hair the way he said he liked. He rewarded her by closing his mouth over the hot wetness of her folds, and she let out a groan of satisfaction. His hands traveled up her thighs to spread her farther as he tasted her, delving deep, tightening the coil of pleasure inside of her. She'd missed the sensation so much, missed the intimacy of being with him like that. The trust that it took for her to open herself to him, to let him slide his tongue along her most intimate parts, was more potent than any raw pleasure.

She'd been too long without him, without this kind of love in her life, and when he circled his tongue over the fiery nub of her desire, completion rushed through her before she could control it. Her body burst into life, filling with liquid pleasure, as her inner muscles throbbed with her climax. But as beautiful as it was, it was incomplete.

"I love you, Peter," she called out as the tremors continued to shake her. "I love you."

He pulled himself up the length of her body to look into her eyes. The combination of joy and surprise that she saw there broke her heart. "You do?"

"How could you doubt it?" she asked.

When he hesitated, she arched up to kiss him, putting her whole heart into it. She circled him with her arms and legs, wanting nothing more than to be one with him so that he could see just how much he meant to her. She dug her fingers into the firm muscles of his back as he smoothed a hand over her side, lifting her hips to meet his. The hard length of him rubbed right where she wanted him, and she sighed at the sensation.

"Yes," she sighed. "I need you, Peter. I need you inside of me."

"I love you," he murmured, close to a growl, and pushed inside of her.

It was bliss. He felt so perfect filling her, stretching her. She lifted her leg and ground against him, working to find the perfect way for their bodies to join. He let out a groan of pleasure as she moved in just the right way, taking him in deeply. He moved inside of her, slow at first as he kissed her lips, her neck. His hand cradled her breast, his thumb teasing her nipple. Every sensation was heavenly.

And then he grew more insistent, thrusting faster and with more purpose. She arched her hips to meet each thrust, which only encouraged him. The languid pleasure he was giving and taking turned to something more urgent. She could feel the muscles of his arms, back and thighs harden as he took her in earnest. She moved her hands lower to cup his backside, digging her nails in to encourage him.

"Mariah." He breathed her name as an urgent cry while something primal took over. Tension raced through him, and as it did she squeezed her inner muscles around him. Nothing had ever felt so good, so whole, and so wonderful as holding him and giving him pleasure. The whirlwind of her own pleasure swirled harder and harder as he abandoned everything staid and refined to make love to her with the power of instinct alone, and in no time she was crying out with each of his thrusts until completion swallowed her whole once more.

He let go moments later, letting out a rough cry as he came inside of her. She clung more tightly to him as his body tensed, then slowly, beautifully relaxed. Everything about the moment was perfect. Everything except the twinge of regret she felt over having wasted so much time not being with him.

Never again, she swore as he collapsed to her side, weary and spent. She rolled with him, keeping her arms around him and her body nestled against his as they floated down from the heights they had reached together.

"I love you too, my dearest darling," she panted, threading her fingers through his.

His arms tightened around her, and happiness seemed to tingle in every part of her. Never again would she let anyone or anything come between her and the man she loved.

CHAPTER 19

The sense of calm that pervaded Mariah when she awoke the next morning, nestled against Peter's side, her hand on his steadily rising and falling chest, was like returning home after a long and arduous journey. She smiled, snuggling closer to Peter, saying a quick prayer of thanks that what was wrong had been righted. She wouldn't have given up the way she felt, body and soul, for the world.

Although improvements could always be made.

Her smile grew mischievous as she drew her hand downward from Peter's chest to his stomach. She understood so much more about him after all they'd been through, painful though it'd been. He craved affection, needed it expressed boldly. And having seen his body in motion as he tackled not only sparring matches with Lord Malcolm, but riding and banging about his estate with the energy of a man half his age, she was eager to learn more. Where many men his age had turned plump and let their waistline grow and their muscles soften, Peter had only grown leaner, harder.

The muscles of his stomach and thighs weren't the only things growing harder as she explored his body. She had to bite her lip to keep from giggling as his staff stirred and came to life the closer she came to touching it. It seemed unspeakably bold for her to caress that part of him, to learn his feel and reactions, but everything her mother had told her about asking for what she wanted came back to her. Peter was her husband, and she had every right to signal that she wanted to be intimate with him.

Holding her breath, she let her wandering hand slip between his legs, cupping the sack beneath his staff. She had so little experience with male anatomy that this part of him was a mystery to her. He twitched slightly, drawing in a breath as she tested the weight of him, rolled him through her hands. His skin was hot, the contrast of textures alluring as her hand moved from his sack to the rigid length of his penis. She knew what his instrument was capable of, the memories of being filled by him making her ache and shiver in expectation.

She brushed her fingertips along the underside of his shaft, which had hardened to the point of standing straight up against his abdomen, then circled around his head. The involuntary groan that escaped from him betrayed that he was awake at last, but he said nothing as she continued her exploration. She wriggled closer to him, hooking her leg over his and grinding against his hip as her hand traveled down to the base of his staff once more. She closed her hand around him, a jolt of longing zipping through her at the thought of how thick he was and how amazing he felt inside of her, then began moving up and down with lazy strokes.

He let out a deep sound of pleasure and raised one arm above his head, as if signaling that he wouldn't stop her, whatever she wanted to do. Heat radiated from his body.

"Do you like that?" she asked in a hopeful whisper.

"So much," he sighed.

She continued to stroke him with one hand, but shifted so that she could look at his face as she pleasured him. The heavy-lidded look of bliss that he wore sent spirals of longing through her. He was so easy to please, so patient with her, even though she didn't know what she was doing. He could easily have grown bored with her, or worse, disliked her boldness. She couldn't forget what he'd said about Anne, the way she pursued him, and the inequality of their interactions. She suspected he'd only glanced the surface of what was a painful chapter in his life. But all of that seemed forgotten now. The only thing she saw as she watched him react to the way she sought to give him pleasure was enjoyment.

She wanted more. She wanted to give herself to him as much as she wanted him to feel pleasure. With a nervous swirl low in her stomach at what she was about to attempt, she drew her hand away and lifted her body up to straddle him. The bedcovers slipped down to her waist, exposing her breasts, her stomach, even her spread thighs and her sex to his view. He sucked in a breath and drank in the sight.

"You're so beautiful," he whispered.

She blushed from head to toe. "I feel beautiful when I'm with you."

He lifted toward her, and she bent to kiss him. Their mouths met in a dance that was becoming familiar, yet ever new. Her heart sang as their tongues twined. He relaxed back against his pillows, his hands sliding across her sides, up to knead her breasts. When he pinched her nipples just enough to send a jolt of sensation through her, she gasped and arched toward him. But it was when his hands traveled down her back to take possessive hold of her backside, that her desire reached a fevered pitch.

"I want to...." she started, not knowing how to communicate what she wanted. She flexed her hips, rubbing across his rigid staff in a way that sent unexpected spears of pleasure through her. "I want...how do I...."

Pleasuring herself against him felt divine, but he knew what she truly wanted. He took hold of her hips and moved her to the right position, then grasped himself, bringing his erection to her entrance. She bore down on him, gasping as he slid inside, filling her to the fullest.

It was different, joining with him that way, than it had been with them before. Mariah felt awkward and uncertain, but she wanted him so desperately that she pushed on. She sheathed him to his root, gasping as his tip pressed against something deep inside of her. The sensation made her restless, but she wasn't sure where to go next.

Without words, Peter stroked her spread thighs for a moment, then took hold of her hips, urging her to lift up. She followed his lead, moving over him until he almost came free of her. Then he pushed her down. The friction was so heady that she wanted more, and, with his guidance, she found herself moving slowly into a rhythm that turned her blood to fire.

Her inexperience melted away as she became used to the movements and gradually sped up. Peter's breath became deep and ragged, and he moved his hands from her hips, up her sides, to cradle her breasts. The combined sensations of him stretching her from the inside and holding her breasts was magical. She tilted her head back and let out a sound so wanton that she never thought she'd hear it from her own lips.

Peter made a matching sound, which sent the coil of tension building inside of her spiraling tighter and tighter. She moved on him at a frantic pace, suddenly aware that he had a full view of her body in the throes of passion. And from the sound of things, he loved what he was seeing.

That thought tipped her over the edge, and her body burst into shimmering, throbbing pleasure. She cried out, bearing down on him hard as the tremors turned her into a being of pure pleasure and light. Peter grasped her hips again, pushing into her with a few more, pounding strokes until he, too seemed to ripple with tension, then release, then satisfaction.

Mariah lost all will to hold herself upright and spilled across his chest, burying her head on the pillow next to him. He closed his arms around her as they lay panting and sweating together, his hands stroking her back and backside.

"That was magnificent," she gasped as she tried to catch her breath.

"Better than anything I've experienced before," he said, equally exhausted.

Mariah raised herself enough to look at him. "Really?"

His lips twitched into a wicked grin. "By far."

"Oh my."

She rested on top of him, so happy she burst into a giggle. She half expected him to scold her and tell her to stop, but he laughed as well, rolling until they lay on their sides, facing each other. He kissed her for a long, lingering moment, and the two of them basked in the glow of pleasure and love. It was a love like Mariah had never imagined before.

She wasn't sure how much lazy, beautiful time passed with the two of them entwined together like that, but the sound of movement from the dressing rooms eventually shook them out of their affectionate stupor. Peter pried himself reluctantly away from her and climbed out of bed, fetching his robe before heading into the dressing room. Mariah nestled back into the bed, eyes closed, for a few moments, breathing in the scent of Peter and their love-making before forcing herself to start the day.

She and Peter were both in such an obviously good mood when they joined Captain Tennant, Domenica, and Lord Malcolm in the breakfast room that she was sure their friends knew exactly what had made them so late coming down. Domenica sent Mariah a knowing grin, which had Mariah's cheeks bright pink in no time. The men launched straight into a chat about the headlines in the day's newspaper with such stoic concentration that Mariah was sure Lord Malcolm and Captain Tennant were tweaking Peter's nose in some mysteriously male way.

It wasn't until Mariah had finished half her breakfast that she blinked and asked, "Where is everyone else? Where is Victoria?"

The men's conversation hushed.

"Poole and Robinson never returned to the house yesterday," Lord Malcolm said.

"And Victoria?"

"Is she the kind to keep to her room in a snit?" Domenica asked.

Mariah let out an uneasy breath. "Yes, she is." But that didn't feel like the right answer to her.

"Where is William?" Peter asked with a grim frown.

The footman waiting in attendance cleared his throat. All eyes turned to him. Mariah had seen the young man around the house over the last month, but assumed he had been promoted to Davy's position on short notice.

"Christopher, isn't it?" Peter asked.

"Yes, my lord." Christopher bowed, his face red. "And Lord William was spotted leaving the house long after midnight last night."

"I see." Peter nodded in approval.

"I should probably check on Victoria," Mariah said, standing. Peter stood with her, but rather than being a show of respect, his movement was in reaction to Mr. Snyder rushing into the room.

"My lord, I'm terribly sorry," Mr. Snyder said, more ruffled than usual. "But these were just discovered behind the large vase in the front hall." He held out two envelopes.

"What are they?" Peter asked, his frown as anxious as the knot forming in Mariah's gut.

Mr. Snyder continued forward, handing one of the letters to Peter and the other to Mariah. The bottom fell out of Mariah's stomach as she looked at the letter. It was addressed simply, "Mariah" in Victoria's flowery handwriting.

"It's from Victoria," Mariah said, sitting down heavily as she opened the envelope.

"And this one is from William." Peter remained standing as he tore the pages from his envelope and read.

Mariah swallowed and took out Victoria's missive.

"My dearest sister," it read. "I don't care what you say, I'm in love. William is the most wonderful, handsome, passionate, exciting man I've ever met, and he adores me. I refuse to listen to you say anything bad about him, or to have you tell me I'm ruined. I'm not ruined, and I'll prove it. William and I are to be married. We're leaving tonight, in grand romantic style, and you won't be able to stop us. It looks as though I will be in line to be Countess of Dunsford after you in the end. But don't worry, I shall be gracious and generous with you. Your loving Victoria."

"Oh, Victoria," Mariah groaned, folding her letter and tossing it and the envelope on the table.

"What does it say?" Domenica asked.

"She believes she is eloping with William."

Domenica paled. "Would William actually do that? Would he marry her?"

"No," Peter said, his frown darker than ever. "He's holding her for ransom."

"What?" Mariah and Domenica gasped at the same time.

"Where have they gone?" Malcolm asked, standing and looking as though he would ride off single-handedly to bring them back.

"He said we can find them at the County Arms Inn in Truro," Peter said. "I'm to come alone tonight, and I'm to bring a note giving him five hundred thousand pounds."

"Five hundred thousand pounds?" Mariah gaped in disbelief.

"Does he say what he'll do if you don't come?"

Captain Tennant rose, and Domenica and Mariah stood as well.

Peter shot a quick, apologetic look to Mariah. "He says he's already ruined her, and that he'll do worse if I don't pay up."

"Oh, Victoria." Mariah shook her head, unsure whether she was more furious or terrified for her sister. "What do we do?" she asked Peter, glancing to Lord Malcolm.

"We go after her, of course," Lord Malcolm said.

Peter nodded in agreement. "But we go prepared."

It was the last straw. For years, decades, Peter had carried a burden of responsibility in his heart where William was concerned. He'd spent too long thinking he could have changed the young man, steered him away from a path of self-destruction. But William hurting Mariah, ruining her sister, was where Peter's guilt ended. He'd lived his life going out of his way to care for Anne at the cost of his own happiness. William had no qualms about destroying a young woman's chance at happiness at best and killing her at worst. Peter could see now that his nephew's moral compass was shattered, and as far from his own code of honor as could be. The time had come to stop trying to reform him and to instead bring him to justice.

"If he sees the two of you, he'll run," Peter said to Albert and Malcolm as they gathered in the stable, mounting Charger and the horses Harry had prepared for the other two.

"If he tries, he won't get far," Malcolm said, flashing the revolver that was hidden under his coat.

Peter sent his friend a flat look. "I'd like to avoid murdering the last family member I have."

"Peter." Malcolm nudged his horse to walk closer to Charger. "Do you honestly think that William will go into this encounter without some kind of weapon at the ready?"

"If he's capable of burning my ship, he's capable of much more," Albert added.

It tore at the core of everything Peter believed in, but Malcolm was right. Worse still, when his friend reached into the saddlebag behind him and handed him a second revolver, Peter took it.

"I'm not going to use it unless I feel like my life or either of yours is in danger," he said, stashing the pistol in his own saddlebag and half wishing they were in the Wild West of America, where everyone wore gun holsters and could draw and fire at a moment's notice.

"Come on," Albert said, turning his horse toward the road. "Let's get this over with."

Peter sighed and nodded, then tapped Charger into motion. His body ached as though he were too old for riding around Cornwall after dark, pretending to deliver a ransom but actually intent on rescuing a woman. But it was his soul that was weary as they rode across the estate and onto the road that would take them into Truro. As glorious as it was that a new part of his life had begun with Mariah and, God willing, their child, it was still painful to watch the entire first half of his life fold to a close.

Truro was a longer ride than Peter would have liked. The land attached to Starcross Castle was vast enough to give the castle itself the feeling of being isolated. They rode over and around hills, and Peter's thoughts turned to his mines, to the people who depended on him for their living. He was doing this for them as much as for himself or Mariah. If it were left to him, William would squander the lives and resources of Starcross. The promise of a new chapter that reports from the surveyor hinted at would be dashed. Peter couldn't let that happen.

"Someone's coming," Malcolm muttered as they rounded a bend to see the spire of Truro Cathedral and the lights of the town.

The three of them pulled their mounts to a stop and turned to watch a lone figure riding after them. Peter flashed from grim determination to alarm as Mariah rode up to join them.

"What are you doing here?" he asked, fear making him sound harsher than he intended to.

"You left without me," Mariah fired back.

As much as he admired her strength, considering her condition, her stubbornness needed to be addressed. "Mariah, this could be dangerous. There's no telling what William has waiting for us, or how he'll react when he sees I haven't come alone."

"And Victoria will be caught in the middle of it all," Mariah said as though she agreed with every statement he'd made. "She'll be confused and frightened."

"It's true that we might need someone to keep the young woman out of harm if William causes trouble," Albert said.

"This whole endeavor could be dangerous, Mariah." Peter guided Charger closer to her. "I don't want you to be hurt."

"Don't worry," she said, her impish grin apparent even in the dark. "I've come armed."

Peter's brow flew up, but when she twisted to show him the sword tied to her saddle, he nearly laughed in spite of himself.

"Perhaps a hundred years ago that would have protected you," he said, "but not tonight."

"Then you'll protect me," she said.

She could have kissed him square on the lips and thrown her arms around him and he wouldn't have felt as powerful and loved as he did in that moment. He didn't know how he'd lived so much of his life without her spirit, her confidence, and her joy. He didn't want to live another day without her, and as soon as they finished the business with William, he would never let her out of his sight again.

"I'm worried about the baby," he said.

Mariah gripped the reins of her horse tightly to steady her. "It's so early for the baby that I doubt it will be hurt at all."

Peter arched a brow. He'd rather have a doctor's opinion on that assumption than a guess. In fact, as soon as they had an opportunity, he would take her to London to have the finest medical minds on Harley Street examine her to make sure she was healthy. But for now, sending her home was likely to cause a fight they didn't have time for.

"Stay back if things get complicated," he warned her.

The smile she rewarded him with was enough to convince Peter he was doing the right thing. Although it would have been more right to take her back to the castle, back to their bed, and ravish her. But first things first.

"Come on," he said.

They continued down the road and into Truro. The town was well-lit and bustling. It was a pleasant June night, and the pubs seemed to be doing a generous amount of business. The County Arms stood at the top of the hill where the train station was. Peter and Malcolm dismounted and headed inside the noisy inn while Albert waited with Mariah outside, ready to jump into action at the drop of a hat if needed.

But as crowded and noisy as the inn was, William was nowhere to be found.

"Can I get you a pint, my lord?" the innkeeper, a man Peter vaguely recognized, asked from behind the bar in the common room.

Peter gestured to Malcolm, and the two of them approached the bar. "Have you seen my nephew, William?"

The innkeeper made a grim noise and shook his head. "That blight on decent society lit out of here without paying his bill not more than two or three hours ago. Begging your pardon, my lord."

Peter was convinced William was just as much of a blight as the innkeeper said. He exchanged a look with Malcolm.

"Do you know where he went?" Malcolm asked.

"He and his friends talked about heading on to St. Austell."

"Friends?" A tight knot formed in Peter's gut.

"Yeah, a balding bloke and a tall man with reddish hair."

The knot in Peter's gut rose to his throat. "Poole and Robinson."

"That's them." The innkeeper nodded.

"Did they have a woman with them?" Malcolm asked.

The innkeeper grimaced. "They did, my lord, and I'm worried for her. She was posh-looking and crying. I tried to step in and help her, but Lord William told me to mind my own business."

"Thank you, sir." Peter did his best to give the man a grateful smile and pushed some money across the bar for his troubles before turning to Malcolm. "They could still be on the road to St. Austell."

"If they are, we'll catch them."

They pushed their way out of the inn and back to where Albert and Mariah were still mounted.

"They've gone to St. Austell," Peter said. "We need to catch them before it's too late." He mounted Charger, then maneuvered closer to Mariah. "I'm afraid there could be some hard riding. Are you ready for it?"

"I am," she said. "Anything to find my sister."

He nodded to her, deep, pervasive love working its way up through the seriousness of the situation. Then he glanced to Malcolm and Albert to make sure they were ready before nudging Charger into a fast run.

The road to St. Austell was wide and well-traveled during the day, but as soon as they were a mile outside of town, darkness closed in. The landscape was hilly and wild, with patches of trees whose leaves rattled in the warm, summer breeze. On any other night, he would have enjoyed the rugged, Cornish feel of it all, but things weren't settling right with him. Why would William tell them to bring ransom to the County Arms but leave before they got there? And what were Poole and Robinson doing with him? Most importantly of all, was Victoria in harm's way? Judging by the innkeeper's report of her tears, Peter didn't think things were good.

He was in the middle of calculating how long it would take them to get to St. Austell and whether he should try to send Mariah back to Starcross, when three dark shadows appeared on the road in front of them.

"Whoa," he shouted, pulling Charger out of his run.

Malcolm, Albert, and Mariah did the same. Their horses were still restless, dancing and huffing in the night.

The shadows became more definite as they got closer, three men in billowing cloaks.

But it wasn't until the click of pistols being cocked and William declaring, "Stand and deliver, Uncle," that Peter realized the trap he'd walked into.

CHAPTER 20

"Mariah, get back," Peter ordered. He held out a hand, hoping it looked like he was warning Mariah off, when, in fact, he was reaching for the saddlebag behind him and the revolver it carried.

"No, no, Mariah. Stay," William said, mocking and tense. "This will make things so much easier for me. Having my uncle *and* his wife both killed by highwaymen in the dead of night will save me the trouble of, oh, say, pushing Mariah down the stairs later."

"You would stoop to murder?" Mariah gasped. Her horse danced sideways, coming closer to Peter instead of taking her out of harm's way. Yet, there was something deliberate about the move.

Peter hardly had time to think of it. Beneath the rush of danger that snapped his nerves taut lay a deep well of disappointment, of failure. "I've done wrong by you,

William," he said in a low voice, hoping to buy his friends time to plan a counterattack.

"You have," William answered, looking surprised. "You should have given me what was mine ages ago, then we wouldn't be in this mess." He cast furtive looks at his companions.

Peter glanced between the two other men, Poole and Robinson, who held a gun in each hand. They were deadly serious and had the calculating look of men who had killed before in their eyes, but they weren't just aiming at Peter and his friends. One of Poole's revolvers was pointed at William.

Peter pretended not to notice, shaking his head and slumping in his saddle, still trying to reach for his saddlebag without being seen. "No. I should have given you better guidance, taught you to be a better man."

William snorted. "What, a better man like you? Who drove his wife to her grave, only to go out and find a newer, younger cow to breed?"

It took self-control he hadn't drawn on since the war in Crimea not to lash out at William. "I'm sorry that it's come to this."

"So am I," William barked. "You could have lived if you hadn't driven my associates here to murder. But they want their money, and they've seen for themselves that the only way they're going to get it is if I inherit immediately. So goodbye, Uncle."

Time slowed down. William cocked his gun, took aim, and fired, but for a man who had spent his younger years in the army, the amount of time Peter had to react was more than enough. He rolled out of his saddle as the crack of William's shot filled the air, landing on his feet beside his horse.

Mariah screamed, and Peter lunged for her horse before she could do anything more. Behind him, he heard Malcolm shout, "Now!" More cracks of gunfire filled the air as Poole and Robinson fired. Peter pushed Mariah's horse hard, hoping that the would-be assassins wouldn't be able to hit a moving target. As he did, he caught sight of the one thing that could save his and Mariah's life.

The sword Mariah had brought with her was tied loosely to her saddle and came free easily when he pulled on the handle. He didn't stop to think about the ridiculousness of wielding a sword in a gunfight, not when Mariah's life was at stake. He could tell from the feel of the hilt in his hand that it wasn't a practice sword either, but one of the functional, military swords that Snyder kept in top condition for him.

Sword in hand, he wheeled around to find Robinson crumpling over and falling off his horse, Poole charging toward Albert, and William stared at the melee with wide-eyed panic, gun lowered. Peter charged toward his nephew.

"Drop your revolver, William," he demanded.

William snapped out of his panic and raised his gun to Peter. He fired, but the gun didn't go off. With a wordless cry, he hit the gun several times, then pointed it at Peter again.

Peter was close enough to strike. He swung his blade with all his might, slicing across William's raised arm. The revolver and William's hand tumbled to the ground.

William's face curled into a rictus of horror, his mouth falling open as he stared at the bleeding stump where his hand had been. His silent scream found voice at last, and William spilled from his saddle, sprawling to the ground and writhing in agony as he screamed.

Heart pounding, Peter dropped his sword and rushed to his nephew's side. He fell to his knees, gathering William in his arms. "It's all right, it's all right," he panted, holding William tight even though he fought and thrashed. "We'll call for a doctor. You'll be all right. We'll start over."

William continued to scream, his eyes rolling back in his head.

"Hold still, hold still, now," Peter urged him, terrified by the wild, wounded animal that William had become. "It will be all right."

A split-second later, another shot was fired. William jerked, then was still and silent. A dark hole appeared in his forehead, blood streaming down his face. Peter's throat closed over the cry that wanted to rip out of him. He jerked his head up, eyes wide.

Poole stood a few feet away, smoking pistol raised. "Dead men tell no—"

Another shot rang out, and Poole dropped.

"Tales," Malcolm finished, lowering his revolver.

The shots still rang in Peter's ears, forming a high-pitched ringing that he would never forget. Surely, Malcolm had saved his life, but the dark glint in his friend's eyes gave Peter pause.

He blinked, and sense started to return to him. He dropped William's lifeless body and rocked back to his haunches. "Where's Mariah?" he asked, voice hoarse.

"Up ahead." Malcolm nodded down the road.

"Is she...."

"Unharmed. Go to her, and we'll take care of this."

Peter pushed to his feet, staggering a few steps. William's body lay at his feet, Poole's a few yards farther away. Robinson's lifeless form was sprawled by the side of the road. The dead men's horses had scattered at the sound of gunfire, but hadn't gone farther than the field beside the road. Far ahead, Peter could see Mariah's horse in the moonlight, beside a tree.

He launched into a jog, then a run. Too many parts of him were still numb, but his heart knew what it needed. He had to be sure Mariah was safe. He had to have her in his arms.

MARIAH SCREAMED WHEN THE FIRST SHOTS WERE fired. The way Peter fell from his horse convinced her he'd been shot. But when he landed on his feet and jumped toward her, those fears vanished. She opened her mouth, ready to help him fight, but he pushed her horse instead. The sword Mr. Snyder had armed her with when she announced she was going after the men flashed in the moonlight, but as Peter drew it, he must have nicked her mount's backside. Her horse shouted and leapt forward, running for its life.

Mariah could do nothing but hold tight, leaning forward over the horse's neck. A volley of shots followed, and fear filled her. She clenched her jaw and used all of her strength just to stay seated.

But that fear shifted at the sound of a woman screaming farther along the road. She knew in an instant it was Victoria, and urged her horse to go faster. The shots behind her stopped, and she pulled up on the reins as she neared a cluster of trees by the side of the road.

"Victoria?"

The terrified cries changed to panicked shouts of, "Mariah! Mariah!"

Mariah managed to control her mount enough to bring her to a stop. As soon as she unhooked her leg and slid to the ground, though, the injured animal danced away, bobbing its head. As much as Mariah wanted to see to it, she had Victoria to worry about.

Her sister sat at the base of one of the trees, her hands behind her back. The moonlight was bright enough for her to see the look of terror in Victoria's eyes, as well as a rough gag that now hung loose around Victoria's neck.

"Help me, help me," Victoria yelped, panicked beyond the point of sense. "Help."

Mariah rushed to her, crouching by her side and pulling Victoria into her arms. "I've got you. You're safe."

When Victoria didn't hug her back, Mariah realized

that her sister's hands had been tied. Not only that, she had a bruise on her tear-streaked cheeks.

"What did he do to you?" Mariah demanded, moving so that she could work free whatever was binding Victoria's hands. The knot in the rough rope around her sister's wrists was so tight she wasn't sure she'd be able to untie it.

"He doesn't love me," Victoria wailed. "He said he did, but he said such cruel things to me once we left Starcross Castle, and he...he wouldn't stop when I told him to stop."

White-hot rage filled Mariah's gut. She had half a mind to find Peter's sword and run William through, but she needed to free Victoria from her bonds first. Another shot split the air, then a final one moments later. At last the knot holding Victoria's wrists together began to loosen.

"What about the other two?" Mariah asked, not wanting to know the answer. "Did they hurt you?"

Victoria shook her head, but burst into a fresh round of weeping instead of saying more. The moment her arms were free, she threw them around Mariah, clinging to her as if her life depended on it.

"It's all right," she said, smoothing her hand over her sister's hair. "I've got you now. It's over."

"Mariah?" She heard Peter's frantic cry before his shape materialized in the darkness. "Mariah!"

Mariah kissed her sister's cheek then stood just as Peter reached them. He crashed into her with so much force that for a moment she thought she would fall over.

But Peter caught her and held her close, so tightly that she couldn't breathe. But she didn't care. Peter was safe and whole and in her arms.

"You're alive," she panted, brushing her hands over his face, then kissing him.

He kissed her back hard, not out of passion, but with a relief that was so potent it had her aching for him.

"So are you," he gasped, touching her face, her hair, her arms, every part of her he could.

"Victoria's been hurt," Mariah said at last, turning to her sister as Victoria tried to stand.

When Victoria stumbled and Mariah caught her, she realized her sister's feet were still tied together. Victoria wailed and grasped tightly onto Mariah again with a grip that nearly strangled her. Mariah let her squeeze though. Victoria needed the comfort far more than she needed the air.

"Let me untie your feet," Peter said, his voice calming as he crouched by Victoria's side.

Once Victoria's bonds were disposed of, the three of them waited where they were until Malcolm came for them.

"Albert's gone to fetch the constable," he said, looking grim and exhausted. "I'll stay with the bodies until they return, but in the meantime, I suggest you take the ladies back to Starcross Castle."

"Bodies?" Victoria squeaked.

Peter let out a weary breath. "Poole and Robinson... and William. They're all dead."

"Oh, Peter, I'm so sorry." Mariah reached for him with one arm as Victoria continued to cling to her, weeping.

Peter took her hand and squeezed it, shaking his head. "I'll fetch the horses."

The ride back to Starcross Castle seemed to last forever, and yet Mariah felt as though she were drifting through unreality as they rode in silence. When they arrived at the castle, Mr. Snyder was there to greet them.

"I knew no good would come of this," he said, gesturing for the stable-hands and footmen, all of whom were still awake even though it was well after midnight, to take the horses. "Mrs. Wilson has tea waiting, my lord."

As they dragged themselves into the house, Peter paused to ask Mr. Snyder, "Did you send the sword with her?"

Mr. Snyder nodded once. "I thought you might need it."

Peter nodded, but said no more. Mariah wanted to ask what happened to the sword, but the weary, drawn look of grief in Peter's eyes kept her silent.

Ginny and Poppy were waiting in the front hall, and came to take Victoria up to her room. Mariah went with them, helping to strip Victoria from her tattered and dirty clothes and to bathe her before dressing her in a clean nightgown and putting her into bed. Victoria cried herself to sleep, but at least she slept.

"I'll stay with her, my lady," Poppy said, taking a seat in the chair by the window.

Mariah nodded to the faithful maid, then dragged her weary body out into the hall.

"Do you need my help, my lady?" Ginny asked.

"I probably will tomorrow," Mariah told her as they walked down the hall to the door to Peter's room. "But tonight, I just want to be with my husband."

Ginny nodded in understanding, curtsied, then left as Mariah retreated to the bedroom.

Peter sat hunched over at his desk, his head in his hands. He looked up when Mariah entered, and she could tell he'd been weeping. He covered it with a sharp sniff, wiping his face and rising from his chair.

"Go on," she sighed, crossing to take him into her arms. "You can cry. He was your family, the last of your family."

"No." Peter shook his head, resting his cheek against her head. "You are my family. Our children are my family."

Mariah smiled in spite of herself, though her joy was dulled by the grief she could feel radiating from Peter. "Come on, let's go to bed."

They shed their clothes, not bothering to hang or fold them, and climbed into bed together. They were too exhausted to make love, but just lying together, giving each other comfort and affection was all either of them needed.

It was well into the morning by the time Mariah

awoke. The bed was warm, but Peter had already gotten up. He sat at his desk in his robe, rubbing his forehead as he studied a letter in his hand. Mariah stretched awake, scooted to the edge of the bed, and turned to her side. She watched him in silence for a while, her emotions a tempestuous mix of grief on his behalf, anger for Victoria, relief that William was gone, and a calm, steady joy, like the dawn after a storm.

He must have felt her gaze. He glanced up, and a weary smile spread across his lips, bringing a hint of new life to his lined face.

"What are you reading?" she asked.

He blew out a breath, then stood and walked to the bed. "It's a report from Malcolm about his dealings with the constable last night." He sat on the bed.

Mariah pushed herself to a sitting position, not bothering to cover herself when the bedcovers dropped to her waist. "What does he say?"

Peter showed her the short letter. "The constable acknowledges that the men who were killed were killed in self-defense. Poole and Robinson were wanted in London, and Scotland Yard has been informed." He lowered the letter. "Snyder has already started going through William's things. The ambush was planned more than a week ago. It was the reason Poole and Robinson came to Starcross Castle. William's creditors put a price on his head, but somehow William convinced them to settle for my death instead of his."

"That's awful." Mariah put her arm around him, resting her head on his shoulder.

"It's over now," he said, his voice hollow.

"It's over," Mariah repeated, pushing aside his robe to kiss his bare shoulder. "And as horrible as the ending was, all we can do is look to the future. A future where nothing is keeping us apart and no one will stop us from having a long, happy life together."

He smiled, twisting so that he could draw her into his arms and kiss her. Through the shock and the grief, Mariah could feel that the two of them would move forward, happier than ever.

"I was going to write to your parents," Peter said at length, "but I thought you might want to write instead."

"I will." Mariah sighed, filling with sadness at the thought of everything she'd have to say. "I don't know if it's what she would want, but perhaps we could offer to have Victoria stay here for a while."

"Here?" Peter blinked at her. "Wouldn't this place be filled with painful memories?"

"Possibly. But at least she wouldn't have to face all the people who know her at home. It's quiet here. And if she stays long enough, she'll have a nephew or niece to lift her spirits."

"She will." Peter rested his hand on Mariah's belly. "I still can't believe we've been so lucky so soon. I worry, though...."

His words trailed off, but Mariah knew exactly what he was thinking. She rested her hand on top of his. "This baby will be born," she said, so firm it was as if she were scolding him. "I know it. And after this one, there will be more. As many as you'd like."

He smiled, so much happiness in his eyes, in spite of the pain, that the years seemed to drop away. "I want whatever you want," he said. "I could be content with just you in my arms for the rest of my life."

Mariah laughed. "No, you couldn't." She brushed her hand along his stubbly jaw, then kissed his lips. "You need love, Peter. You need mountains of affection, a house full of children who adore their papa. And nothing will make me happier than giving you that life. It's what I was made for."

"I love you," he said, emotion thick in his voice.

"And I love you," she answered. "I always will."

EPILOGUE

The winter wind howling against the walls of Starcross Castle, swirling fresh snow through the grey skies, was bitter, but it was the least of Peter's worries. He paced from his desk to the door and back again, nearly knocking his shin against the corner of the bed as he went.

"There, there, old friend." Edmund caught him in the middle of one pass and thumped his back. "She'll be just fine. She's a strong girl, always has been."

Before Peter could reply, a cry sounded from Mariah's room. A cry of pain. Peter's gut twisted, and he marched toward the door to his dressing room.

Again, Edmund caught him and stopped him. "There's nothing you can do in there but get in the way."

"I can be there," Peter said, shaking out of Edmund's grip and storming into his dressing room.

In spite of protests from everyone from Snyder to the

midwife to Mrs. Travers, from the moment Mariah had gone into labor, he had insisted every one of the doors from her room, through the dressing rooms, to his room remain open. In exchange, he'd promised to stay in his room and not get in the way. But that promise had become impossible as Mariah's cries and grunts grew louder and more anxious.

They'd made it through nine months of pregnancy together, faced the turmoil of William's sudden death together, and helped each other and Victoria recover from the ordeal together. He couldn't stand by and let Mariah go through the most important moment of their life alone.

"There you are, my dear. I see the head," the midwife was in the middle of saying as Peter marched into the room.

He stopped short at the sight that met him. Mariah sat on the edge of the bed, her mother and a pile of pillows supporting her back. The midwife sat on a stool in front of her, reaching between her legs. Victoria stood next to the midwife with a towel ready and waiting. Ginny and Poppy hovered on either side of the bed, looking as though they were ready for anything. But it was Mariah who instantly had his full attention. She was drenched in sweat, her dark hair plastered to her head, face red and contorted in pain. The sight broke his heart.

Until she looked his way.

"Peter," she shouted through her panting, and reached out for him.

He didn't hesitate. He ran to her, sliding onto the bed by her side and looping an arm around her back. He was only marginally conscious of knocking Mrs. Travers out of the way. When he opened his mouth to ask how Mariah was, nothing but wordless sound came out.

"Easy now, easy. We're almost there," the midwife said, shooting him a nasty look.

"My lord, what are you doing here?" Mrs. Travers gasped, looking mortally offended. "Fathers do not attend births."

"This one does," Peter said.

"But—"

"It's coming. Push now, dearie."

Everything else was forgotten as Mariah gritted her teeth and pushed. The sound she made was excruciating for Peter to listen to, but he ignored it like he'd ignored the sounds of battle ages ago, giving Mariah his hand to squeeze. Which she did. So hard he nearly cried out along with her.

"Here we go, here we go." The midwife shifted, intent on the miracle in process.

There was a strange sound, Mariah let out a final cry, then collapsed in exhaustion, and Victoria rushed forward.

Then a tiny, furious wail rent the air.

The midwife did something Peter couldn't see, then said, "Congratulations, my lord. It's a boy." She held up a screaming, red-mottled, sticky infant with a cord hanging from his belly.

Peter had never seen anything so horrifyingly beautiful in his life. He was stunned, mesmerized as his son—*his son*—flailed his tiny fists in the air. Peter's eyes stung and his throat closed, but he had never been happier in his life.

The midwife slid the baby onto Mariah's belly while she continued her work with the afterbirth. Mariah wept openly as she embraced their son. "He's so perfect," she said, blinking back tears.

"You're perfect," Peter insisted. He scooted farther onto the bed so that he could embrace her and their son together. The moment was so beautiful that he could hardly keep his thoughts together, but one thing jumped to the front of his mind. "Are you well?" he asked, kissing Mariah's forehead and brushing back her sweat-dampened hair.

"I'm fine," Mariah wept. "Tired, but I don't care. Look at him."

"Mother and baby came through beautifully, my lord," the midwife said as she stood. She briefly took the baby to wrap him in a towel, tucking his tied cord inside the bundle. "Easy as pie. They'll both be on their feet in no time."

"Thank you," Peter told her from the bottom of his heart, then turned his full attention to Mariah. "And thank you."

"Me?" She laughed, dragging her eyes away from the baby to gaze up at him with so much love that Peter felt warm all over.

"For agreeing to marry a broken old man," he said. "For giving me hope."

"You've given me so much more than I could ever repay," she said, tilting her head up to kiss him.

He kissed her in return, holding her and the baby in an embrace that he never wanted to end. She'd given him so much more than he could ever have hoped for—an heir, a family, a future. But more than anything, she'd opened his heart and filled his world with love.

THE ROMANCE OF STARCROSS CASTLE IS NOT OVER yet! Are you curious about maid Ginny Davis and stableman Harry Pond? What about the charming, if clumsy, maid Poppy Miller and handsome gardener Nick Parsons? Don't worry! All of your romantic questions will be answered. You can learn all about Ginny and Harry in *Starcross Lovers*. And once you've smiled and sighed and fanned yourself over those two, it'll be time for *Starcross Dreams*, Poppy and Nick's story. Both novellas are available now. That's right, for every full-length novel in the *Silver Foxes* series, there will be a series of companion novellas about the servants in the household of whichever house the main novel takes place in.

SPEAKING OF THOSE FULL-LENGTH NOVELS, BOOK two in *The Silver Foxes of Westminster* is available now!

August Sunrise tells the story of industrial heiress, Marigold Bellowes, and rising star of Parliament, Alexander Croydon. You remember Alex from *A Place to Belong*, right? Is Alex still grieving over the death of his long-time mistress? Has he been able to open his heart to his illegitimate son, James, yet? And how will Marigold react when she learns her new husband already has a son? Especially when a horrible miscarriage leaves her barren, and James may be the only child Alex will ever have? *August Sunrise* is a tale of heartbreak and forgiveness, and finding love against all odds. And when you're finished with Alex and Marigold, be sure to read the companion novellas which take place at Winterberry Park, *Winterberry Spark* and *Winterberry Fire*.

Wanna keep in touch with me in the fastest way possible without having to check your email or go on social media? Text DECEMBER to +1 215-486-0270 today!

If you enjoyed this book and would like to hear more from me, please sign up for my newsletter! When you sign up, you'll get a free, full-length novella, *A Passionate Deception*. Victorian identity theft has never been so exciting in this story of hope, tricks, and starting over. Part of my *West Meets East* series, *A Passionate Deception* can be read as a stand-alone. Pick up your free copy today by signing up to receive my newsletter (which I only send out when I have a new release)!

Sign up here: http://eepurl.com/cbaVMH

Are you on social media? I am! Come and join the fun on Facebook: http://www.facebook.com/merryfarmerreaders

I'm also a huge fan of Instagram and post lots of original content there: https://www.instagram.com/merryfarmer/

AND NOW, GET STARTED ON AUGUST SUNRISE...

Chapter One

London – May, 1879

Miss Marigold Bellowes turned heads wherever she went. It was a fact of life she'd lived with since emerging from the schoolroom into society. She was well aware that she possessed a figure men stared at and coloring that women envied. Her blonde hair had just a touch of copper to it, proving that her parents had named her well, and her green eyes were the sort that unnerved those she stared at for too long. But Marigold wasn't foolish enough to believe her looks were what enthralled people. That honor went to her father's money.

"Is Lord Kendrick staring again?" she whispered to her best friend, Lady Lavinia Prior, as the two crossed St. Stephen's Hall, heading toward the stairs that would take them to the Strangers' Gallery overlooking the House of Commons Chamber.

Lavinia—who was younger than Marigold by five years and quite pretty herself, with thick, chestnut hair and dark eyes—glanced over her shoulder, then sniggered. "He is, poor thing."

Marigold's answering sigh quickly turned to a giggle. "I've refused his proposal three times. You'd think the man would go and sniff up another tree."

Lavinia laughed out loud, then raised a hand to cover her mouth, her cheeks going pink. "I don't know whether it's cruel of you to say that or if you're doing the man a favor by snubbing him."

"I'm doing him a favor," Marigold answered as they joined the queue to the gallery stairs. "Clearly, Lord Kendrick is only interested in marrying a woman who can bolster the sagging fortunes of his estate, if rumors are to be believed."

Lavinia hummed sagely. "They are to be believed,

according to Mama. That's why she hasn't tried to thrust me at him."

Marigold winced for her friend and rested a gloved hand on her arm before they started up the narrow stairs to the gallery. "Is she still trying to snag a titled husband for you?"

Lavinia let out an ironic laugh. "She's trying to match me with anyone prominent and influential enough to meet her exacting standards, no matter what I think of things. Lord Kendrick doesn't come close to meeting her mark. Not when his chances of bankruptcy are so high."

"And I suppose that's why he hasn't given up on me," Marigold sighed, feeling far guiltier than she should. But as more than a few men needed to understand, financial difficulty on their part did not necessitate feelings of love and a desire to wed on the part of whatever female they set their hearts, or rather, their billfolds, on.

They reached the top of the crowded stairs and stepped out into the Strangers' Gallery, a stretch of tiered seats in the balconies above the House of Commons chamber floor. The gallery was open to any members of the public who cared to observe the proceedings of government, but women rarely attended. At least, they rarely attended when it was business as usual. But change was afoot. A group of men, both in the House of Commons and in the House of Lords, had been making noise about passing a bill that would increase the rights of women. It was a long way from granting them equal standing with men or the vote, as Marigold wanted, but anything that would secure a woman's right to her own property and her life was a step in the right direction.

The bill was due to be debated that day, so more than a few women had taken up seats at the very front of the gallery. Marigold tapped Lavinia's arm and pointed to a section of seats at the front, then made her way toward them.

"To be honest," she said, continuing their conversation, "I've reached the end of my tether when it comes to men hoping to win my hand, as though it's some sort of prize. The fact that my father has made a smashing success of his business should not preclude me from having a real marriage based on love."

They reached the front row amidst the hubbub of dozens of conversations, but Marigold had been loud enough to catch the attention of Lady Stanhope, who glanced up at her with shrewd, calculating eyes.

"Well, that's quite an introduction," Lady Stanhope said, her lips twitching into a smile. She scooted to one side, patting the bench beside her. "Do sit next to me."

"Lady Stanhope." Marigold greeted the woman with a fond grin.

Everyone who had spent any time observing Parliament or getting involved in political circles knew Katya Marlowe, the Countess of Stanhope. She was regarded by many as the most powerful widow in England. Her husband, the Earl of Stanhope, had died fifteen years before, leaving her with three children, a title, vast estates, and, reportedly, a huge sum of money. Her son,

Rupert, the current earl, was not yet eighteen and was still at university, so Lady Stanhope continued to manage the Stanhope legacy. At a year shy of forty, she was a strikingly handsome woman, with sharp, bold features, dark hair, and piercing blue eyes. She was rumored to have had a string of lovers after her husband's death, and was considered to be friends with several prominent politicians.

"Still batting fortune hunters away with a stick?" she asked as Marigold settled onto the bench beside her.

Marigold laughed. "I can't fault them for trying. I just wish they would try somewhere else."

Lady Stanhope smiled. "Good for you for not giving in and marrying one just to make the others go away."

"Believe me, there have been times when I've been tempted," Marigold said with an ironic twist of her lips. "If I could find just one man who I thought I could be happy with, who would appreciate me for myself and not what I can do for him, then I'd fasten the leg-shackles tomorrow."

Lady Stanhope arched one severe eyebrow. "Why not seek out a man who can do something for you?"

Marigold paused in the process of settling her reticule and parasol by her side. "How would I do that?"

Lady Stanhope raised her shoulders slightly in a shrug and glanced out over the chamber. "Simple. Think about matrimony the way a man does. Consider what your aims and goals in life are and set your sights on a man who can fulfill those goals."

"That's rather mercenary, isn't it?" Lavinia asked, glancing around Marigold to study Lady Stanhope.

"Men do it all the time," Lady Stanhope said with a wave. "Robert only married me because my mother was a Romanov, and he wanted his children to have royal blood. Why shouldn't we marry for similar reasons?"

"Why is it that you never remarried, Lady Stanhope?" Lavinia asked.

Marigold felt a flush of embarrassment for her friend's impertinent question, but Lady Stanhope merely chuckled.

"There are a great many reasons I haven't remarried, my dear," she told Lavinia, then leaned closer to Marigold, as if sharing a secret. "I have too much power, too much influence, on my own. And besides." She inched closer still and lowered her voice to whisper to both women, "I am not the sort to be unfaithful, which would vastly limit my ability to sample the many delicacies that the men of the world have to offer."

"Oh, my!" Lavinia pressed a hand to her mouth and snapped straight, her face turning bright puce.

Marigold, on the other hand, laughed so loud that several sets of eyes—both male and female—turned to them. Only then did she cover her mouth, blushing with merriment as much as embarrassment. "I like the way you think, Lady Stanhope," she whispered.

Lady Stanhope sat a little straighter, beaming with pride and mischief. She tilted her head and studied

Marigold. "So what are your goals, my dear? Who do you want to be?"

Marigold blinked rapidly under the assault of such an important question. "I'm not sure. I don't think I've ever thought about it."

"Yes you have," Lady Stanhope countered immediately. "A woman like you, who has turned down half a dozen offers of marriage, who continues to receive those offers even as she approaches thirty, and who attends sessions of Parliament when the rights of women are being discussed, has most definitely considered what she wants from life."

Marigold's startled expression melted into a cunning grin. "I suppose you're right." She darted a glance around to gauge if anyone was eavesdropping. Since ministers were flooding into the gallery below and taking their seats, as if the session were about to start, their conversation went unnoticed. "I want to be the wife of a powerful man," she confided, mischief bubbling up inside of her.

"I thought so." Lady Stanhope nodded in approval.

"I want to have a say in the world," Marigold went on. "At the moment, the only way to do that is as the wife of a powerful man and the mother of his children, but I want to align myself with those who are fighting to give women power of their own."

"Would you enter politics yourself if you could?" Lady Stanhope pressed her.

Marigold hesitated. She glanced to the gallery as the Sargent at Arms called the room to order. The men crowding the benches on either side of the room seemed worn and full of cares to her. They were a stern, grey mass of seriousness.

"Perhaps it would be more enjoyable to be the power behind the throne," she said in a circumspect voice, tilting her head to one side.

"A wise observation," Lady Stanhope said.

A different swirl of emotion filled Marigold's heart. "And I have always wanted to be a mother." She took a breath after her statement, caught by the seeming paradox that wanting to give birth and hold public power seemed to present.

"You can be a mother and a powerful woman," Lady Stanhope told her, in a hushed voice as the men below began to speak. "In fact, I'm certain my children would argue that I'm frightfully powerful, in spite of and because of them." There was a mischievous glint in her eyes as she glanced to Marigold.

"Does your son think so?" Lavinia whispered.

"More than my daughters," Lady Stanhope answered.

Marigold wanted to laugh again, but the gallery had settled in to watch proceedings below. She smiled to herself all the same, her heart beating with excitement and promise that had nothing to do with the drone of parliamentary business below. She'd always considered motherhood and ambition to be two separate beasts, and believed she could only feed one of them. But if Lady

Stanhope could wield influence and raise children as well, then so could she.

However, Lady Stanhope was right about something else, though she had hinted at it more than stating it outright. If she wanted to be the woman she'd dreamed of being, she would have to choose a husband for what he could do for her, the same way men tried to pitch woo to her because of what her father's money could do for them.

In the true way of men, Marigold had to sit through a lot of unnecessary business and debate about topics that made about as much sense as corsets for puppies before the bill to advance the rights of women was brought up. As soon as the issue of extending the budget for rail lines in Surrey was finished and voted on, the MP from Bury St. Edmunds introduced the bill for women's rights. A flurry of activity ensued as both the men on the floor and the observers in the gallery prepared for the fight.

Marigold watched the Liberal side of the aisle with interest. The bill was supported by several Liberal MPs and fiercely opposed by the Conservatives, as was just about every other bill that extended the rights of women, the working class, or anyone not currently enfranchised. Lord Hartington, the Leader of the Opposition, stood in a huddle with a handful of other MPs, looking ready to stand up and debate. But he wasn't the one who broke away from the group to approach the box.

A shiver of something warm and exciting swirled in

Marigold's gut. "Who is that?" she whispered to Lady Stanhope.

A fond smile spread across Lady Stanhope's lips. "That, my dear, is Mr. Alexander Croydon."

"Who is he when he's at home?" Marigold went on, her eyes trained on him. She couldn't account for the way her heart suddenly beat faster and harder, other than the man's obvious good looks. He was tall, with broad shoulders and a fit physique. His hair was graying at the temples, but he didn't seem particularly old, all things considered. His confident grin as he took the podium and cleared his throat made Marigold want to lean in to listen.

"My lord Speaker, members of the House, and especially my distinguished colleagues on the other side of the aisle," he began. "What would any of us be without the women in our lives?"

His question was met by various grunts and guffaws.

"We would be nowhere," he went on. "And nowhere is precisely where these brave and valiant women who form and shape us are in the eyes of the government of this kingdom. They are the very backbone of our society, and yet, in the eyes of the law, they are reduced to the status of servants or children. They are not even entitled to the property that they bring into a marriage. If they should choose to break free from a union that is abusive or degrading, they are left with nothing. We propose to change all of that. Therefore, we are introducing this bill to extend the rights and legal protection of women, their persons, and their property."

Both sides of the chamber erupted into shouts of encouragement or derision. Mr. Croydon allowed it to continue for a moment, as if building up for his next assault. He glanced straight up into the gallery as he waited, directly at Lady Stanhope. Out of the corner of her eye, Marigold watched Lady Stanhope raise an eyebrow and nod in approval. A thousand questions about what the relationship between the wily widow and Mr. Croydon could be popped to Marigold's mind.

Then Mr. Croydon's gaze shifted to her.

Their eyes met. Marigold's breath caught in her throat. Mr. Croydon's eyes were almond-shaped and blue. They burned with cleverness and confidence...and something new. The clamor in the room faded to the background, and for a moment, all she saw was his handsome, self-assured expression, his poised smile. She smiled back before she could stop herself, pressing a hand to her heart.

A moment later, he turned back to the men around him and continued. "The bill we propose encompasses the three major legally sanctioned offenses against women: property rights, legal recourse in cases of divorce, and the right to maintain custody of children in case of abandonment or neglect."

Marigold's breath came rushing out. Whatever connection she and Mr. Croydon had had in that split-second of wonder, it was gone. The electric energy that had coursed through her ebbed as he dove into a long, complicated speech spelling out the laws and changes that needed to come. As desperately as Marigold wanted to hang on his every word, she was buzzing with the need to know so much more than he was saying. How had she never noticed the man before? Why hadn't he attended any number of social events that made up the season? Had he been in attendance and she just hadn't noticed him? That seemed impossible.

WANT TO READ MORE?
PICK UP AUGUST SUNRISE TODAY!

Click here for a complete list of other works by Merry Farmer.

ABOUT THE AUTHOR

I hope you have enjoyed *December Heart*. If you'd like to be the first to learn about when new books in the series come out and more, please sign up for my newsletter here: http://eepurl.com/cbaVMH And remember, Read it, Review it, Share it! For a complete list of works by Merry Farmer with links, please visit http://wp.me/P5ttjb-14F.

Merry Farmer is an award-winning novelist who lives in suburban Philadelphia with her cats, Torpedo, her grumpy old man, and Justine, her hyperactive new baby. She has been writing since she was ten years old and realized one day that she didn't have to wait for the teacher to assign a creative writing project to write something. It was the best day of her life. She then went on to earn not one but two degrees in History so that she would always have something to write about. Her books have reached the Top 100 at Amazon, iBooks, and Barnes & Noble, and have been named finalists in the prestigious RONE and Rom Com Reader's Crown awards.

ACKNOWLEDGMENTS

I owe a huge debt of gratitude to my awesome beta-readers, Caroline Lee, Sylvia McDaniel, and Jolene Stewart, for their suggestions and advice. And double thanks to Julie Tague, for being a truly excellent editor and assistant!

[Click here for a complete list of other works by Merry Farmer.](#)

ALSO BY MERRY FARMER

The Noble Hearts Trilogy (Medieval Romance)

Montana Romance (Historical Western Romance – 1890s)

Hot on the Trail (Oregon Trail Romance – 1860s)

The Brides of Paradise Ranch –

Spicy and Sweet Versions (Wyoming Western Historical Romance – 1870s)

Willow: Bride of Pennsylvania (Part of the American Mail-Order Brides series)

Second Chances (contemporary romance)

Nerds of Paradise (contemporary romance)

The Culpepper Cowboys (Contemporary Western - written in partnership with Kirsten Osbourne)

New Church Inspiration (Historical Inspirational Romance – 1880s)

Grace's Moon (Science Fiction)

Printed in Great Britain
by Amazon